A SENSE FOR MURDER

Also by Leslie Karst

The Sally Solari Mysteries

DYING FOR A TASTE
A MEASURE OF MURDER
DEATH AL FRESCO
MURDER FROM SCRATCH
THE FRAGRANCE OF DEATH

JUSTICE IS SERVED:
A TALE OF SCALLOPS, THE LAW, AND
COOKING FOR RBG

A SENSE FOR MURDER

Leslie Karst

SEVERN
HOUSE

First world edition published in Great Britain and the USA in 2023
by Severn House, an imprint of Canongate Books Ltd,
14 High Street, Edinburgh EH1 1TE.

severnhouse.com

British Library Cataloguing-in-Publication Data
A CIP catalogue record for this title is available from the British Library.

ISBN-13: 978-1-4483-0905-4 (cased)
ISBN-13: 978-1-4483-0906-1 (e-book)

All Severn House titles are printed on acid-free paper.

Typeset by Palimpsest Book Production Ltd., Falkirk, Stirlingshire, Scotland.
Printed and bound in Great Britain by TJ Books, Padstow, Cornwall.

Praise for the Sally Solari novels

"Enjoyable . . . This well-done culinary cozy should win new
fans for the ever enterprising Sally"
Publishers Weekly on *The Fragrance of Death*

"Lots of suspects and even more food"
Kirkus Reviews on *The Fragrance of Death*

"Engaging . . . Will have readers of Rita Mae Brown and Darci
Hannah dining out on a delicious mystery"
Booklist on *Murder from Scratch*

"Cover-to-cover fun for culinary cozy fans"
Publishers Weekly on *Murder from Scratch*

"A tasty combination of culinary tidbits, an unusual motive for
murder, and appended recipes for ambitious cooks"
Kirkus Reviews on *Death al Fresco*

"Cozy fans should have fun"
Publishers Weekly on *Death al Fresco*

"Engaging characters, terrific writing, and a savory blend of
musical and culinary erudition . . . Karst is a dab hand
with the red herrings"
Publishers Weekly Starred Review of *A Measure of Murder*

"Fans of Joanne Fluke, Edith Maxwell, and Lucy Burdette will
savor this food-oriented debut, seasoned with well-done plotting
and characters, complete with tasty recipes"
Library Journal on *Dying for a Taste*

For Erin, who believed in an untested author.

ONE

If not for the clatter of my bicycle bouncing down the wooden planks of the Santa Cruz Municipal Wharf, I felt certain that every tourist I whizzed past would have been startled by the loud rumblings emanating from my empty stomach.

I'd set off on my morning ride with only a cup of coffee for sustenance, and the effects of the initial caffeine buzz had now been replaced by a severe case of low blood sugar. As a result – notwithstanding the million-dollar view of the historic fisherman's wharf stretching out from the sparkling beach and the iconic roller coaster rising up behind – the only thing on my mind at that moment was the prospect of biting into one of my father's famous ricotta-and-mascarpone-filled cannoli.

I spotted Dad's tall, stocky figure standing in front of Solari's Restaurant as soon as I rounded the bend near the end of the wharf. He was turned toward me, waving, so I waved back, then quickly grabbed hold of my handlebars as I hit a nasty bump in the road. Once closer, however, I realized he wasn't waving at me. He hadn't even noticed my arrival. Rather, he was shouting and gesticulating at a form sprawled on the sidewalk at the corner of the building.

'Why the hell do you insist on camping out *here?*' I heard him yell as I approached. 'You and your kind are driving away my business!'

Wheeling up to the front entrance, I clipped out of my pedals and leaned my red-and-white road bike against the restaurant's whitewashed wood siding. Through the neon Budweiser and Amstel Light signs hanging in the window above, I could see a table of early lunchers chowing down on plates of crab salads and linguine.

'Hey, Dad. What's going on?'

'Sally.' He turned to me with a frown. 'I didn't hear you ride up.'

'Probably because you were making quite a bit of racket yourself.'

The person at his feet – a thin, gray-haired man wrapped in a dark green sleeping bag – pushed himself to an upright position and regarded the two of us with dull eyes. A fat seagull pecked at a discarded French fry not three feet from where he sat.

Dad returned the man's gaze with an angry stare. 'I've been trying for five full minutes to get this guy to move his sorry ass away from my restaurant, but he pretends like he doesn't even hear me. Maybe I should just call the cops on you,' he said to the cocooned man, 'and let *them* deal with it.'

'Maybe if you tried treating him like a human being, your powers of persuasion would be a little more effective,' I responded. 'I mean, really: "you and *your kind*"?' But my father merely shook his head and turned to walk back inside Solari's, clearly now annoyed not only with the guy in the sleeping bag but also his only daughter.

'Sorry about that,' I said to the man, who shrugged and snuggled back down, then closed his eyes. Walking my bicycle around the building to the back entrance, I wheeled it past the kitchen and into the tiny office behind the dry storage room. Dad stood at the metal desk, scowling at a sheet of paper.

'I don't need you sticking your nose into my business,' he said as I leaned my bike against the green filing cabinet in the corner of the room. 'I've managed to get by just fine for many years without having to listen to all your politically correct views on how I should run my restaurant.'

Like the time you insisted on celebrating Columbus Day at Solari's against my advice, resulting in a pack of protesters convening outside the building? was my immediate thought. Which I judiciously kept to myself.

Ever since I'd left Solari's to run Gauguin, the French-Polynesian restaurant I'd inherited from my Aunt Letta the previous year, this sort of issue had been a sore subject between my father and me. 'You think your hoity-toity foodie friends are better than me and the restaurant that put you through college and law school,' he'd told me soon after Letta had died. And although things had improved since then, I knew Dad was still sensitive to any suggestion that his traditional Italian-seafood restaurant might have become out-of-date and somehow irrelevant.

'I'm not trying to tell you how to run Solari's,' I said, taking a seat in the folding chair next to the desk. 'I just think it might help to consider the other side – what's going on from the perspective of a guy who finds himself in the position of *needing* to camp out next to your restaurant.'

Dad swiveled around to face me. 'You don't think I've considered that? Who do you take me for? Of course I've thought about all the reasons he might have ended up there. But that doesn't help any when my customers trip over him on their way to the front door. Or worse yet, when they start avoiding the place because of all the transients hanging about.'

Thrusting out the paper he'd been reading, he jabbed a finger at it. 'Just look at this – the profit-and-loss statement I got this morning from the accountant. We were down fifteen percent last month, and it's the height of the tourist season. It's gotta be 'cause of all the homeless who've descended on the wharf over the last few months.'

'Well, you can't be sure that's the reason—'

'And you can't be sure it's not,' he interrupted. 'In any case, I don't see *you* doing a whole lot about the issue. Griping to me that I'm not "nice" or "understanding" enough to some guy who hasn't had a shower in six months and who insists on blocking my doorway doesn't do zip to fix the problem. Maybe you should take your concerns to someone who could actually do something about the whole mess. Or better yet, do something *yourself.*'

I stared past my father at the poster of pasta from *Anelli* to *Ziti* tacked to the wall and swallowed. He was right. What *had* I done, other than talking about how sad it was, people losing their homes for a variety of reasons often completely beyond their control? But talking was easy. And it certainly didn't fix anything.

Before I could articulate these thoughts, however, Dad smiled and laid a beefy arm across my shoulders. 'It's okay, *bambina*. I get it. It's just a lousy situation all around. You want a cannoli? 'Cause I know that's the real reason you showed up here today.'

'Thanks. That would be great.' I stood and headed for the walk-in fridge to fetch one of his decadent pastries. My father knew me all too well.

An hour later, I was cruising down West Cliff Drive in my 1957 Thunderbird. The classic, creamy-yellow car had belonged to my Aunt Letta, and whenever I drove it, I experienced a combination of both glee and melancholy. And today, since I'd neglected to use the scrunchie I kept in the convertible for when the top was down, I was experiencing the additional sensation of strands of dark brown hair whipping into my eyes as I drove.

Luckily, it wasn't far to the Westside of Santa Cruz. I could probably have made it there faster on my bike, but I didn't like to lock the valuable Specialized Roubaix outside, and doubted the restaurant I was headed to would appreciate my bringing it indoors.

Allison was standing outside Pages and Plums when I pulled into an empty spot right in front of the place. 'I swear that car brings you good luck,' she said as I hoisted my tall body from the T-Bird's bucket seat. 'Though you should know there is, in fact, a parking lot on the side of the building.' This part of town – once home to a Wrigley's gum and Lipton's tea factory among other industrial concerns – had now been transformed into a bustling hive of wineries and brew pubs, bakeries, trendy grocery stores, and upscale eateries. As a result, parking was often at a premium in the neighborhood.

'Well, this is an even better spot,' I replied, giving my friend a hug and kiss on the cheek. 'It's the Luck of Letta. She always seemed to find the best parking space. Remember how back in high school she drove us up to San Francisco to see the Foo Fighters and found a spot just around the corner from the Fillmore?'

'Ha! I'd totally forgotten about that. And what a saint she was to take a couple goofy teenagers to a concert like that in the first place.'

'I know. Letta was way more into classic rock and jazz than grunge, that's for sure. A saint, indeed.' With an affectionate pat to the car's gleaming hood, I turned and followed Allison into the restaurant. Though 'restaurant' didn't fully describe the establishment. Pages and Plums had been open for only a month, but it was already garnering big buzz around town with its eclectic combination of café, wine bar, and culinary-themed bookshop. So when Allison, who was a friend of the owners, had invited me to try it out with her for lunch, I'd been only too happy to oblige.

As we walked through the bookstore area of the establishment, I peered at the categories posted above each of the tall wooden shelves: 'Cookbooks', 'Travel', 'Memoirs and Essays', 'History' and 'Biography', the signs read. Stopping to examine the titles on the memoir shelf, I pulled out a volume and flipped through its pages.

Allison leaned over to see what I was reading. 'It's *Tender at the Bone* by Ruth Reichl,' I said, showing her the cover. 'You know, the gal who was a restaurant critic at the *Times* and then the editor of *Gourmet* magazine? Aunt Letta absolutely adored this book and gave me her copy years ago – a first edition. But then like a dork I went and left it on the plane on my way home from college one time.' Turning to the copyright page, I smiled. 'Aha! Check it out – a first edition. Kismet. I gotta get this.'

After waiting for me to pay for the book, Allison led the way to the restaurant portion of the large room. At a quarter to one that Saturday afternoon, the dining area was packed – some folks finishing up their lunches with an espresso and biscotti, others just settling down to scan their menus. We were seated at the corner table by a lithe man in a tight black T-shirt and multiple rings on his slender fingers, who asked if we'd like still or sparkling water, then left us alone with the card stock menus.

I perused the lunch offerings. 'Oh, check it out: they have merguez sausage on a toasted baguette with onions, roasted pepper, and harissa. Looks delicious, though probably more than I want to eat right now. But the ham on rye looks good, as does the mushroom omelet with summer savory and Comté cheese.' And then I set down the menu with a sigh.

'What?' asked Allison.

'It's Aunt Letta again. For whatever reason, this place' – I waved my hand in the general direction of the kitchen and the bookshop area – 'it keeps reminding me of her. Like the book I just bought, and now this omelet special here. She used to make one a lot like it for me when I'd come to dinner.'

'Maybe it's 'cause of us talking about her earlier, so she's just on your mind right now.'

'Maybe.' I fiddled with my place setting and napkin, then sat back as the guy who'd seated us returned with our waters and asked if we had any questions about the menu. Once we'd ordered – the omelet for me and a Caprese salad with toasted sourdough bread and house-churned sweet butter for Allison – I asked how she'd come to know the owners of this new business.

'I only know one of them very well,' she replied. 'Lucinda, who runs the book side of the biz. Though I haven't seen her here yet today. I met her in grad school – she was doing the moderns like Eliot and Joyce, while I was focused on the old geezers from the Renaissance and Reformation. But after she discovered Alice B. Toklas and then MFK Fisher, Lucinda got totally hooked on food writing and changed her dissertation subject to women and the politics of eating in literature.'

'Sounds like heady stuff. So, what about the other owner? What's his – or her – deal?'

'Her.' Allison jabbed a thumb in the direction of a woman in green chef's pants and a long white apron, who was talking animatedly to a four-top on the other side of the restaurant. 'That's Kamila, Lucinda's partner, though I've only met her a few times. She used to cook for a Spanish place in Monterey, down the block from the bookstore Lucinda worked at, and I think they met by patronizing each other's businesses.'

'So by "partner", do you mean "business partner" or, you know, "*partner* partner"?'

Allison chuckled. 'Business only, unless there's something going on I haven't heard about. She's single now, but Lucinda's always been with men, and I think she told me that Kamila used to be involved with the guy who manages the dining room here. Him, I bet,' Allison added, nodding towards a slender man in a blue-and-white brocade vest and long-sleeved white shirt, who was now engaged in what looked to be a tense conversation with the woman in the apron.

As we watched, Kamila patted him on the shoulder before turning to push through the swinging door into the kitchen. The man frowned at the spot where she'd touched him, then shook his head and strode across the floor and disappeared around the corner into the wait station.

'I guess their split wasn't all that amicable,' said Allison, and I shrugged.

'Who knows? Things can get pretty stressful at a restaurant, especially one that's only been open a few weeks. But I bet having recently broken up with your co-worker – especially if one of them is the boss – could only make it that much worse.'

'True.' Allison flashed me a sly smile. 'So . . . speaking of romantic involvements, what's going on with you and Eric? How's it working out, you two being back together again after so long?'

I returned her look with an exaggerated eyebrow wag. 'Let's just say it's going quite well. I'd forgotten how nice it can be – on so many levels – to have a boyfriend in your life.'

'So you haven't returned to the ho-hum stage of your old relationship yet. That's nice.' Allison let out a soft laugh. 'Not that we're having any problems or anything, but maybe Greg and I should split up just so we can experience the excitement of getting back together again.'

'You know,' I said, 'I always thought it would be fun to have a divorce party with a black-iced cake, and the couple could hold the same knife – you know, like for a wedding – and cut the cake in half right down the middle.'

Allison appeared to be seriously considering this idea when our food arrived, at which point we both fell silent, she occupied with slathering her toast with butter and me admiring the custardy texture of my perfectly cooked eggs. After I'd taken several bites – yes, the omelet tasted as good as it looked – I finally came up for air and asked Allison how her salad was.

'Simply scrumptious!'

'A phrase you picked up in England, I gather?'

'Spot on!' she replied with a grin. Allison, a lit professor at the University of California, Santa Cruz, had recently spent a sabbatical year in London, researching her forthcoming book on what she considered the questionable historicity of the Bard of Stratford having penned the plays attributed to Shakespeare. I wisely kept out of the fray, but did enjoy listening to her passionate arguments regarding Edward de Vere, the Earl of Oxford, having been the 'true Bard'.

'Allison,' a voice came from behind me. 'I thought that was you.'

We both looked up to see a tall woman – close to my height of six feet, I guessed – who'd come up to our table. She had a swath of dark hair pulled back into a braid and wore a white T-shirt depicting an open book with a vibrant, purple plum on one of its pages.

'Lucinda!' Allison jumped up, and as the two hugged, I smiled at the difference in height, my petite friend barely reaching the other's shoulders. She turned to me. 'This is Sally Solari, who I was telling you about – the one who runs Gauguin.'

'Ah, right.' Lucinda smiled and extended a large hand. 'So glad to meet you. Do you mind?' she asked with a nod at the empty chair at our table.

'Please,' I said, and she took a seat.

'So it looks like the place is doing well.' Allison indicated the large crowd of diners around us. 'Congrats.'

'Thanks. It's been pretty intense, but so far so good. The restaurant has been doing over forty covers a day, and we've been selling a fair amount of books, so we'll see . . .' Lucinda shrugged. 'Oh, and we're even hosting our first big event in a few days – a farm-to-table dinner to benefit that Teens' Table organization.' She turned to me. 'Have you heard of it? I know some of the other restaurants around town have been helping them out, too.'

'Uh, I have heard the name, but can't say I know a whole lot about what it is. They teach kids to cook, right?'

'Yeah, that's a big part of it. But what's super cool is that the kids not only learn cooking skills, but the meals they prepare are donated to needy causes like Meals on Wheels and various homeless shelters around town.'

Allison was nodding vigorously. 'Eleanor's a member of Teens' Table,' she said, 'and absolutely loves it. Last week they made lasagne for two hundred and then distributed it to the Grey Bears.'

'It's actually partly 'cause of Allison telling me about her daughter's involvement that I got interested in the whole thing,' Lucinda explained. 'So when Alan – he's our dining-room manager – suggested doing a benefit for them, I thought it would be a great way to help out the community and also hopefully garner some good publicity for Pages and Plums at the same time.'

As the two women started discussing a mutual friend whose child was also involved with the Teens' Table organization, I savored more of my tasty omelet and mused about what Lucinda had just said. Was it mere coincidence that the issue of homelessness had come up in two separate conversations within a couple of hours today – first with my dad and now with Lucinda and Allison?

No doubt. The subject had become disturbingly common of late, as the number of folks living in tents or their vehicles seemed to increase every single day in Santa Cruz. But still . . .

I couldn't help thinking about what my father had said about not seeing *me* doing anything to help solve the problem. And he'd been right. What had I done to deserve the benefits of inheriting a fancy restaurant in a wealthy town, while others were scrambling simply to find money for food and a place to live?

Kismet, indeed.

I waited for a break in the other two's conversation, then asked, 'So when is this farm-to-table dinner you're hosting?'

'This coming Monday,' Lucinda said. 'The night Pages and Plums is usually closed for business.'

'As is Gauguin,' I said. 'You need any help with the event?'

TWO

Lucinda glanced at Allison as if to ask, 'Is she for real?' then turned to me, a slow smile spreading across her broad face. 'Heck, *yeah*. We could use all the help we can get, especially from the head chef of Santa Cruz's premier fine-dining establishment.'

'Well,' I said, with an exaggerated clearing of the throat, 'I think my co-owner and executive chef, Javier, might have some qualms about that description of me, but certainly not of the restaurant. Thanks.' After taking a sip of sparkling water to soothe my larynx, which I'd irritated with my theatrics, I asked Lucinda, 'So are you in charge of the event?'

'Heavens, no. I'm pretty useless about anything to do with food. The dinner is mostly Alan and Kamila's baby, but I'm absolutely doing everything I can to help out. So far I've mostly just been tasked with soliciting items for the auction that we'll be holding that night. Oh,' she said, touching Allison on the hand, 'and you'll love this. One of the items is this amazing book I'm thinking might fetch well over a thousand dollars. Though Sally's probably going to be more interested,' she added with a glance my way, 'since it's a cookbook.'

'Oh, yeah?' I was trying to imagine a cookbook that could be worth that much money. *Maybe a first-edition Escoffier?* 'Which one?' I asked.

'It's technically two books – a rare boxed set of *Mastering the Art of French Cooking*, Volumes One and Two, each signed by both Julia Child and Simone Beck. They belonged to the father of the guy who donated it, who I gather knew Julia's husband Paul back when they lived in Boston.'

'Wow. That's a pretty generous gift for him to donate.'

'I know. But he's apparently a big supporter of Teens' Table. I think he has a son with a drug problem who went through the program, got clean, and then went on to some fancy-schmancy cooking school. Anyway, the books are in that locked case over there. I can show them to you sometime, if you want.'

Looking up, Lucinda spied the guy in the brocade vest standing at the host stand and waved him over to our table. 'Alan,' she said, 'this is Sally Solari, who owns—'

'Co-owns,' I put in.

'Right, co-owns Gauguin, and she's offered to help out at our big dinner Monday night.'

Alan, who'd been wearing the polite but mildly bored expression of someone being introduced to a person of small import, straightened his shoulders and graced me with a bright smile. 'Is that so? That's marvelous! We'd love to have your assistance. Were you thinking of prep work, or cooking the night of the event, or . . .?'

'Whatever you need, just so long as it's not during a time Gauguin is open. Though I'm thinking that cooking at the event itself would be the most fun. Will it be held here, or somewhere else?'

'Here. We're gonna set out long tables in the parking lot, since the dining room only seats about thirty people and we're expecting double that. And that way, the cooking can all happen in our own kitchen. Not as atmospheric as those farm-to-table events held at actual farms, but far easier logistically. And I'm having some friends come string lights and put up other decorations, so it should be quite the festive affair.'

He glanced around the dining room, which had started to thin out. A couple of tables were still working on their lunches, but it didn't look as if anyone was waiting for their meal to arrive. 'If you want,' Alan said, 'why don't you come on into the kitchen when you're done eating, and Kamila can show you around and talk to you about the best way you can be of help. She's the boss with regard to all the cooking around these parts.'

I nodded agreement. 'Sounds like a plan.'

'Good. I'll let her know to expect you. And thanks again.'

'I should go, too,' said Lucinda, rising from her seat. 'There's just me and one other guy in the bookstore today, so I should make sure he's okay. But I'll see you soon. And you, too, I hope,' she added, giving Allison a quick hug.

After they'd both left, Allison reached across the table and squeezed my hand. 'That was so nice of you to offer to help out like that, Sal. Especially since I know it's not like you have a ton of free time on your hands. But I think it should be fun. And you'll get to work with Eleanor – how cool is that?'

At my blank look, she elaborated. 'The kids with Teens' Table – they'll be helping out at the benefit. It's part of the whole deal, to get them involved as well.'

'Ah . . .' But what I was really thinking was, *cooking with a bunch of kids? Yikes.* What on earth had I gotten myself into?

Once we'd topped off our delicious lunches with a shared crème brûlée and dainty cups of espresso, Allison and I paid our bill, then headed across the dining room to peer in through the pass. Kamila was wiping down the griddle with a wet side towel, but when she saw our faces at the window, she set it down and waved for us to come on in.

Ever curious about other restaurant kitchens, I looked about me. A six-burner range with two ovens sat below the pass, above which hung racks of pots, pans, whisks, ladles, and tongs. Next to this was the *mise en place* cart, with ten inserts for the *à la minute* cooking ingredients, then, farther down the line, I spotted the flat-top griddle and an electric grill station. Against the opposite wall of the long, narrow room ran a stainless-steel table with a work-space and row of appliances: a food processor, stand mixer, slicer and microwave. Shelves below the table held mixing bowls, hotel pans, and an array of different-size containers.

'Nice set-up,' I remarked. 'And I love the yellow KitchenAid – it's almost the exact same color as my car.'

'Perhaps we should introduce them,' said Kamila with a laugh. 'Though Gertrude can be quite snobbish about her pedigree, so you may not approve of the match.'

'Well, my T-Bird can be rather temperamental when she wants, so perhaps they'd be perfect together.' Hands on hips, I gazed admiringly at the shiny yellow-and-chrome mixer. 'And now you've made me wonder why I've never given a name to my car.'

'Well, Gertrude pretty much named herself. It just popped into my head the first time I used her, as I was whipping up a batch of German spritz cookies.'

'I like it,' said Allison. 'Though if she's anything like her name-sake in *Hamlet*, I'd be cautious about letting her spend too much time with your T-Bird, Sally.'

Kamila's uncertain smile suggested she wasn't all that familiar with the story of the Prince of Denmark's faithless mother. Turning to me once more, she changed the subject. 'So, I hear tell you're going to help out this Monday at our farm-to-table dinner. It's very generous of you to offer your time and your expertise for this great cause.'

'Well, I figured it was the least I could do . . .' Was my face turning red? Because I certainly didn't feel that I deserved a whole lot of praise for making the offer, especially as it was largely due to the shaming of my decidedly not-progressive father.

The cook didn't appear to notice anything awry, however, and beckoned us to follow her to a tiny office just off the kitchen. Sifting through a pile of papers on the small desk that took up most of the available space, she pulled one out and handed it to me. 'Here, take a look at the menu for the meal.'

I set down my Ruth Reichl book and read the items aloud for the benefit of Allison. It was an impressive list: curried carrot soup drizzled with ginger crème fraîche; spinach, fennel, and plum salad with a bleu cheese and shallot vinaigrette; a choice of blackened Chinook salmon with lemon-butter sauce, sautéed collard greens and garlic mashed potatoes, Duroc pork medallions in a brandy-plum glaze with a sautéed string bean medley and roasted fingerling potatoes, or risotto with chanterelles, parmesan cheese, peas, and thyme; and for dessert, grilled peaches with fresh-churned vanilla bean ice cream and a balsamic-plum-black-pepper reduction.

'Dang,' I said when finished. 'I just ate an enormous lunch, but this makes me hungry all over again. And I like how you got plums in there several times.'

'Yeah, well, we do have to promote Pages and Plums as much as possible, right? And of course we'll include the names of all the various farms providing the fruits and vegetables, as well as the meat and seafood purveyors, on the printed menus for the dinner.'

'Of course.'

Kamila nodded at the paper in my hand. 'So what do you think? Anything on there you feel especially drawn to working on? I'm going to have the kids do the salad and soup prep the afternoon before the dinner, and the ice-cream churning, as well.'

Ah, good. So I likely wouldn't be actually cooking alongside a bunch of children. 'Do you have all the folks you need on the hot line? If not, I'd be happy to lend a hand there.'

'I was hoping you'd say exactly that,' said Kamila with a grin, 'as I was thinking I'd have to be on the line by myself. My assistant cook is going to be supervising the older Teens' Table kids with the soup and salads, and the prep cook will have his hands rather full with all the veg and cold food preparation, so we're actually fairly short-staffed in the kitchen. You came to our rescue at the perfect time.'

'Glad to hear it.' I handed her the menu back. 'What time would you like me to show up? I have the whole day off, so I could come by anytime.'

Kamila thought a moment. 'Well, the event starts at five, so how about two o'clock? That way, if there are any last-minute fires to put out – hopefully not literally – you'll be here to help out.'

'Okay, sounds good,' I said, picking up my book. 'And I'll see if I can drum up some more customers for you, too. Unless it's already sold out?'

'We have a few more spots open, but not many. So tell them to go online soon and buy their tickets if they want to come.'

'Will do. Oh, and let's exchange numbers in case you need to get hold of me, like if you want me here earlier or something.'

'Good idea,' said Kamila. 'You never know.'

Once Kamila and I entered our cell numbers into one another's phone, Allison and I headed back into the dining room and through the bookstore. 'I think I'll ask Eric if he wants to come,' I said as we emerged into the bright sunlight. 'I'm assuming he can sit with you and Greg? That is, if you're going . . .'

'Absolutely, on both counts. And that way I can pump him about what he thinks about your newly ignited romance.'

'Great. Let me know what you find out.'

'Maybe, maybe not, girlfriend.'

It had now been well over a year since I'd taken over Gauguin from my aunt – and since the brutal murder that had resulted in my inheriting the place. But rarely did a day go by when I didn't think of Letta. Her essence was imprinted in virtually every object I'd pass moving from room to room in what had been her beloved restaurant: the woodblock prints of sugar cane and taro plants that she'd brought home from a trip to Hawai'i. The carbon steel sauté pans she'd splurged on when first opening the restaurant, because that's what she'd seen the chefs use in Parisian bistros and brasseries. The case full of cookbooks, travelogues and food memoirs upstairs in her office.

No, Javier's and my *office, now.*

Even the coffee station reminded me of Letta. 'No way would I ever serve that wimpy, drip coffee to my customers,' she'd loved to say. 'Only espresso and cappuccino here at Gauguin. And if someone insists on a "regular" cup of coffee, well then, they'll just have to settle for an Americano.'

This afternoon, even more than usual, my aunt was on my mind as I pulled into the Gauguin parking lot and gazed at the building's bright orange walls and pale violet trim. 'Mango' and 'orchid', she'd called the colors. And as I stepped through the side door into the cold food preparation area, I couldn't help glancing down at the spot on the floor where Letta's body had been discovered that blustery day in April.

Doing my best to shake off this grisly memory, I greeted Tomás, who was at the long, wooden cutting board deboning a bluefin tuna for tonight's fish special. 'That's a real beauty,' I said as he cut into its ruby-red flesh. 'Was it caught here in the bay?'

'Uh-huh. There's been a run on 'em the past two days, is what I heard.'

I watched as he deftly sliced off the inky-black blood line and tossed it into the garbage. 'Well, I hope we don't sell out tonight, 'cause I think I know what I want for a late-night supper after closing.'

'Ha! That's just what Javier said, too.' The prep cook set down his filleting knife, then wiped his hands on the towel that hung from his apron tie. 'So, by the way, Javier told me he might give me some more training on the line tonight. That is, if it's okay with you . . .'

'Absolutely. We've been talking about getting you more time there, and since both Brandon and Kris are on tonight, there'll be plenty of hands on deck to cover the stuff you usually do. And hey, I don't mind being a runner and plating up appetizers and salads, if need be. It'd be a good refresher course.'

Tomás smiled. 'You're the best, Sally. Thanks.'

I meant what I'd said. Tomás was going to make an excellent line cook, and perhaps even a sous chef someday. The downside, however, was that once he was fully trained on the line and grill stations, we'd have to look for another person to fill his shoes as prep cook – no easy task these days. Rent was ridiculously expensive in Santa Cruz, which meant that those who could afford to live in our town on a prep cook's salary – even one at the high end of the scale – were scarce, indeed. Many workers in the service industry either lived with their extended family or a large group of friends, or else they were forced to make long commutes from towns as far away as Castroville and Salinas.

But I couldn't worry about that right now. We'd be open for business in an hour and a half, and I had plenty of my own prep work to focus on without stressing about hiring new employees down the road. With a nod to Tomás, I headed upstairs to change into my chef's whites, my thoughts already moving on to seared ahi with cauliflower-celeriac purée and coq au vin au Gauguin.

Five hours later, however, once the tickets had finally slowed down after a busy Saturday night, I found myself again pondering the dilemma of finding new workers. And also the more far-reaching ramifications of the worsening housing crisis in our town. If someone like Tomás, a smart, hardworking guy in his late twenties, had to live with his parents and grandparents in order to remain in Santa Cruz, it was no wonder we had so many people living on the streets. The only reason I had such a lovely house to live in was because my father – who'd inherited the place from his sister, Letta – rented it out to me at far below the market value.

But what was the answer? The cost of housing was unlikely to go down anytime soon. Not with our temperate climate, glorious coastline and towering redwoods – not to mention all those nouveau-riche techies from Silicon Valley clamoring to move over the hill to our bucolic beach town now that telecommuting had become the norm. If the current upward trend in prices was any indication, the crisis was only going to get far worse in the coming years.

Squeezing behind Javier and Tomás, I checked to make sure none of the hot-line inserts needed replenishing, my jaw clenched in frustration. But as I glanced out through the pass, all gloomy thoughts were swept away at the sight of Eric, sitting at the small table nearest the kitchen working on a crossword puzzle. As if detecting my gaze, he looked up, and the vision of his tousled, blond hair and boyish grin sent a shiver of pleasure down my spine.

I walked out to his table, and he stood to give me a light kiss on the lips. 'Hey, babe. Thought I'd come in for some coffee and dessert in the hope you'd be able to join me for a bit, once things slow down.'

As if on cue, Brandon appeared at the table and set down a slice of olallieberry-lemon tart, the special our dessert chef, Amy, had created for the night. The dollop of whipped cream spiked with lemon zest and ginger that nestled against the warm pastry was already beginning to melt into a pool of creamy deliciousness.

'*Mangia, mangia*,' I encouraged Eric, waving at him to sit back down. 'Eat while it's still hot. I've got a few more things to do right now, but I can join you for a few minutes after that.'

'Awesome. You go work while I enjoy this hella dessert.'

I left him to it and returned to the kitchen to help wrap up the unused food and stow it in the walk-in fridge, cart the dirty pots and pans to the dish room, and wipe down the counters in the *garde manger*. Since I hadn't been on the line that night, I was thankfully spared the chore of cleaning all the spills and grease off the Wolf range.

Twenty minutes later I joined Eric again at the small table. He started to rise when I emerged into the dining room, but then quickly sat back down.

'Thanks,' I said, taking a seat.

'Huh?'

'For restraining yourself from pulling out my chair. I appreciate the effort it took.'

Eric shook his head with a bemused smile as he sipped from his espresso. It had taken years of training, but I'd finally managed to cure him of this chivalric impulse, something ingrained in him from a young age by his socially conscious mother, and which I found tremendously annoying.

'I got a ticket to that dinner thing Monday night,' he said, wisely changing the subject. 'Looks like a great cause, and an even better meal. Did you check out the menu they posted online? I opted for the pork.'

'Of course you did.' Eric had quite the love affair with meat. 'And yeah, I've seen the menu. Kamila – that's the head cook at Pages and Plums – she showed it to me this afternoon. Kinda made me wish I was attending the event instead of cooking.'

'I'll see if I can try and save you some of mine for a doggie bag.'

'Right. That'd be a first, you not finishing every single morsel on your plate. But thanks for the sentiment. Oh, hey, Brandon,' I said as the server passed by, 'could you see if there's any of that tart left, and if so, snag me a piece?' We'd sold out of the tuna, but a flaky, fruity pastry drowning in cream would make for a fine consolation prize.

'Sure thing, Sally.'

I turned back to Eric. 'So, was there a specific reason you came by tonight – other than the burning need to see me again after what, twelve long hours?'

'Only that, my dear, only that.' He removed his horn-rim glasses and wiped them on his white cloth napkin, all the while avoiding my gaze.

There is something else, I decided.

'Okay, out with it. What's going on? Is it that new case you got? The one with the guy who clobbered his drinking buddy with a bottle of St Pauli Girl?' Eric was a prosecutor with the district attorney's office and had been growing ever more dissatisfied with what he considered to be the small-time cases he'd been assigned over the past few months.

'Allegedly clobbered,' he said. 'And it was a Newcastle Brown Ale. But no, that's not it. I actually want to talk about something far more enjoyable.'

'Oh, yeah?'

He turned his demitasse cup around on its tiny saucer a few times, then finally looked up into my eyes. 'I'm thinking it might be time for us to move in together. You know . . . again. What do you think?'

What *did* I think? I loved spending time with Eric and, in particular, had grown quite fond of our evenings – and nights – together. But to move in with him?

'Where would we live?' I asked.

He sighed. 'Yeah, that's the five-billion-dollar question. Your place or mine? And I've been thinking about that, as well. It makes sense to me that, since I actually own my place and you're only renting, you should move in with me. That way I don't lose the equity I've accrued.'

'Huh-uh. No way. I love where I live. It's my *home*. And what about Buster? He's lived in that house ever since he was a puppy. Plus, it would be crazy to live on the second floor of a condo with a dog. What about when he needs to go out in the middle of the night?'

'You have to do that now,' Eric replied. 'Or I do. I seem to remember it was me who took him outside to pee at about three a.m. last night.'

'Yeah, well, I'm thinking of getting a dog door installed at my place.'

'Uh-huh . . .'

'And besides, I don't think *I* could stand to live somewhere without my own backyard to hang out in, even ignoring Buster.'

'So, impasse.' Eric finished his coffee, a decided droop now to his shoulders.

I reached over and took his hand. 'For now. We'll figure something out.'

'Uh-huh,' he said again.

THREE

At a quarter to two on Monday afternoon, I pulled into the exact same parking spot outside Pages and Plums that I'd scored two days earlier. The front door was locked, so I headed around to the side, where a host of people were scurrying about the parking lot. Six long tables had been set up, as well as several pop-up pavilions, and two teenage girls were busy distributing the folding chairs. Several other kids were dragging utility carts loaded down with cardboard boxes from the kitchen into the parking lot.

Spotting Eleanor, I walked over to where she was helping unload wine glasses and placing them atop the white tablecloths. 'Hey, Sally!' she said, and raced over to give me a hug. 'Mom said you'd be cooking tonight. It's totally *sick*, us getting to work together!'

'I know, super rad,' I responded, hoping my attempt at Gen Z lexicon wasn't too far off. It must have passed some sort of muster, because the thirteen-year-old merely grinned and took my arm, leading me over to where several of her cohorts were trying to figure out the mechanics of a pair of old-school ice-cream makers.

'Hey, guys,' Eleanor announced to the group. 'This is Sally, the celebrity chef I was telling you about who's a friend of my mom's.'

'Well, I'm not really a—'

'Do you know how to put this together?' interrupted a boy with short, curly hair and a mild case of acne.

'Uh, yeah, I think so . . .' I knelt to examine the contraption. My mother had loved using her father's ancient hand-crank machine when I was a kid, but after Mom died, Dad had bought one of those electric models with an insert that went in the freezer. So it had been a while since I'd put one of the old-fashioned churns together.

It only took a minute, however, before it all came back to me. *Good.* The 'celebrity chef' would pass the test.

'Right,' I said. 'So you pour alternating layers of ice and salt into this outside area here and pour the custard – the ice-cream mixture – into the middle container. Then you put on the lid, attach this crank here, and start cranking away. And as the ice melts, you have to pour in more ice and salt.'

'How come you need to use salt?' asked Eleanor. 'That seems weird.'

'It's 'cause cream doesn't freeze until it's colder than the temperature of melting ice. But if you add salt to the ice, it lowers its melting point, so everything can get cold enough to turn into ice cream.'

'Okay . . .' she said, her frown telling me she didn't really understand.

'Look, all you gotta know is that it has to do with the chemistry of the different freezing points of the cream compared to the water. And you don't really even need to understand that in order to make the stuff. But feel free to Google it if you want to know more. Oh, look. Great,' I said, the relief no doubt evident in my voice. 'Here comes Alan. I'll let him help you get started.'

As the dining-room manager got the kids going with the ice cream, I headed inside to the kitchen, where I found Kamila in the pantry sorting through a box of potatoes. A tall, gawky girl of about fifteen stood at her side, watching as the cook pulled out one of the fingerlings – which bore more than a passing resemblance to the gnarled digits of an old man – and held it up for display.

'This one, see? It's got a big rotten spot here.'

The girl nodded as Kamila tossed the bad potato into a bucket with 'compost' written in black magic marker on its side.

'Okay, I'll leave you to it. Once you're done sorting, wash them all, then coat them with olive oil and spread 'em out on those baking trays over there.' Turning to me, she smiled. 'Oh boy, I am *so* glad you're here, Sally. We've had a bit of a mix-up, and my other line cook didn't show. You up for prepping the risotto?'

'Sure, no problem. We make it at Gauguin all the time: cook the rice about three quarters of the way done, then chill it down till time to fire the orders, and finish each off with a ladle of stock, then the cheese and peas.'

'Right. Except all the plates will need to be ready at once.'

'Duh.' I slapped my forehead. 'Of course, since it's banquet service.'

'But it looks like it's only fifteen people who've opted for the vegetarian main, so it should be no big deal.'

'Easy-peasy,' I said. 'Pun intended. You got the ingredient list handy?'

I set to work on the risotto and, once that was prepped, moved on to the balsamic-plum-black-pepper reduction for the dessert, and then the garlic mashed potatoes, which I set atop a pot of simmering water to keep warm till service. At five o'clock, the guests started streaming into the parking lot, where they headed for the bar set up under one of the pavilions, then stood around sipping wines donated to the event by a local winery up in the Santa Cruz Mountains.

Since I wouldn't be needed again until we started firing the first course, I took the opportunity to step outside and, spying Eric, Allison, and Greg chatting with Lucinda, joined their group. I declined the glass of bubbly Eric offered me, but did accept some fizzy water.

They were looking over the silent auction items set out under another pavilion: four rounds of golf from a course down in Carmel; a double magnum of Pinot Noir from the winery who'd donated tonight's wines; dinner for two at several local restaurants (including Gauguin); six day-passes for the Boardwalk; a set of blown-glass bowls; several watercolors and monotype prints; and a handful of other items.

'Dude, check this out,' said Eric, peering down at a sheet of paper. 'Someone bid *two grand* for a couple cookbooks.'

I glanced over at Lucinda, who was beaming. 'And I'm hoping it will go even higher after folks have had a few more glasses of wine,' she said.

'I see the books aren't here, so where are they?' Eric was still staring in amazement at the auction paper.

'Inside the store, in a locked cabinet.' Lucinda patted her pants pocket, then winked at Eric as he looked up. 'But anyone who's interested in bidding on them is welcome to see the gorgeous books. Feel like bumping up the current bid? You've got until right before dessert is served, when we'll announce all the winners.'

Eric backed quickly away from the auction table, as if afraid of accidentally committing himself to spending a couple of grand on the rare volumes, and in the process barely missed colliding with a tall, gray-haired man in a turquoise blazer.

'Oops, sorry,' he said.

The newcomer smiled and held up his unspilled glass of red

wine. 'No harm no foul.' Turning to Lucinda, he graced her with
a toothy smile. 'Hello, my dear.'

'*So* good to see you, Saul,' she said, the exuberance in her eyes
reminding me of Buster when he'd just spotted a squirrel. 'Your
gift has been a very big hit, as you can see.'

Ahhh . . . The guy who donated the Julia Child books.

Lucinda introduced us all around, then, spotting Alan gesturing
to her from the side door into the dining room and bookstore, she
waved back. 'I better go see what he wants,' she said, and excused
herself from our group.

'I hear tell from Lucinda that your dad knew Paul Child
back in Boston,' I said to Saul. 'Was he as marvelous as he appeared
in *Julie and Julia*?'

Saul chuckled. 'Well, if you mean, did he *look* like Stanley
Tucci, then I hate to disappoint you, but no. But if you're asking
about his personality, the answer is an emphatic yes. Perhaps even
more so. I was only a kid at the time, but I could tell that Paul
was a real mensch.'

I was about to ask Saul to elaborate, eager to hear more about
the charming man who'd captured Julia Child's heart, when we
were interrupted by the clinking of a glass calling us all to attention. The chattering of the crowd slowed, then finally ceased, and
Lucinda stepped up to a mic that had been placed next to the auction
table. After introducing herself, Kamila, and Alan, she spoke briefly
about Pages and Plums, then invited the executive director of Teens'
Table, Stephanie Pham, to say a few words.

'Hi, all, and welcome,' said Stephanie. 'Thank you all so very
much for coming here tonight, and for bidding on all these fabulous
auction items. I'm not going to take up much of your time, but I
will say that these youngsters' – she waved at the group of about
a dozen teenagers standing at attention – 'are some of the most
enthusiastic and hardworking people I've ever had the pleasure of
working with. And the support they provide for our community is
beyond compare. Just last week, Teens' Table prepared over one
hundred hot meals and helped deliver them to the Sunshine Center
for Health and Housing. So, please join me in giving them a hand
to thank them for all they do.'

We all applauded, with a few hoots and hollers thrown in for
good measure, and at a nod from Stephanie, the kids bowed in
unison with a practiced air.

'So, in conclusion,' the executive director said once we'd quieted down again, 'the best way you can thank them for all their hard work is to make fabulously high bids on all of these wonderful items that have been so generously donated by our local businesses. Thank you very much.'

With a nod to the crowd, she stepped away from the mic and was replaced by Alan. 'Okay!' he said with a flourish. 'Please take your seats now, as it's time to eat!'

My cue to get back inside.

The young gal who'd been tasked with prepping the potatoes was at the long counter in the kitchen, ladling soup into white ceramic bowls. Kamila followed behind, squirting a spiral of ginger crème fraîche atop each bowl, then finishing it with a scattering of chopped chives. A trio of Pages and Plums servers stood by to place the bowls on banquet trays as soon as they were garnished.

Looking up at my approach, Kamila held out the squirt bottle and container of chives. 'You wanna take this over? That way I can get started on plating up the salads for the next course.'

'Sure thing,' I said, and set to work.

In between the soup and the salad course, I popped over to the bookstore area to take a gander at that boxed set of cookbooks signed by Julia Child and Simone Beck. (The project initially had a third author as well, Louisette Bertholle, who bowed out soon after the first volume of *Mastering the Art of French Cooking* went to press.) Several others were milling about the locked cabinet, peering inside to see what could possibly be so valuable as to garner what had now shot up to a $2,500 bid.

'Seems pretty ridiculous for a couple of cookbooks,' said a man with a mass of dark hair pulled back into a ponytail. He had on a loose-fitting Hawaiian shirt which had seen better days, and from the look of his faded cotton pants and slip-on canvas shoes, I got the impression that this constituted 'dressing up' for the guy.

'Oh, c'mon, Phillip,' said the woman next to him, 'they're first editions, signed by *Julia Child*!' Unlike the other, she wore meticulously styled hair, a tailored jacket and slacks, and a pair of shiny leather pumps.

The man shrugged, unimpressed. 'Whatever you say, Meg.'

I got the distinct impression that this was not the first time he'd said those words to her. *They must be a couple*, I concluded.

'But at least it's all going to a good cause,' Phillip added by way of concession.

The woman next to me piped up: 'I used to watch Julia Child on TV with my mother when I was a little girl. Mom would take notes and then try out the recipes at dinner parties she and my dad hosted for their friends.'

Another gal added her account of trying out Julia's detailed recipe for cassoulet, and before long we were all trading stories about the culinary icon who'd almost single-handedly brought French cooking into American homes in the 1960s. Even Phillip had something to contribute – about having once visited the town where Julia and Paul famously ate the sole meunière she claimed to have been the catalyst for her lifelong passion for food and cooking.

As we were standing there chatting, Lucinda strode into the room, followed by a man in a silk Tommy Bahama shirt, cream-colored linen slacks, and what looked to be some very expensive hair implants. *The Yin to Phillip's Yang*, was my amused thought.

'Here, let me show the books to you, Julian. They're simply exquisite!' Pulling a keychain from her pocket, Lucinda unlocked the wood-and-glass cabinet and carefully removed the boxed set. 'You have clean hands, yes?' she asked.

'Of course.'

She placed volume one into his eager fingers. As Julian opened the book to the title page, we all crowded around to see the cooking diva's signature, scrawled in blue ink. Below it was that of Simone Beck, the flourishes of her S and B far more exotic than Julia's decorous handwriting. But it was the French Chef's autograph over which we all oohed and ahed.

'It looks to be in fairly good condition,' the potential buyer remarked, flipping through the pages. 'And the other volume is the same?' I wasn't positive, but I thought I detected a slight British accent – of the upper crust variety.

'Absolutely,' said Lucinda. 'Would you care to see?'

'No, that's all right.' He handed the book back, gracing her with an ingratiating smile. 'Thank you. I truly appreciate your taking the time to speak with me and show me the books.'

After the man had left, the woman with Phillip asked who he was. 'Julian owns a small used and antiquarian bookstore here in town,' Lucinda replied. 'B-J Booksellers, which has an online as well as bricks-and-mortar store.'

Ah, so that's why he looked familiar. I'd been in his shop several times, though it had been a while since my last visit.

'So I'm thinking he must believe the Julia Child books are worth even more than twenty-five-hundred dollars,' Lucinda went on with a grin, 'else he wouldn't have asked me to let him have a look at them. And he certainly was eager to get me away from the crowd to talk to me about the books.'

'Can I have a look, too?' one of the women asked. When the rest of us voiced the same request, Lucinda – after carefully inspecting our hands – allowed us to take turns holding the precious book and gawking at the famous signatures. Once we'd all had our fun, she replaced the boxed set into the cabinet and locked the door.

I then returned to the kitchen, where I set about making sure the *mise en place* for the three main courses was in order. This is the set-up – generally a collection of stainless-steel inserts – for the prepped ingredients needed for the various dishes, all within easy reach of the sauté cooks. I studied the menu and then the items before me: blackened seasoning, sliced plums, brandy, clarified butter, lemon quarters, chanterelles, grated cheese, shelled peas, minced thyme, and chopped chives.

Check.

In addition, I needed a pot of heated vegetable broth, so I fetched the liquid from the reach-in fridge, poured it into a stock pot which I set over a medium flame. The salmon steaks, pork medallions and par-cooked risotto were all at hand, ready to go. And someone else would be on the collard greens, string beans and potatoes, so I didn't need to worry about the sides.

Kamila joined me at the line as I was stirring the broth. 'We've got twenty-one fish, twenty-five pork, and fourteen risotto,' she said, 'but best to make a few extra of each, just in case.'

'Gotcha.'

Pulling several large skillets from the rack above us, she ran a side towel over their surfaces, then set them on the stove. 'How 'bout I take the pork and you take the salmon, and we can each do half of the risotto?'

'Sounds good. How soon till we fire everything?'

'Alan says they've already cleared about half the salad plates, so we can go ahead and start now.'

And with that, the show began. Wielding our sauté pans as if in a well-choreographed *pas de deux*, Kamila and I flipped our salmon steaks and pork medallions, reached for ladles of butter and handfuls of plums, and splashed in lemon juice and brandy, all the while stirring our pots of creamy risotto.

Then, the first round of dishes plated up, we wiped down the pans with paper towels and started all over again, with barely a moment to take a breath in between. But no matter. As restaurant nights went, this was a cake walk – only thirty covers apiece. And Kamila and I worked well as a team, the result of the countless hours we'd both spent at the stoves of commercial kitchens, dancing adroitly around other cooks as they performed their magic at the stove.

Once the mains had all been taken outdoors to be distributed to the eager diners, Kamila and I leaned against the stainless-steel counter and wiped the sweat from our faces. It was probably close to ninety degrees in the kitchen, what with the heat from the ovens and all six burners having been going full blast for the past thirty minutes.

'How about a beer?' Kamila asked. 'I think we've earned one. Or maybe three.'

'Sounds good to me.' Following her over to the wait station, I selected a Sierra Nevada pale ale from the drinks fridge. We opened our bottles, then wandered over to the screened kitchen door and peered out at the goings-on in the parking lot. What with everyone excitedly digging into their salmon, pork, and risotto, the crowd was momentarily quiet, the clinking of flatware on ceramic plates rising above the low murmur of those few who were talking.

The Teens' Table kids had an area to themselves and were just sitting down to eat the mac 'n' cheese and tossed salad that comprised their meal, having now completed all their duties, save the serving of the dessert course. Over at the auction table, Lucinda was studying the bids that had been made, alternatively nodding and frowning as she moved from sheet to sheet.

At a sudden noise, I looked over to see Alan standing at the table farthest from the kitchen. He was shouting at one of the guests, who had swiveled around in their chair and appeared to be giving their own back in return.

'What on earth?' said Kamila, setting down her beer to push open the screen door. But seeing Lucinda spring into action, she stayed put. Lucinda strode between the tables, gripped Alan by the elbow, and steered him to the edge of the parking lot, all the while talking intently in his ear.

Once she'd dragged him away from the crowd, many of whom had turned to see what the commotion was all about, Lucinda stood, hands on hips, giving what looked to be a stern lecture to her dining-room manager. He pointed feebly toward the person at the table, who I could now see was a thirty-something woman. She had short blonde hair and was wearing a navy-and-white-striped shirt in the style of a French sailor's jersey.

But Lucinda was having none of it. Shaking her head at whatever excuse Alan had given her, she said a few more words, then headed over to speak with the woman in the striped jersey. Alan was clearly not pleased. He glared at the two of them for a moment, then stalked off toward the bar, helped himself to a large glass of wine, and stood there sulking between swigs.

Kamila and I watched as Lucinda made her apologies to the dinner guest, then returned to where she'd been standing before the ruckus had begun. The cook picked up her beer and drained the bottle. 'I so don't need that,' she said, letting out a slow breath.

I responded with a sympathetic smile. 'No fun when the staff gets into it with a guest, that's for sure.'

'Nope.' Kamila walked back into the kitchen, hefted a stack of dessert plates, and began spreading them out on the counter. 'Wanna grab the peaches from the warming oven?' she asked me, and I complied.

It thankfully wasn't a common problem, restaurant workers arguing with their customers, but it happened often enough to be the stuff of nightmares for any owner or boss in the service industry. Incidents like this pretty much guaranteed a scathing one-star review on Yelp.

Working without speaking, we prepped the dessert course. While Kamila arranged the peaches on the plates, I reheated the balsamic-plum-black-pepper reduction that would be drizzled atop the grilled fruit. After about ten minutes, Lucinda popped her head through the screen door. 'I'm gonna announce the winners of the auction, if you want to come on out and be there for it,' she said.

I turned off the flame under the plum reduction, and we followed her outside. Lucinda tapped several times on the mic to make sure it was working, then called everyone to attention.

'We'll be serving our tantalizing dessert course in a little bit, but before that, it's time to announce the winners of our fabulous auction items.' Lucinda cleared her throat, then held up the sheets of papers in her hand for display. 'And here they are! The first item is a three-course dinner for two at Tamarind. And the winning bid of one hundred seventy-five dollars goes to . . . Tracy Eriksen!'

A woman with long silky gray hair stood up and waved, and we all gave her a round of applause.

'Oh, and by the way,' said Lucinda, once the crowd had quieted down, 'all the winners should come see me at the auction table after I've finished my announcing here, where you can pay for your items. Okay, on to the round of golf . . .'

She was clearly saving the cookbooks for last, and I knew there were quite a few items to go before them, so I dragged a folding chair over to where Eric, Allison and Greg were sitting. Eric again offered me a glass of bubbly, and this time I gratefully accepted.

After about fifteen minutes, Lucinda held up the last remaining paper in her hand. 'And now for the *pièce de résistance*,' she said, flashing a cat-who-ate-the-canary grin. 'The magnificent first edition boxed set of volumes one and two of *Mastering the Art of French Cooking*, signed by both Julia Child and Simone Beck. Oh, Kamila,' she said, turning to where the cook still leaned against the kitchen door. 'You want to fetch the beautiful books from the cabinet before I announce the winning bid?'

Kamila caught the set of keys that Lucinda tossed her way and headed inside.

While we waited for her to return, I asked Eric what he'd thought of the meal. 'Not bad,' he said. 'Though the pork was slightly overcooked, to my taste.'

'Ah, well I was on the salmon, so not my fault.'

'Well, the salmon was cooked perfectly,' said Greg. 'Crispy outside but still nice and tender with a bit of pink in the center. In fact, it—'

Allison's husband didn't get a chance to finish his sentence, as a collective gasp rose from the crowd, drowning him out. I swiveled around in my seat to see Kamila at the side door from the parking lot into the bookstore, a look of horror in her eyes.

'Alan's dead,' she said. 'And the books are gone.'

FOUR

There was a moment of silence – probably only a second or two, though it seemed longer – before the crowd erupted into chaos: chairs thrown back, pushing and shoving, panicked shouting, and people charging this way and that like a colony of frenzied ants. Most were headed away from the building, but a fair number crowded toward the door, and I was afraid they might trample poor Kamila, who still stood there as if frozen in place.

'Stop!' I yelled at the top of my lungs. This served to slow everyone down, but I knew the pause would be only momentary. I glanced at Eric, who nodded back, and the two of us pushed our way through the throng toward the door.

Eric stepped up on to the doorstep next to Kamila and raised his hands above his head. 'Okay, everyone!' he boomed. 'You need to settle down right now and listen to me.'

'Why should we listen to you?' someone called out.

'Because he's a district attorney,' I shouted in return, 'and because you're all acting like a bunch of *lunatics*.'

Okay, maybe not the best response.

Eric gave me a look saying exactly that, then cleared his throat and turned back to the crowd. 'As she said, yes, I am in fact a DA, but more importantly, you need to settle down because you could hurt yourselves, and because there's nothing you can do to help inside. Unless we have a medical doctor in attendance tonight?'

Lucinda, who must have gone inside through the kitchen, appeared behind Eric and Kamila. She was shaking her head, and her pale face said it all. 'No need for a doctor, I'm afraid. I called nine-one-one.'

Eric bit his lip, then leaned down and spoke in my ear. 'Why don't you go on inside and see if anyone else is in there, then lock the kitchen door to make sure the scene is secured. I'll hold the fort here till the cops arrive.'

'Got it.'

Slipping under his arm, I heard Eric continue to address the dinner guests. 'I'm sure the police would like to talk to all of you,' he said, 'so if you could please take your seats once again . . .'

Fat lot of good that's going to do, I thought. *Everyone but the lookie-loos are gonna skedaddle out of here as fast as possible, rather than spend the entire night waiting to be interviewed by the police.*

Once inside, I stopped for a deep breath before proceeding. I'd seen dead bodies before. Too many, in fact. But that didn't make this any easier. I could see the book cabinet from where I stood, its glass door smashed open. A body lay among the glass shards on the red and black carpet next to the cabinet.

Not just a 'body'. Alan.

No one else appeared to be inside, but I made a quick check nevertheless, walking between the bookshelves and glancing behind the checkout counter. Nobody.

Next I made my way slowly to where Alan lay on the floor. He was on his back, eyes open, arms and legs splayed. Fighting back the urge to close those staring eyes, I knelt down to examine the gash on the right side of his head. Could he have been struck by a baseball bat or some other weapon? But then I noticed the blood on the edge of the cabinet. Standing up, I saw that it was a little below my eye level, which would correspond with the forehead of the slightly shorter Alan.

He must have hit his head on the sharp wooden edge. But how? A fall?

No. The broken glass in the cabinet and on the floor, as well as the space where the boxed set of cookbooks had once been, meant that someone else had to have been here, too. A quick look around told me the missing books were not in the immediate vicinity.

Unless they were under Alan's body? But again, no. He appeared to be lying completely flat upon the floor. *Maybe he was shoved by whoever stole the books. But if so, it must have been quite a push to kill him like that.*

The sound of a siren jolted me from my thoughts. Better get out of there and go lock the kitchen door, as Eric had instructed. But before leaving the scene, I pulled out my phone and snapped a few photos.

You never knew.

*   *   *

Turns out that – although they interviewed all of the Pages and Plums staff, as well as the Teens' Table adults and me – the police only wanted to talk to a few of the dinner guests that night.

'There were so many at the event,' Eric told me while I was waiting for my turn with Detective Vargas, 'that they realized it wasn't feasible to keep everyone here that long. But they did get a list of all the guests and their contact info from Lucinda.'

Vargas had spoken with all those who'd made a bid on the cookbooks, as well as the woman who'd gotten into the argument with Alan during the dinner, and a couple of others whose relationship to Alan and the restaurant was unclear to me. It was now past midnight, and the only people left were Kamila, Lucinda, Eric, me, and several servers and kitchen helpers who had stayed on to help with the clean-up.

Once the forensic team had finished their work in the bookstore, Alan's body had been transported to the morgue for an autopsy. Though it seemed pretty likely they'd conclude the cause of death was a blow to the head from the sharp corner of that book cabinet. The only question was how had *that* happened?

Eric was currently polishing off a plate of grilled peaches topped with homemade vanilla ice cream and my balsamic-plum-black-pepper reduction. 'No reason to skip dessert when you've gone to all the trouble to prepare it,' he'd commented on spying the plates of abandoned peaches lined up on the kitchen counter where Kamila and I had left them. I couldn't disagree, though at the moment I couldn't bring myself to eat anything. But nothing ever seems to stem Eric's appetite. Which I guess is one of the reasons I love him so.

The door into the Pages and Plums office opened and the shaved head of Martin Vargas popped out. 'I'm ready for you now, Sally,' he said with a glance in Eric's direction. 'Sorry about the wait.'

'No problem. I had to stick around to help clean up, in any event.' Turning to Eric, I gave him a kiss on the cheek. 'Thanks for sticking around, babe. I think I'm gonna go back to my place tonight, have some alone time after all this. So you might as well head on home now – no need to wait here for me.'

'Sure, I understand. I'm gonna get up early and get in some surfing before work, anyway, so probably for the best. But I'll call you when I get to the office.'

'Sounds good. See ya.'

Wondering how he felt about seeing me with Eric, I followed the detective into the office. Martin and I had been an 'item' for several months the previous winter, but we'd soon realized it wasn't a good match. He lived his life in an ordered, protective kind of way, whereas I . . .? Well, I kept getting involved in his murder investigations, for one thing. And I was definitely not one to always follow the rules, a trait which drove Vargas slightly bonkers.

But although we'd parted as friends, this was the first time Martin had seen Eric and me together since we'd rekindled our romance after several years' hiatus. If the detective had any issues with my current relationship status, however, he was doing a good job of keeping it to himself.

'Have a seat,' he said, and settled his burly frame on to the chair he'd claimed for the night behind the office desk. 'So we meet again at the scene of what appears to be yet another homicide. Getting to be a little weird, don't ya think?'

'Tell me about it. Even I'm starting to believe I might be an "angel of death", like some of Javier's friends now call me.'

Martin's smile was wry but warm. 'If so, then I must be the *arch*angel of death.'

'Yeah, but you're a cop, so at least you have an excuse.'

'Maybe.' He shuffled through the papers on the desk, found the one he was looking for, and picked up a pen. 'Well, I guess we should get to it. So first off, what the heck were you doing here tonight, anyway? I heard the story from the head chef . . .'

'Kamila,' I filled in.

'Right. Kamila. But I'd like to hear it from your end, as well.'

'I guess you could call it serendipity. Though it kind of seems like the opposite now, in retrospect. Is there a word for that?'

'Bad juju,' Martin said quickly, then shook his head. 'Sorry. You don't deserve that.'

'I don't know; maybe I do.' Why *did* I keep stumbling upon dead bodies? It was as if I were single-handedly turning our lovely town of Santa Cruz into a real-life Cabot Cove.

Martin's dry smile suggested that maybe he didn't disagree.

'Anyway,' I went on, 'I had lunch here last week with my friend Allison, and when I heard they were putting on this dinner, I offered to help out. 'Cause, well, it seemed like a good cause . . .' I trailed off, not wanting to get into how I'd been shamed earlier that same day by my father about not giving back to our community.

'Okay. So, can you take me through the events of this evening, from when you arrived to when Alan Keeting's body was discovered?'

Ah, so that was his last name. I'd only known the guy as 'Alan'. As I gave my account, I paid attention to which parts caused him to take notes and ask questions, as opposed to merely listening and nodding encouragingly. He seemed particularly interested in Lucinda, but that could have merely been because, unlike Kamila, who'd been in my presence for much of the evening, the bookseller's comings-and-goings were more of a mystery. But also, I realized, she'd been one of the last people to speak with Alan before he'd been killed – and that conversation had clearly not been a pleasant one.

After about a half-hour, Martin declared the interview over and told me to go home and get some sleep. 'I may have more questions later, but that's all for now.' Standing up, he came around to my side of the desk and there was a moment's awkwardness, neither of us sure what to do. Should we hug, given how close we'd once been?

I solved the dilemma by placing a hand on his shoulder and giving him a warm squeeze. 'It is good to see you, Martin. Even if it is like this. Again.'

'You, too,' he said, opening the office door for me. 'But I want you to promise that you're not going to get involved in this. We've got it all covered, okay?'

'Got it.' I stepped into the hallway, then turned back around. 'Oh, but I do have one question. Who was winning bidder on those Julia Child cookbooks?'

Martin just shook his head and closed the door.

I was awakened the next morning by the buzz of my cell phone on the walnut dresser next to my bed. *Who the heck is calling so early?* It had taken me a long time to finally nod off the night before, and I'd been hoping to sleep in till at least nine. *What time is it anyway?* Eight-oh-seven, the screen said. And 'Unknown Caller'. I was about to hit the 'decline call' button, but then realized it might have something to do with what had happened last night.

'Hullo?' I said, making no attempt to hide the sleepiness or annoyance in my voice.

'Is this Sally Solari?' a woman's voice asked.

'Uh-huh, yeah, it is.'

'Oh, good. I'm calling on behalf of Eric Byrne. He's had a bit of an accident.'

Sitting up, I was now fully awake. 'What? Is he okay? Who is this?'

'I'm Yolanda Lopez, a nurse down here at the hospital, and Mr Byrne has you listed to call as his contact person. He hit his head surfing this morning and lost consciousness for a bit, so some friends brought him in to be checked out. It appears that he's suffered a mild TBI – a concussion, that is – so his treating doctor has ordered an MRI, and we're going to keep him under observation until the results come back. But he's alert and talking and, unless the MRI shows something amiss, he should be ready to be taken home later today. Sorry, could you hold on a sec?'

I heard Eric saying something in the background which prompted a laugh from the nurse. After a moment, she came back on the line. 'He's asking for you to call his work to let them know what's going on, since he doesn't have his phone, and to also bring him some clothes when you come get him. That is, if you can come?'

'Yeah, absolutely. I can do that, no problem. But could I see him before then? Is he allowed visitors?'

'The doctor wants to keep him quiet for the time being, so best to wait until he's released.'

That didn't sound good. 'Okay. Do you know anything about his car – and his surfboard? Are they still at the beach?'

She spoke once more to Eric, then told me that one of his friends had taken them back to his house for him. 'So why don't you call back in the early afternoon, and we should know by then the results of the scan and if he's been cleared for release.' After giving me the number for the nurses' station, she ended the call.

Damn. What else could go wrong?

But at least it seemed like Eric was going to be fine. The fact that he was joking around and thinking about work and his clothes proved he was okay, right? They were simply being cautious by doing the MRI and keeping him for observation, as well they should. And besides, there was nothing I could do about it, in any case.

Lying back on my pillow, I tried to calm the thumping of my heart, which had sped up to about two hundred beats a minute on hearing the news from the nurse. *Try to think about something else. What had I been dreaming about when my phone jarred me awake?*

Right. Letta. My aunt had been showing me how to prepare a soufflé made with Gruyère cheese, smoked salmon, and plum jelly, and I'd been overcome with her brilliance at coming up with such a perfect combination of flavors.

Now, in the light of day, however, the dish seemed merely odd.

But the dream had been so very real. To have Aunt Letta here again in this house, laughing and reminiscing about her days as a chef in Berkeley, her travels in the South Pacific . . . What a marvelous feeling that had been. Could I get it back?

Closing my eyes, I mentally placed myself at the red Formica kitchen table downstairs. Letta was standing at the counter, a wire whisk in her hand, channeling Julia Child's booming voice as she 'scoffed at lumps and curdles'. I could feel the touch of her hand on mine as she bent over to tell me about the special butter she'd sourced from a dairy up in Marin County . . . But why was her hand so rough? And *wet*?

Buster.

It was no use; the moment was gone. Sitting up once again, I patted the bed and the big brown dog jumped up next to me, tail thumping in greeting. 'You miss her, too, don't ya, bud.' A kiss to my cheek was his response.

Clutching Buster in a tight hug, I allowed the feelings to wash over me. First a few tears, then slow, silent sobs as the heartache of her loss seared through me again like a hot poker to the gut. It was likely a combination of what had happened the night before, the news about Eric this morning, and the vivid dream I'd had this morning, but my emotions were overflowing, and all I could think about was the loss of my beloved aunt: why had she been taken so soon, when we'd only just begun to reconnect after all those years she'd been away? And why now, a year and a half after her death, was she coming to me so frequently in both my waking life and dreams?

Buster's body began to squirm as mine finally calmed down. 'Okay, boy, I know what you want.' I swung my legs out of the bed and pulled on some clothes. Then, his nose bumping every few seconds on the back of my calf, Buster followed me down the stairs and into the kitchen, where I opened the back door to let him outside.

I watched as the dog made his morning round of the perimeter of the yard, leaving his mark at the usual places along the way. Once he was back inside chowing down his breakfast, I fetched my phone. *What had the nurse said Eric had suffered? A TBI?* I typed this into my search bar, then slumped in my chair. 'Traumatic brain injury' is what the initials stood for.

But she'd said it was a 'mild' TBI – a 'concussion', she'd said. They probably used that phrase in the medical profession any time you hit your head.

Now wishing I hadn't Googled the term, I punched in the phone number for the district attorney's office. On being connected to Eric's assistant, I told her what had happened, then attempted to quell her alarm at hearing the news, even though I was experiencing the exact same worries as she.

'I'm sure he'll be fine; they just want to monitor him for a few hours to make sure he's okay. And I bet it's mostly a risk management thing,' I added. From my years as an attorney at a firm that handled a lot of insurance defense cases, I knew this was likely a significant part of the hospital's concern.

'Good point,' she said, appeased.

But I hadn't convinced myself. I was as jittery as a first-year law student taking her first exam, my breath shallow and heart racing – and this was before I'd even had my morning coffee. Add to the mix what had happened last night, and I was in serious need of something to burn off all this pent-up anxiety. A long, hard bike ride, that was the answer. One that would make my legs scream and drown out my brain. Trotting back upstairs, I changed into my cycling gear, performed a few cursory stretches, then pedaled off.

I started the ride along West Cliff Drive which, as its name suggests, hugs the cliffs along the ocean, then turned left on to Bay Street, heading for the UCSC campus. The road up to the university isn't horribly grueling as cycling climbs go, but it provides a healthy workout with a payoff of magnificent views of the Monterey Bay, especially if you descend via the bike path through the Great Meadow.

As I pumped my way uphill, I tried not to think of Eric lying in his hospital bed, waiting to learn whether he'd suffered a truly 'traumatic' brain injury or not. Instead – notwithstanding Detective Vargas's command – I turned my thoughts to Alan's death. Far worse than a concussion, of course, but at least it didn't concern me personally.

Could his death have been intentional? The missing books certainly suggested that he hadn't merely tripped and hit his head against the cabinet by accident. But who would be willing to commit so heinous a crime for a couple of books? Sure, they were valuable, but would someone really risk a murder conviction for a mere twenty-five-hundred dollars? Plus, they'd be difficult to sell, so it didn't seem like a random killing by someone merely looking for quick cash.

And what had Alan even been doing in the bookstore at that time, when he should have been outdoors helping with the dinner?

I ran through the events that I'd witnessed right before his body had been discovered: Alan had argued with that woman in the striped jersey, had been chastised by Lucinda, and then went to sulk over by the bar. At that point, Kamila and I had retreated to the kitchen until being called outside again about ten minutes later for the results of the silent auction. So, Alan had to have gone into the bookstore during that time, and whoever shoved him into the cabinet must have already been in there or had followed him inside.

A pair of deer wandering into the road rousted me from my thoughts. This being summer, the students were largely absent from the campus, and the wildlife up there – deer, turkeys, coyotes, and a host of other critters – could become quite brazen without many humans about. I gave the deer, which paid me no heed whatsoever, a wide berth, and continued on.

Once I reached the end of the climb, I turned my trusty red-and-white steed downhill, marveling once again at the beauty of this place I called home. From the top of the bike path, I could see the town of Santa Cruz spread along the north coast of the bay, with its Boardwalk and iconic Giant Dipper roller coaster gleaming in the morning sunshine. Out in the water bobbed several fishing boats, not unlike the one my grandfather and his father before him had used to bring in ling cod, squid, and salmon for the daily specials at Solari's.

Across the bay, due south of where I was barreling downhill, rose the Santa Lucia Range, whose rugged chain runs from Carmel all the way down to San Luis Obispo. The day was exceptionally clear, and their brown peaks stood out sharply against the azure sky.

A flash of fur darting across the path at my wheels startled me from my sightseeing, and with an oath worthy of the line cook that I was, I swerved sharply, then touched my brakes to slow down. It was generally still foggy this time of day up at UCSC in August, but the sun warming the asphalt was bringing out early the pesky ground squirrels – bane of cyclists' existence in these parts.

The near-accident brought Eric back to mind. That was all I needed, for the both of us to end up in the hospital on the same day. Proceeding more cautiously now, I made my way down to the base of campus and back home.

Time for coffee. I stowed my bike in its usual spot in the corner of the living room, kicked off my cycling cleats, and headed for the kitchen. Pulling out my phone, I switched it from vibrate back to its ring setting and saw that I'd missed a call from Allison.

She picked up on the first ring, her voice near frantic. 'Ohmygod, Sally, I'm so glad you called back!'

'What is it? Is Eleanor okay? Or Greg?'

'No, no, they're both fine. It's Lucinda. She called this morning to tell me the cops are convinced she killed Alan, and she's totally freaking out. I know you're not a practicing lawyer anymore, but you're the first person I thought of to call. We need your help.'

FIVE

I leaned my head against the cupboard above the coffee maker. What more could this day possibly bring?

'Sal, are you there?'

'Yeah, yeah. Sorry. I've just had kind of a bad morning, is all. Eric's in the hospital with a concussion he got surfing, and I'm waiting to hear back on the results of his MRI.'

'Oh, no, that's awful! I'm sorry to unload this on you right now. You so don't need that. Look, why don't I call you back sometime later, when you're not so stressed.'

'No, it's okay,' I said, taking a seat at the kitchen table. 'There's nothing I can do about Eric right now, and it's probably good to have something to take my mind off it, anyway. But the first thing you need to do is call Lucinda back right now and tell her not to talk to the cops or anyone else about anything to do with Alan's death.'

'She knows that already. They asked her to come down to the station to talk sometime today, and she said no.'

'Good.' I stood up again and fetched the bag of French roast from the freezer. 'So why does she think they suspect her of his death?' I asked, pouring coffee into the grinder. 'Wait, hold on. Don't answer that yet.' The racket of blades on beans filled the room for several seconds, then subsided. 'Sorry, but I truly need some caffeine ASAP. Okay, you can talk now.'

As I dumped the coffee into the filter, filled the water reservoir, and punched the on switch, Allison told me what she knew. 'It's partly 'cause of how they're treating her compared to Kamila and the other staff,' she said. 'The questions they asked Lucinda last night, for instance, were different from what they asked Kamila. They compared notes this morning, and Kamila says no one asked *her* about where she was between the time Alan got in the argument with that woman and when his body was discovered.'

'Well, I'm sure that's only because Vargas already knew Kamila was with me, so I'm her alibi for that entire time.'

'Maybe,' said Allison, not meaning it. 'But also, it's gotta have to do with Lucinda chewing Alan out right before he died.'

'But if that's their angle, then you'd think that woman Alan was arguing with would be a far better suspect than Lucinda.'

'Tell that to Detective Vargas. Only figuratively, that is,' she quickly added. 'I don't really expect you to talk to him.'

I snorted. 'Not that he'd want to hear anything from me, in any event. The good detective made it quite clear last night that he wanted me to keep my nose far, far away from this whole thing.'

'Oh,' Allison said quietly, then grew silent.

'What?'

'It's just that Lucinda really wants to talk to you. Do you think that would run afoul of Vargas's mandate?'

No doubt it would, was my thought. And I also wondered if I even *wanted* to talk to her. Lucinda would, of course, have heard about my helping solve those other cases over the past two years, and she likely hoped that I could pull another rabbit out of my white chef's hat and prove her innocence, as well. Was that what I wanted? Another murder to solve? And was I willing to defy – yet again – the unequivocal directive of Martin Vargas?

A prickle of something akin to electricity shot up my spine as a slow smile formed on my lips.

'Well,' I said to Allison, 'he can't very well prohibit me from having lunch with my good friend, can he? And if my good friend's friend just happens to be working at that same place we're eating and comes over to talk to us, what am I supposed to do? It would be rude to simply tell her to go away, right?'

Allison laughed. 'Right,' she said. 'How 'bout lunch tomorrow at, say, Pages and Plums?'

'Perfect.'

At three o'clock I was finally able to get through to someone about Eric's status. Yolanda had gone off duty, and a new nurse, Simon, had taken over her patients. 'We got back the results of Mr Byrne's MRI,' he said once I got the nurse on the line, 'and the results are inconclusive, I'm afraid. His treating doctor wants to keep him overnight for observation, and if he doesn't show any sign of complications from his concussion, then he should be released in the morning.'

'What are the signs of "complications"?' I asked.

'The list is fairly long . . . things like seizures, reduced thinking skills, issues with memory, slurred speech. But I don't mean to frighten you,' he added on hearing my intake of breath. 'Other than having a headache – which is quite normal, given the injury he suffered – he's asymptomatic as of now. We just want to be very cautious, since he did lose consciousness for a bit and the location of the blow he received is a concern. Blunt injury to the temple is unfortunately not infrequently followed by internal damage from leakage of blood or cerebrospinal fluid getting trapped in the skull. So we just need to monitor him a bit longer. But it should be far clearer by the morning whether any complications develop.'

'Oh, boy.' I took a deep breath. Simon's attempt not to frighten me was having the exact opposite effect. 'Okay,' I said. 'I understand. And I appreciate all you're doing for him. I take it he still can't have visitors?'

'I'm afraid not. We want to keep him calm and undisturbed for the time being. He's sleeping comfortably now, in fact. But I will tell him you called. And hopefully tomorrow you'll be able to not only see him, but take him home, as well.'

Setting down my phone, I reached out to stroke Buster's rough fur. The dog, lying next to me on the living-room couch, rolled over on to his back, and I obliged, providing the belly rub he was requesting. I was tempted to Google 'injuries to the temple' but resisted the urge. It would only make me more worried than I already was, seeing the list of all the worst-case scenarios that would surely pop up from the search.

Instead, I got up and headed for the kitchen, with Buster jumping down to follow after me. Peering into the fridge, I pulled out a to-go container of coq au vin and roasted Brussels sprouts I'd brought home from Gauguin Sunday night. Best to eat something before heading off to work.

And there was nothing like food to distract one from the misfortunes of life.

Bzrzrzrzr . . .

'What the . . .?' Reaching out a hand before I was even conscious of what I was doing, I grabbed hold of the phone rattling on the wooden dresser to silence the maddening buzz. I really needed to remember to place it on a piece of fabric or something at night, since simply setting it on vibrate was clearly not enough. And so once again, after a late night on the line at Gauguin, here I was being awoken at . . . what time was it, anyway?

But as I came fully awake, I realized the call could be important. Without a glance at who it was from, I punched 'accept' and said, 'Hello? This is Sally.'

'Oh, hi. This is Yolanda calling from the hospital with good news. Eric did fine last night, and he's been cleared to go home after nine this morning. They're doing the paperwork for his release right now.'

Muscles I hadn't even realized were tense began to immediately relax as a wave of relief swept through my body. 'Thank God,' I said, lying back down on my pillow. 'That is such great news. I'll be there then to pick him up. And thank you so much for calling to let me know.'

It was only seven thirty, so I had time to take Buster for a walk and brew some coffee. Then, both of those vital tasks accomplished, I fired up the T-Bird and headed to Eric's place in Capitola to pick up some clothes for him to wear home.

His condo wasn't in the picture-postcard village where stucco homes reflected their pastel-colored paint in the lagoon, but rather, in a more mundane subdivision behind the shopping mall. But at least parking was easy to find in his neighborhood, I thought as I pulled up in front of the building.

Letting myself in with the key he'd given me after we'd gotten back together, I stood in the living room and surveyed Eric's digs. Off-white paint, white wall-to-wall carpet (*why on earth would anyone want a carpet virtually guaranteed to call attention to any speck of food or wine spilled upon it?*), enormous flat-screen TV, and framed photos of beach scenes and surfers on the walls. Pretty darn antiseptic, in a bachelor pad kind of way.

The furniture was comfy, though. I plopped down onto his La-Z-Boy recliner and ran a finger along its silky-soft black leather. And he did have a passable – albeit tiny – kitchen, with a gorgeous butcher-block counter and state-of-the-art fridge and gas range.

But could I live here?

I thought not. It was too much like a hotel, with its new, almost unlived-in ambience of Ethan Allen cabinets and Crate & Barrel kitchenware. Perfectly nice, but nothing like my aunt's well-worn sofas and vintage O'Keefe and Merritt stove. And Eric's condo contained no memories of birthday celebrations in Letta's comfy living room, or summer barbecues in her backyard, or of late-night dinners at her red Formica kitchen table.

And then I sighed. Eric had just had a near-death experience, for goodness' sake. Why was I looking for reasons not to share this space with him before he even returned home from the hospital? Maybe I'd just need to give it time, and some beautiful new memories could be made here, as well.

With a grunt, I stood up from the recliner and wandered into the bedroom. The king-size bed had been made and there were no clothes strewn about, even though Eric must have left the house near the crack of dawn to be able to get in his morning surfing before work the day before. With a wry smile, I opened the chest of drawers to perfectly folded shirts and pants. Selecting a Johnny Rice Surfboards T-shirt, a pair of jeans, boxer shorts, socks, and Eric's black-and-white checked skate sneakers, I tucked them into a cloth grocery bag I found in the kitchen closet, then made my way down the stairs and back out to my car.

Eric was seated in his bleak hospital room's one plastic chair when I arrived, staring morosely at the TV. Slouching there in his cotton gown, he seemed simultaneously vulnerable and bored stiff. On the floor next to the chair was a white plastic bag containing his wetsuit – the clothes he'd had on when brought into the ER the day before.

'Hey, kiddo,' I said, knocking lightly at the door. 'Whatcha watching?'

At the sound of my voice, his scowl became a wide smile. 'Sally! You came!' Standing up as I crossed the room, he gave me a tight hug.

'Of course I came. And I've been worried sick about you. How you doing?'

Eric sat back down, and I perched on the edge of the bed. 'Here, lemme shut this off,' he said, grabbing the remote. The talking head in a blue suit and yellow tie faded from view. 'Much better now that you're here. Did you bring my clothes?'

I handed him the bag and he immediately began to pull on the boxers and jeans. 'How's your head feel?' I asked as he tossed the discarded gown aside.

'Well, I've got a pretty constant headache, and even though it's only a low-grade one, I have to be careful about moving my head too quickly or I get kind of dizzy. But they say that's normal, given what happened. Other than that, I feel okay.'

We were interrupted by the entrance of a middle-aged woman

in a white lab coat. 'Good morning,' she said, extending a hand to shake with me. 'I'm Doctor Singh, Eric's neurologist.'

'Pleased to meet you.' I introduced myself and offered her a seat next to me on the bed, which she declined.

'I've approved Eric for release today, but there are a few things that he's been instructed about, and which I'd like you to be aware of, as well. That is, assuming you'll be his primary caretaker?'

'Uh . . .' *He's going to need a caretaker?* I glanced from the doctor to Eric. 'Yeah, I guess I'm that person, unless you want someone else?'

'No,' he said. 'It should be you, Sal.'

'Okay, then I'm it. So what do I need to know?'

Dr Singh tapped a slender finger on the clipboard she carried. 'Well, as you know, Eric sustained a fairly serious blow to the head and lost consciousness for some twenty seconds, according to those who pulled him from the water. Add the vertigo, and he got sent for an MRI, though the imaging results were, unfortunately, inconclusive. As a result, although I'm allowing him to return home, I've ordered that he stay as still as possible for the next several days – possibly more, depending on how he progresses. I don't think he needs complete bedrest, but he should definitely take it easy until his follow-up appointment. He shouldn't leave home, and no strenuous activities such as standing for long periods of time to cook, or do house- or yard-work, or anything of that sort.'

Eric snorted. 'Not that I much like to do housework or cook to begin with, so that shouldn't be any problem.' But I could tell he was merely putting on an act. His eyes told the true story – he was frustrated and annoyed. And maybe a little scared, too.

'What about his work?' I asked, knowing this was likely high up there among Eric's concerns.

'Well, I certainly don't want you going in to the office for the time being,' she said to Eric. 'And I'd prefer that you not allow yourself to become agitated working, even from home. You're a lawyer, correct?' she asked, peering down at her clipboard. 'Ah, right, an assistant district attorney. Not the most calming of professions. But I'll leave that to you to decide.'

'Right.' Eric raised himself slowly from the chair, trying his best to make it look as if this were his normal manner of moving. 'Anything else, or can we head out?'

The doctor handed him the clipboard and a pen. 'I just need you to sign here, and we're done for now. But I'd like to get daily updates on your progress, find out how you're feeling and if you develop any further symptoms.'

'Such as . . .?' I asked.

'Well,' she said, 'it's possible, for instance, that you may find that your ability to concentrate seems diminished or that you're more forgetful than usual. And if that's the case, I'd certainly want to know.' The doctor accepted back the signed release form, then flipped through the pages underneath it on the clipboard. 'Here,' she said, pulling out a sheet and handing it to me. 'This is a list of symptoms that may develop from a TBI, a concussion, that is. I'd like you to be on the lookout for any of these and to let me know if anything worsens or if something new develops. My number is at the top of the page.'

I read through the list: memory issues such as loss, confusion or difficulty concentrating; headaches; dizziness or loss of balance; fatigue or drowsiness; nausea; vomiting; ringing in the ears; trouble speaking; loss of coordination; weakness or numbness in parts of the body; irritability and moodiness; sensitivity to light and sound; restlessness; change in dilation of pupils; double vision; seizures.

Oh, boy . . .

Forcing a smile, I thanked Dr Singh, then took Eric by the arm. 'C'mon, kiddo, let's split this joint.'

He didn't speak much on the way home. I wasn't sure if it was because of his headache, or simply the blues he was experiencing about his plight. But I didn't push him to chat. Once inside, he made a bee-line for the bedroom. 'I'm kinda tired,' he said, kicking off his Vans and settling on to the bed. And then he flashed a crooked grin. 'Is that one of the symptoms?'

'It is, actually. But I'd say, under the circumstances, that fatigue is probably nothing to fret about. And speaking of symptoms, I'm thinking that maybe I should stay with you for a few days – or you with me. I'd still have to leave to go to work, of course, but at least I'd be around at night and in the mornings to make sure you're doing okay.'

'No, that's all right,' Eric said. 'I mean, I do appreciate the offer, but I don't think it's necessary. The doctor would have told me if she thought I needed someone with me. And besides,' he added, 'I'd much rather be here at my own place, and I wouldn't want you to have to come stay at my second-floor condo with no yard . . .'

Although he punctuated this last bit with a laugh, it was clear neither of us thought it was all that funny.

'Right,' I said, then glanced toward the kitchen. 'You hungry?'

He shook his head, then grimaced at the pain the sudden movement caused. 'I had a large breakfast of cold pancakes, sausage, and freeze-dried scrambled eggs.'

'Sounds, uh . . . filling,' I said. 'So, would you at least like me to stay with you a while right now, or would you rather I go so you can take a nap?'

'Stay a bit, if you can. Tell me what's been going on with you while I've been held hostage at the hospital.'

What to tell him? Talking about Alan's death certainly wasn't a 'calming' subject. 'Well, I've been having dreams about Letta the past few nights,' I said.

'What kind of dreams?'

'Super realistic ones, where she's with me at the house cooking or talking about her travels in the South Pacific. It's really . . . I dunno. Unsettling.'

Eric raised himself up slowly, gingerly placing the pillow behind his back. 'Unsettling because . . .?'

'Because it seems so wonderful and *real* having her back again. But then when I wake up, I realize it's not true – that she's still gone.' I could feel the tears wanting to come once again and closed my eyes, trying to keep it together. Eric did not need someone else to take care of right now. But then again, maybe hearing about someone else's issues might be a good thing to take his mind off his own troubles.

'It's just that I miss Letta so much,' I went on, settling down next to him on the bed. 'And she was taken from me so soon – right when we'd just started to really get close. It's not fair.'

And that's all it took. As the tears streamed down my cheeks, Eric wrapped his arms about me and held me close.

'Life's not always fair,' he said.

SIX

I met Allison at Pages and Plums at half-past twelve, and while we waited for our table, I filled her in on the latest about Eric. After a few minutes, we were seated by the same young man with multiple rings on his fingers, who then dashed back to the host stand to welcome another group of hungry lunch-goers waiting for a table.

'I wonder if he's taking over the dining-room manager duties, now that Alan's gone,' I said with a nod in his direction. 'Looks like it.'

'I'm actually surprised they're even open,' said Allison. 'Seems kind of soon, given all that happened.'

I tried to keep from staring behind her at the area of the bookstore where I'd seen Alan's body splayed out on the floor, but it was hard not to do so. The glass cabinet had been removed – taken into custody by the police, perhaps? – and the carpet betrayed no sign of the ugly event that had occurred on its red and black surface.

'They likely had little choice,' I answered. 'Restaurants run on such a tight margin, even missing a few days could mean the difference between eking out a profit or going belly-up. Especially for one that's just opened, like Pages and Plums.'

'And I thought making tenure was hard. Oof. I don't know how you do it, girl.'

I laughed. 'Yeah, well, it takes a special kind of crazy to want to own a restaurant. And sometimes I do indeed wonder why I keep at it.'

Because of Letta, I thought to myself. *It's a way of keeping her alive.* But I didn't speak this aloud. Instead, I opened my menu and concentrated on what I wanted to eat. I considered ordering that delicious omelet again, but then decided to try the ham-on-rye that had tempted me the last time we'd been here for lunch.

Once we'd ordered – Allison having opted for the salade Niçoise – I looked about me to see if I could spot Lucinda. She was at the register in the bookstore and, as if sensing my gaze, looked up at that moment and gave me a 'just a sec' sign. Then, after completing the sale, she crossed to the dining room to where we sat.

'I only have a few minutes,' she said, ''cause Ellen has her lunch break at one, and I'll have to go spell her. But I really appreciate your taking the time to talk to me, Sally.' Taking a seat at the table, Lucinda put her hands in her lap, and I could see the muscles in her upper body tense up. 'Uh, I'm not really sure where to start . . .'

'How about with why you wanted to meet with me?' I offered. 'Allison said you thought the police might suspect you for Alan's death?'

She nodded. 'I'm almost certain of it. They asked me different questions from the other staff I talked to, and now they want me to come in and talk to them again – which I said I wasn't going to do,' she quickly added. 'I've watched enough TV to know I don't have to talk to them if I don't want to. But I have to say, it does make me worry they'll suspect me even more if I refuse to speak with them again.'

'Don't worry about that,' I said with a wave of the hand. 'It's completely within your rights, and they know that.'

'Right,' she said, then swallowed. 'But mostly it's because of that . . . discussion I had with Alan right before he died, I'm sure. You know, when I pulled him away from the argument he was having with that woman at the dinner. It definitely doesn't look good when you're not only the last person to talk with a dead man, but also when that conversation consisted of you chewing the guy out.'

'Yeah, I can see how that would be worrisome,' I said. 'But it seems to me they have far more reason to suspect the woman Alan was arguing with than you. Which begs the question, do you know what that was about?'

'According to Alan, she was getting in his ear about his being involved in some homeless advocates group, and I gather she's one of those types who wish they'd all simply go away – the homeless, that is.'

'Wait.' I made a timeout sign with my hands. 'Alan was involved in a homeless advocacy group?'

'Right. That's one of the reasons he wanted to host the benefit for Teens' Table, since they provide meals for the homeless.'

'Ah, got it. Okay, go on.'

'So anyway, I'm not sure why that woman even paid to come to the dinner, given how much of a NIMBY she seems to be, but maybe she didn't realize exactly who the kids in the program were cooking for. In any case, she apparently recognized Alan from when he spoke at a city council meeting about the camping ban a while back, and decided that a farm-to-table benefit dinner was an appropriate time to get into it with him about their difference of opinion.'

'You sound like you take Alan's side on the issue,' I said.

Lucinda gave me a *duh* look.

'I mean, not that that's surprising or anything,' I amended. 'It's only because of how you chewed Alan out about his arguing with the woman, is all.'

'That was because he was the *host* and she was a *customer* at our restaurant. If it had occurred somewhere else, I would have absolutely taken his side. You of all people must understand that.'

'You're right. And I do. Sorry.'

Lucinda leaned forward and placed her head in her hands. 'But that's exactly what I'm afraid the police won't understand, either. That it was a simple, garden-variety interaction about customer–staff relations, not the result of some bitter, angry feud.'

'Do they think that – that you'd been having a feud with Alan?' asked Allison quietly. When Lucinda didn't answer, she put a hand on her forearm. '*Did* you have an ongoing issue with him?'

'It certainly wasn't a feud, that's for sure. It was more of a power struggle, I guess you could call it.' Lucinda sat back up and looked, first Allison, then me, in the eye. 'Alan was sure he knew better than me how to run the bookstore end of the business, which was absolutely not true. And when he'd try to butt in and tell me what to do, well, I didn't appreciate it.'

Not good. 'Did you tell this to the police?' I asked, and she shook her head.

'They mostly wanted to know about what happened that night. You know, the logistics of everything, where people were and when. Especially me. But I wouldn't be surprised if my relationship with Alan is something they want to ask about now. Who knows, maybe someone else mentioned it to them? It wasn't as if our spats were always private.'

Allison glanced quickly my way, then drummed her fingers on the table. I was trying to think what exactly to say in response to this revelation when we were granted a moment's respite by the arrival of our lunches.

'Ah, thanks,' I said, leaning back to allow the server to set down my plate. At the sight of the sandwich, my mouth began to water, and I realized I'd had no breakfast that morning. A mound of paper-thin ham and slices of Swiss cheese sat atop Jewish rye flecked with caraway seeds, with leaves of Bibb lettuce, tomato, a dill pickle, and ramekins of house-made mayo and honey-mustard on the plate next to the sandwich.

Digging into the mayo and slathering it on my bread, I decided to move the conversation on from Lucinda's relationship with Alan. 'So, I was wondering who ended up winning the bid on those cookbooks,' I asked. 'Was it that book buyer you showed them to? What was his name . . .?'

'Julian,' she said. 'And yes, he did make the highest bid, of twenty-seven hundred dollars. Which money of course we'll never see, since the books are now gone.'

Allison swallowed her bite of seared tuna and baby string beans. 'What do you know about him?' she asked. 'Any chance he did it, and then absconded with the books free of charge?'

'Not likely,' said Lucinda. 'He couldn't very well advertise them for sale after what happened. But then again . . .'

We all had the simultaneous thought. 'But if he already had a buyer lined up who didn't care if they were stolen,' Allison managed to get in before anyone else.

'Exactly.' I set down my sandwich. 'Do you have a list of all the guests from the farm-to-table dinner?' I asked Lucinda. 'Preferably one with their contact info?'

'I do. I already gave a copy to the cops, but I'd be happy to let you have it, too.' A hopeful look sprang into her eyes. 'So does that mean you're going to investigate the murder?'

'I might just have a little gander . . .'

Work that night proved to be a welcome distraction. For no sooner had I said those words to Lucinda than the seriousness of the decision settled over me like a thousand-pound weight.

I'd been telling myself I wasn't worried about Martin Vargas finding out if I did a little snooping around about Alan's death, but – truth be told – I was very concerned, if the churning in my stomach was any clue. Not to mention the anxiety caused by the thought of putting myself in the sights of whoever had killed Alan by poking my nose where it shouldn't be. Which, of course, was one of the primary reasons Vargas didn't want me involved. *How could he not find out?* Especially if I decided to talk to people who'd been at the benefit dinner once I got hold of that guest list.

Adding to my stress that night was Eric. I'd stopped by his place on my way to Gauguin to drop off the sandwich I'd bought for him at Pages and Plums, and had been surprised by his lack of interest in the food.

Eric was *always* hungry.

'Are you feeling okay?' I'd asked him.

'I'm fine. Just a little tired. I'll eat it later.'

He denied feeling dizzy or nauseated and pooh-poohed my concerns, telling me to not worry and to go to work. Nevertheless, I arrived at Gauguin with an ever-growing pit in my stomach.

Luckily, it was farmers' market day downtown, which always provided an early dinner crowd. Nothing like wandering through stalls offering farmstead cheeses, crusty loaves of sourdough bread, vine-ripened tomatoes, and rotisserie chickens dripping their luscious fat onto roast potatoes to prime one's belly for dinner. And since we were only a few blocks from the weekly market, Wednesdays were always a big night at Gauguin.

So I didn't have a whole lot of time to spend stressing about Eric, my own safety, or my questionable behavior in even considering taking on another clandestine investigation. Instead, I concentrated on searing bok choy with rice wine, soy sauce, mirin, and sesame oil; brushing salmon steaks with tarragon butter; and keeping an eye on the béarnaise sauce atop the warmer at the back of the stove.

Javier was in a good mood. He and his new girlfriend, Ana, had been talking about moving in together, and he wanted to tell me all about the house she lived in up in the hills above Soquel Village. I made a show of paying attention, nodding and saying 'Mmmm' at appropriate times, but was in fact thinking about the similar conversation Eric and I had had less than a week earlier – not to mention his sarcastic comment that morning when I'd offered to come stay with him for a few days.

And now I had to worry more about whether I'd even *have* a boyfriend to move in with, than where we might actually live if we did so.

'So, pretty cool, no?'

'Huh?' I yanked myself back into the present. 'Oh, yeah, very cool.'

Javier plated up the spot prawns with citrus and harissa he'd just fired, rang the bell on the pass, then turned to face me. 'So what gives, Sally? You've obviously got something on your mind. You've been acting weird all night.'

I told him about what had happened to Eric, and what the neurologist had said about all the things I needed to be on the lookout for which could still go wrong.

'Oh, wow. I had no idea. Sorry to be on your case. And for going on about Ana, which you clearly don't need to hear about right now. You wanna cut out early to go see how he's doing? There's only a few tickets left, and I can totally handle them.'

'That is so sweet, Javier.' I leaned over to give my head chef a kiss on his fine-boned cheek. 'I would actually like to go check on him, but I don't imagine another half-hour will make much of a difference. How 'bout I stay long enough to get these last orders out and then leave the clean-up to you.'

With a grin, he pulled off the next ticket on the rail and handed it to me. 'Well, since you put it that way, I think this one should be yours.'

I glanced at the printout: six orders of duck two ways, a confit of the leg, with the breast seared rare and served sliced with a lemon and fig glaze. Our most complicated dish. 'Gee, thanks,' I said. 'You're all heart.'

It was a little after ten that night when I crept into Eric's bedroom to see how he was doing. He snorted and rolled over as I leaned over to take a look at him, but didn't wake up, and I was relieved when after a few seconds his breathing returned to normal – slow and steady.

Reassured, I retreated from the room and closed the door behind me. I couldn't stay the night, unless I was willing to drive all the way back to Santa Cruz from Capitola and fetch Buster, which I had no desire to do. But I could stay for an hour or so while I unwound from work, then check on Eric one last time before heading home for some shut-eye.

I went straight to the kitchen, where I pulled the bourbon bottle from the liquor cabinet and poured myself a nightcap. Then, settling into the comfy leather recliner in the living room, I opened my laptop. Some videos of street food vendors in Mumbai, Jacques Pépin preparing something simple and yummy like a fried egg, and maybe even a few of baby monkeys playing with ducklings thrown in for good measure. That seemed like the perfect way to relax.

But before I could type the word YouTube, my eye was caught by a new email in my inbox. It was from Lucinda. 'Here's the list of guests from the dinner,' she wrote, 'and I've added notes regarding the few people I know of who might be relevant/ important. As for the rest, I have no info suggesting they had anything to do with Alan's death, but you never know . . .'

Attached to the message was a PDF, which I opened. It was a spreadsheet of names and phone numbers, with Lucinda's handwriting next to a few of the entries. Eagerly, I leaned closer to read through the names of those with notes:

> Saul Abrams – guy who donated books for auction
> Julian Bartlett-Jones – bookseller who won auction; owns
>   B-J Booksellers, downtown.
> Raquel Santiago – argued with Alan at dinner, turns out she
>   bid $750 on the cookbooks

Only three names; not terribly helpful. And all rather obvious suspects, at that. But it was interesting to see that the woman who'd gotten into that argument with Alan had made a bid on the Julia Child books. Could she have wanted them badly enough to steal them? Or to have killed two birds with one stone, so to speak, and bashed Alan against the side of that cabinet as she was absconding with her prize? She was a pretty big woman – at least from what I'd seen of her sitting down – and certainly larger than the slender Alan had been.

Taking a sip of bourbon and savoring the notes of vanilla, caramel, and wood in its smooth finish, I thought back to the other dinner guests I'd interacted with that night at Pages and Plums. I hadn't had much to do with many of the diners besides the ones I already knew, such as Eric, Allison, and Greg. But there were those people in the group who'd been oohing and ahing over the Julia Child cookbooks with me when Lucinda had come inside to show the books to Julian.

What were their names? I seemed to remember hearing a couple of them during the conversation – a man and the woman he'd been with – but I couldn't recall what they were. I'd have to ask Lucinda if she knew their names.

Plus, there was all the staff who'd been working that night, as well as the Teens' Table folks. Not that I suspected any of the kids of Alan's death – or, for that matter, the director of the organization. Though, of course, you never knew. But I'd definitely have to get hold of a list of the Pages and Plums employees who'd been at the dinner and talk to Lucinda about them, as well.

'Hey, hon.'

I started at the sudden sound from behind me, sloshing some of my drink on to my jeans. 'Eric. You're up.'

He leaned over to give me a kiss on the top of the head. 'I am, indeed. What's that you're reading? Not work, I hope.'

'No, not work,' I said, closing the laptop. 'Just wasting time on social media.'

Eric came around to the front of the chair and gave me a hard stare. 'That most definitely did *not* look like Facebook or Twitter, my dear. And the last thing I need right now is to be gaslighted, Sal. Wait,' he said, his eyes widening. 'Is it something from the neurologist you don't want to tell me about?'

'Oh God, Eric, no. There's absolutely nothing I know besides what she told you, I swear.' I set the computer on the floor. 'I was looking at something completely unrelated to you. A . . . project I'm thinking of taking on.'

He plopped down on to the sofa, then put a hand to his head.

'Is your headache back?' I asked.

'It never went away. But don't change the subject. You said it wasn't work, so what is this "project"?'

I didn't want to lie to Eric, but I was also well aware that if I told him the truth, it would likely serve to agitate him – something his doctor had specifically warned against. Standing up, I walked into the kitchen to pour another drink. And to buy a little time. But he wasn't to be dissuaded. Following me to the liquor cabinet, Eric watched as I pulled the red-topped cork from the bottle of Maker's Mark, his hands clenching and unclenching as he waited for my reply.

So much for not getting him upset. 'Okay, fine,' I said, pouring a healthy glug of bourbon into my glass. 'The cops think Allison's friend Lucinda killed Alan, and I've agreed to help her out.'

Eric's gaze was icy. 'Help her out.'

'Right. That was a list of the guests at the dinner the other night at Pages and Plums you saw, and I was reading through Lucinda's notes about who she thinks might have been the real killer.'

'Oh, lord.' Eric's hand went once more to his head, but I was pretty sure it wasn't due to his headache this time. He returned to the living room and gingerly sat back down on the couch. 'Does Vargas know?'

'Uh . . . no, he doesn't.' Might as well come completely clean, I figured. 'And I'm really hoping you won't say anything to him, 'cause, well . . .'

'He told you to butt out,' he finished for me.

'In so many words, yeah.'

Eric stared at the photo on the wall of sunlight shining through the aquamarine curl of a perfect wave. 'Well,' he said after a bit, 'you don't need to worry about me telling the detective about your antics, because *I* don't want to hear anything about them. And for that matter, I really don't need a nanny coming over all the time to check on me and make sure I'm being a good boy. I can take care of myself just fine.'

With a sharp slap to his knees, he stood. 'I'm going back to sleep.'

SEVEN

That night I clutched Buster tightly in bed – which he seemed to enjoy for a few minutes, then not so much. But I dearly wanted someone to hold, and the dog was going to have to suffice for tonight. Maybe for several nights to come, depending on how angry Eric truly was with me.

I couldn't much blame him – Eric, that is. Not only was I going against the express instructions of an officer of the law, but by doing so I was putting him in an extremely awkward position. As a member of the district attorney's office, Eric worked closely with Detective Vargas – a relationship that was already strained due to his now being involved with the gal who'd only a few months earlier been dating the detective. It was no wonder Eric didn't want to hear anything about what I was doing. What he wanted was plausible deniability.

As Buster's squirming became more urgent, I released him from my grasp. Turning around in several circles to create a nest in the covers, the dog finally settled back down in the exact spot he'd occupied before. But free from my clutch.

Was that what Eric wanted, too? To be free of his 'nannies'? Of what he might feel as others' control over his life right now? It had to be incredibly frustrating for him to lack the agency he normally had over his own actions. And add to that, not knowing how long this would last – when he'd get to go back to his old life? I'd be angry, too, in his situation.

But then I remembered the list Dr Singh had given me of the concussion symptoms I was supposed to be on the lookout for. Rolling on to my back, I startled Buster, who stood and made a few more circles before stretching back out beside me. As I scratched the fur behind his ears, I tried to picture what had been on that list.

Yes, irritability and moodiness were definitely among the symptoms. I remembered thinking at the time that it would make total sense for anyone who'd gone through what Eric had to experience those emotions. So was his anger a sign of concussion, or merely a sign that his girlfriend had truly pissed him off? And would he even talk to me tomorrow if I called to see if his irritability had increased? Did I even *want* to talk to him?

Yes and no . . . Maybe. But either way, I knew that I had to.

The next day, after making a shopping run to Costco for a few Gauguin items (to-go containers, olive oil, milk, butter, and dried figs), I headed over to B-J Booksellers on my way to work. It had been at least a year since I'd last visited the store, so in addition to getting the chance to talk with the fellow who'd made the winning bid for those Julia Child cookbooks, I was also looking forward to browsing through their enticing collection of used and antiquarian books.

But after pulling the T-Bird into a spot around the corner from the store, I pulled my phone from my bag. Time to call Eric first, whether he wanted it or not. I was half expecting him to see my name on his screen and simply send the call directly to voicemail, so I wasn't ready when he actually picked up.

'Sally.' His voice was flat. No sign of either anger or pleasure at my call.

'Eric,' I replied.

There were several seconds with neither of us speaking, until he finally cleared his throat. 'Uh, you're the one who phoned me, so . . .'

'Right. And I'm glad you took the call. You know, after last night.'

More silence on his end.

'So I just wanted to see how you're feeling today.'

'How I'm feeling,' he repeated. 'Would that be regarding the state of my body, or rather the state of my feelings about you?'

Great. He was going to be like this, was he? 'Both, I guess.'

'Both are about the same, I'd say.'

I closed my eyes and attempted to keep my cool. 'Look, Eric, I know you're still mad at me, but I really do want to know how your head is today – physically, not emotionally. I mean . . . you know what I mean.'

'The headache is definitely less today,' he said, his voice still devoid of emotion. 'So that's something. But Dr Singh still doesn't want me to leave the condo or concentrate on any hard thinking, which pretty much precludes me from doing any work. So instead

I'm making the best of it by watching daytime TV and old *Frasier* episodes.'

Not the worst thing in the world, I thought, but I could also see how that would get boring after a while. 'Would you like me to stop by after work tonight?'

'I don't think so. I'll probably go to bed early. Dr Singh says sleep is good for me right now.'

'Oh. Okay. Maybe tomorrow, then.'

'Maybe,' he replied and ended the call.

Not a great result, but at least he did talk to me. And it was good his headache was better. *And who knows, maybe he simply does want to get a good night's sleep tonight.*

Or maybe not.

Unfolding myself from the T-Bird's bucket seat, I climbed out of the car, locked the door with its square-headed, vintage Ford key, and headed around the corner to B-J Booksellers. The tinkle of several tiny bells announced my entrance, and the man at the desk on the far side of the room looked up at the sound.

'Good day,' he said, peering over the tall stack of books before him. 'Is there something specific I can help you with, or are you merely here to browse?'

Definitely a British accent, I decided, recalling my earlier impression of the gentleman. Though it could be simply an affectation, something put on to impress his would-be clients and make them all that more willing to fork out the big bucks for an eighteenth-century calf-hide-bound edition of *Paradise Lost*. In any case, the guy certainly wasn't making any attempt to make me feel particularly comfortable and welcome – not with that dig about being there 'merely' to browse.

'And good day to you,' I replied, feeling the hackles that had risen at the top of my spine. 'I believe you are Julian Bartlett-Jones, correct?'

'That is I,' he said. His eyes, I observed, now exhibited a bit more interest in this newcomer to his store. 'And you are . . .?'

'Sally Solari. We met – well, saw each other, anyway – at that benefit dinner last Monday at Pages and Plums. I was helping cook that night, and was also one of the people admiring those copies of *Mastering the Art of French Cooking* when Lucinda took them out of the cabinet for you.'

'Ah, yes. Dreadful business, that.' With a frown, he looked down at the papers before him. Maybe the man *was* in fact British. If not, he was doing a Masterpiece Theater-worthy job of acting the English peer. 'Do you happen to know if they've discovered anything about . . .?' he asked, still staring down at the desk.

'Who killed Alan Keeting? No. At least there's nothing that I've heard. Though the cops appear to think it was "foul play", as they say.' Nothing in his face appeared to change on hearing this information, so I decided to push my luck. 'And I do know from when I was interviewed by Detective Vargas that they suspect it might have been someone he worked with.' *Was that a slight flicker of his eyes?* 'So, uh, did the police mention anything about who they might suspect when they talked to you?'

'No,' said Julian. 'The good detective kept his hand quite close to his chest, merely querying me about what time I arrived, whether I knew any of the others who'd made bids on the cookbooks, that sort of thing.' His face remained calm, but he'd begun to tap out a slow rhythm on the dark-stained wood desk, only stopping when he noticed my gaze upon his hand.

'And did you?' I asked. 'Know any of the other bidders?'

'I did not. I presume they were all private buyers.' He tapped his finger a few more times, then cleared his throat. 'Speaking of the cookbooks,' he said, 'have they been recovered, do you know?'

I shook my head. 'Again, not that I know of. But if they are found, I'm sure Lucinda will still be willing to let you have them.'

He glanced up briefly, but then a wave of his hand said this was not high on Julian's list of concerns at that moment. Or at least that he didn't want to *appear* to care about such a thing. 'My only interest is that they catch the ruffian who perpetrated such a horrible crime.' Then, as if becoming aware for the first time that he was discussing all of this with a total stranger, he frowned once more. 'So, was there a book-related reason for your visit here today, or did you merely want to gossip about that poor man's death?'

'Uh, yeah, there was,' I lied. 'I actually wanted to look for . . .' *Quick, Sal. What book could you want to buy right now?* 'Something for my boyfriend, who's laid up at home and needs something to read. Preferably a page-turner, if possible. He loves spy novels . . .' I trailed off, realizing this was probably not the sort of reading matter J-B Booksellers specialized in.

Julian studied me for a moment, his thin lips pursed, then stood and walked to one of the tall bookshelves that lined the walls of the store. 'This is our *modern fiction* section,' he said, enunciating the words as if they were ones he was not accustomed to speaking. 'And I do happen to have at the moment several first editions of John le Carré and Graham Greene in very fine condition.'

'Thanks,' I said as he returned to his seat and made a show of picking up a sheet of paper to read. Julian had clearly had enough of me.

Thursday night at Gauguin was relatively slow, and I was able to climb into bed before midnight, a rare luxury in the restaurant business. Of course, not hanging out with Eric after work made for a much earlier bedtime than I'd been experiencing of late. But I did my best not to think about that as I snuggled under the covers with Buster, trying to match his slow, rhythmic breathing.

I was awakened around nine a.m. by bright sunlight streaming through the thin curtains and was surprised to feel so relaxed and refreshed. Maybe I needed to spend more nights alone. Then, troubled by this thought, I reached for my phone and clicked it to life, hoping perhaps Eric had sent me a conciliatory text after he'd gotten up this morning. But no; the only message I had was from my father, asking me to pick up my cousin Evie for Nonna's weekly Sunday dinner the day after tomorrow.

Will do, I wrote Dad back, then threw back the covers and got out of bed. What was on the calendar for today? I had to be at Gauguin at two, to meet with Javier about the fall menu we were starting to plan. But before that time, my day was clear.

Pushing back the curtains, I smiled at the sight of the cloudless blue sky. An invigorating bike ride after a cup of strong coffee seemed like a good way to pass the morning. And then? Perhaps a bit of sleuthing . . .

It was a little after eleven when I pulled up in front of Pages and Plums. I was hoping to get the chance to talk to Kamila before they opened, thinking perhaps the cook knew or had seen something important relating to Alan's death that Lucinda had missed. The front door was still locked, so I made my way along the building to where the side door stood open, letting the late morning sunlight into the bookstore part of the premises. Stepping inside, I stood for a moment to let my eyes adjust to the much darker room.

'Sally!' a voice called out, and I turned to see Lucinda crouched down next to a large box, a stack of books in her hands.

'Oh, hi. I just stopped by in the hopes of talking to Kamila, if she's not busy.'

Lucinda set down the books and came towards me. 'To talk about . . .?'

'Uh-huh. You never know if she might have seen something relevant but didn't think important enough to mention to the police.' I shrugged. 'So, if she's willing to talk to me about it, I figure what can it hurt?'

'No complaints from me on that front,' said Lucinda. 'Ask away.' Then, in a low voice, 'Have you learned anything important since we spoke the other day?' The obvious hope in her eyes made me a little uncomfortable.

'I did stop by yesterday at that antiquarian bookstore Julian owns.'

'Right. J-B Booksellers,' she said. 'And?'

'And, well, he didn't give me any specific information that seemed particularly useful, but I gotta say the guy did seem kind of nervous talking about those cookbooks that he bid on, and about how they went missing.'

'Interesting.' Lucinda stared absently across the room for a bit, deep in thought, then turned back to face me. 'Oh, by the way,' she said, 'I forgot to tell you on Wednesday, but there's going to be a memorial for Alan tomorrow down at Natural Bridges beach. I guess he doesn't have any family in town, so Kamila decided she should do something for him. It's at nine in the morning, so that the staff here can get to work by eleven.'

'Considerate of her,' I said with a snort.

'Yeah, well, at least she's doing something. Though I don't know how many'll actually make it. But I thought you should know in case you wanted to check it out to . . .'

'Spy on the attendees?' And then, at Lucinda's embarrassed look, I smiled. 'No, it's a good idea. I'll definitely be there. And one more thing while I've got you. I was wondering if you'd be able to also give me a list of the employees who were working here that night. Or maybe that'd be some sort of breach of privacy?'

'Technically, yes, I think it probably would be, at least if I gave you their contact info, as well. But . . .' She bit her lip. 'I could just *tell* you who was here, and a little bit about each of them.'

'That works.'

'But let's not do it in here,' Lucinda said, nodding toward the young man who was setting tables in the dining room. 'How 'bout we go outside?'

I followed her outdoors, where we took a seat in the two plastic chairs along the wall – no doubt set there for kitchen staff taking cigarette breaks. 'Let's start with the bookshop,' I said, opening the 'Notes' app on my phone. 'Were any of those employees here that night besides you?'

'There are only ever two besides me, both part-time, and just one was working that night: Ellen. But she just came to help set up and had left by the time the dinner started, so I think we can cross her off our list.'

'Okay, how about the dining-room staff?'

Lucinda thought a moment. 'Besides Alan, there was Sky – you probably remember him; he's our host and is now managing the dining room in Alan's . . . absence. And also Michelle and Antonio – they're both servers. Oh, and our busser Alex was there too.'

I tapped out their names on my phone. 'Anything you can think of that might give any of them reason to dislike Alan?'

She shook her head. 'No, nothing comes to mind. Other than the fact that he could be kind of a prig sometimes. But they all seemed to get along well enough with him, I'd say. Though it's not impossible that Alan might have given them grief at some point. You know, if they didn't clear the tables fast enough, or let dishes sit on the pass for too long.'

I did know. Being dining-room manager was stressful work, and we were supremely lucky at Gauguin to have Brandon, who managed to keep his cool under even difficult circumstances. 'Well, what about the host?' I asked. 'Sky, right? Didn't he benefit from Alan's death – you know, by getting that promotion? It must have come with a pay raise, right?'

'Yeah, but it's also a ton more work, and Sky's already said that he's only willing to take on the extra duties here until we find someone else to be dining manager. He's got another gig at a yoga studio, which is his primary focus in life.'

'Oh. So I guess we can cross him off the list, then.' I made a note next to his name, then looked back up at Lucinda. 'Okay, now for the kitchen staff. Who was here that night?'

'Not many, since Jan – the other line cook – ended up being a no-show.' She held up her hand and ticked off names with her fingers: 'Just the prep cook Enrique, the two dishwashers Neil and Roberto, you, and Kamila. As for Enrique, he barely knows – knew – Alan, since he only started here about two weeks ago and the two probably never said more than a few words to each other. Same goes for the dishwashers. Not that they're brand new, but they didn't have a whole lot of contact with Alan.'

I tapped my finger on my phone then glanced toward the kitchen door which stood open not too far from where we sat. 'And what about Kamila?' I asked in a quiet voice. 'I know you two are friends and business partners, but she did recently break up with Alan, so . . .'

Lucinda drew a slow breath. 'Yeah, I know. But I honestly can't see her doing anything like that. And besides, you were with her the whole time when it happened, right?'

'True. But I've been thinking about that, and I realized it wouldn't have had to be her who actually did it. It could have been someone else . . . on her behalf.'

'No.' Lucinda was shaking her head. 'I just don't believe it.'

I leaned toward her, forearms on my thighs. 'Look. I know this is difficult, but I need you to think really hard about this, because it could be your future on the line here. Is there anything you can think of that might suggest animosity on the part of Kamila toward Alan? Like, why'd she break up with him?'

'Because he was a dick?' Lucinda let out a short bark of laughter, then frowned. 'But seriously, she never told me exactly why. I just figured it was 'cause once they got over the honeymoon period – they'd been together about a year and a half, I'd say – she came to realize about two months ago that maybe they weren't such a good match, after all. So she moved out and got her own place. You know, different interests, different takes on life.'

'Different how?'

'Well, I know Kamila isn't much interested in the whole home-lessness issue, for one. Not that she's indifferent to the problem or anything, but Alan had gotten pretty active of late in the home-less rights movement – the "unhoused," as he preferred to say – and I know Kamila is more one to stay out of politics. She just wanted to do her cooking at the restaurant, then go home and relax with a glass of wine and a movie on Netflix. So they tended to butt heads over that.'

I thought back to the conversation I'd had with my dad the previous weekend. 'Yeah, well, I bet that's not an unusual dynamic these days. Lots of people simply prefer not to think about the issue, and I can't say I always blame them. It can be a real downer. But if your partner is truly involved in something that's important to him, I can see how that would cause a rift in a relationship. Though—'

'Not enough to kill him over it,' Lucinda filled in.

'Right. Probably not. So is there anything else you can think of besides that?'

She gazed out toward the orange dumpster in the corner of the parking lot, where a tabby cat lay in the sun licking its paw. From the way Lucinda was clenching and unclenching her jaw, I got the feeling there *was* something else. But I kept my silence, waiting for her to come to a decision as to whether to share it with me or not.

A slow exhalation told me she'd decided to spill. 'I think there might have been some sort of issue between them about money,' Lucinda finally said, so softly I almost didn't hear.

'He owed her, or vice versa?'

'I don't know. And I'm not even sure there *was* an issue, but from something Kamila said to me right before she broke it off with Alan, that's the feeling I got.' She paused, then, realizing I was expecting her to elaborate, continued on. 'She told me she couldn't believe how much it was costing him to do some kind of remodel at his house, and I got the distinct impression she was annoyed by the whole thing.'

'Huh. Were they serious enough that they were sharing money? Or would she have been annoyed for some other reason? Like maybe she didn't want to live in a construction zone?'

'I have no idea,' said Lucinda. 'And as I said, I'm not positive she was in fact upset about it. I just got that idea from . . . I dunno. Her body language maybe? I can't even remember now what exactly it was.' She stared down at the ground for a moment, then stood. 'Look, I have to get back to work, but I want you to know that I really appreciate your looking into this for me. I've been having a hard time sleeping, worrying that any minute the cops are gonna show up with a warrant for my arrest. So, thanks.

Knowing that you're helping means a lot.' With a quick, forced-looking smile, she headed back indoors.

Well, don't get your hopes up too much, was all I thought as I watched her go.

EIGHT

I sat for a few moments in the sun, trying to figure out what I was going to say to Kamila. The tabby had now made its way to the shade, where it sat eyeing a pair of noisy crows taking turns snatching at a crust of bread at the far end of the dumpster.

I didn't want to come across as interrogating the cook – even though that's exactly what I had in mind. A subtle approach was what the situation called for. Or maybe even the truth – that I was simply trying to help Lucinda out. You tended to get into a lot less trouble if you stuck to the truth. I'd simply omit the bit about my suspicions that Kamila could be the culprit instead of Lucinda . . .

A loud rumbling, accompanied by the stink of garbage mixed with diesel fumes, brought me back to the moment. An enormous truck had entered the parking lot and was lumbering across the asphalt towards the dumpster. A clear sign it was time for me to head indoors and get to it.

Kamila was in the dish room talking to one of the bussers when I popped my head through the back door, so I waited there until she'd finished. 'Sally,' she said, spying me as she turned away from the young man to return to the kitchen. 'What brings you here?' Her voice was friendly, but I thought I detected a hint of suspicion there, as well. Or perhaps it simply was indeed puzzlement at why I might be turning up in her kitchen that morning.

'Hi, Kamila. I was hoping you might have a couple minutes to spare so I could ask you about something.'

'Okay . . .' She gave me a look of curiosity, then crossed the room to the workbench and pulled a chef's knife from the brown canvas roll sitting atop its wooden surface. 'Is it okay if I do some prep work while we talk?'

'Sure, no problem.' A box of brightly colored heirloom tomatoes sat on the counter, and as I came to stand next to her, she selected one with deep creases in its red and green skin and proceeded to cut it into thick slices. 'It's about Lucinda,' I said.

'I gather you're aware she's one of the prime suspects right now in Alan's death?'

Kamila's shoulders appeared to droop as she reached for another tomato. 'I know,' she replied with a slow shake of the head. 'It's just horrible. First his death, and then this? It's like our entire world is collapsing around us.' She set down the knife and looked me in the eye. 'But it couldn't have been her. You know that, right?'

I nodded. 'And that's actually why I came to see you this morning. Lucinda's asked me to see if I can find out anything to prove her innocence, so I thought the first thing to do would be to talk to you. You know, since you two are so close, and also because of how well you knew Alan . . .'

I let that last sentence hang in the air, hoping she'd take up the thread, but Kamila was silent, biting her lip as she stared at the yellow KitchenAid at the far end of the counter. 'Oh, *right*,' she finally said, turning back toward me. 'You do that – solve murder cases. And you think you can solve this one?'

It suddenly hit me that she might have overheard my discussion with Lucinda outside the kitchen door a few minutes earlier, which would explain this last comment. 'Uh . . . I dunno,' I said. Kamila's dark eyes seemed to be searching mine – whether for assurance that I could help her friend, or for a sign that I might in fact suspect her, I could not tell.

After a moment, she picked up the knife and continued slicing her tomatoes. 'So what exactly would you like to know?'

'I guess I'm just wondering if there's anything you know about Alan that might point to anyone wanting to do him harm. Or if there's anything you saw or heard around here at the restaurant, either the night he was killed or before then, that might suggest he had enemies?'

'Alan could be difficult, as I'm sure you've already learned if you've talked to other people about him. And I'm sure that his working for his ex-partner here at the restaurant didn't help any.' Kamila spoke slowly, her eyes focused on her knife work. 'It's the main reason we broke up, his insistence on always being right, on being the one in control of whatever was going on. But he could be very kind, as well.'

'Like his work for the homeless?' I offered.

'Right. He was one hundred percent committed to helping them, and I don't for a second believe it was anything other than pure altruism. But his zeal for the cause could also rub people the wrong way. In part because of that smug assurance that his understanding of the issue was the correct one and that everyone else was sadly misinformed.'

'Yeah, I could see how that would be annoying.' I was thinking of Eric, who shared certain aspects of that know-it-all personality trait. Though thankfully, his default disposition was sweet and easy-going. 'So you think that might have been why Alan was killed?' I asked. 'Because of his position on the homeless issue in Santa Cruz?'

'I have no idea. But it seems as good a reason as any. Just look at how pissed off that woman was at the dinner. He often had that effect on people. He just . . .'

I waited for her to go on, but she instead stopped her cutting and wiped her eyes, then shook out her hands. 'Look,' she said, 'I do appreciate what you're doing for Lucinda, but I don't think I can talk about this right now. Maybe some other time?'

'Sure, no problem. I totally understand. And I'm truly sorry for your loss. And for being a little insensitive just now. I know this must be really hard for you.' Thanking Kamila for her time, I headed through the kitchen's swinging door in search of Lucinda.

The bookseller was standing at one of the dining-room tables talking with a customer who looked vaguely familiar. As I came closer, I saw that it was the same man who'd been in the group with me checking out the Julia Child books in the locked cabinet at the dinner. His dark hair, now released from its ponytail, hung down to his shoulders, but he again wore a Hawaiian shirt, this one sporting an array of tikis and hula girls.

I wasn't sure whether or not to interrupt them, but Lucinda saved me from the decision by waving me over to the table. 'Sally,' she said, 'I want you to meet Phillip, one of our best customers.'

'Howdy,' he said as I came up to the table. 'But I think we've already met, if I'm not mistaken?'

'Indeed,' I said. 'You were the one who thought those cookbooks were being auctioned for a ridiculous price. Though, as I recall, you were happy the money was going to a good cause.'

His grin was easy as he nodded agreement. 'True dat. I can't complain when rich people want to throw their money to those caught in the struggle of injustice and class warfare.'

Lucinda cast a bemused look my way, then gave her customer an affectionate pat on the shoulder. 'I was just telling Phillip here about your helping me out with my plight,' she said.

The man nodded once again, his face now serious. 'And I was telling her that if there's anything I can do, to let me know. I was there the whole evening, so maybe I saw something that could be of assistance. You never know.'

'Have you talked to the police?' I asked.

'Nuh-uh. They asked a few people to stay, but told most of us to just go on home. But I'm more than happy to, if you think it would help,' he added with a glance in Lucinda's direction. 'Or perhaps I could do your reading and that might tell us something helpful.'

'Phillip's a medium ,' Lucinda said. 'He helps people communicate with their loved ones who have now passed on.'

'Oh, really?' I'd always viewed folks who claimed such powers with skepticism and a bit of disdain, but on hearing those words right then I experienced a case of the shivers as I thought about Letta.

He must have sensed something in my demeanor, because the look he gave me was one of sympathy and concern. 'Have you recently lost a loved one?' he asked in a soft voice.

'Uh, no . . . well, yes, but it was a while ago,' I said with a wave of the hand. 'And I don't believe in all that stuff, in any case. No offense.'

'None taken,' said Phillip with a quick smile. He turned back to Lucinda. 'But if you'd like me to see if my . . . clairvoyance can assist in discovering the true culprit responsible for Alan's demise, I'd be more than happy to apply my skills. Just let me know.'

Lucinda patted him one more time. 'Maybe,' she said. 'But right now I really have to get back to work. Enjoy your lunch.'

Bidding Phillip goodbye, I followed her into the bookstore. 'Is he for real?' I asked once we'd gotten far enough away for the man not to hear. 'I mean, not that I believe any of them are for real. But you know, does he believe it himself?'

'He does. And from talking to people he's had sessions with, I gather they believe it as well. Like Sky, for example – our host here. He swears that Phillip's the real deal. So, who knows? And hey, right about now I could use all the help I could get, so maybe I should have him do my reading.'

I stared across the room at the medium, who'd now been joined at his table by the woman I recognized as the gal who'd been with him at the benefit dinner. 'Well, I guess it couldn't hurt,' I said to Lucinda. Then, at the approach of another customer to the cashier stand, I told her I'd be in touch if I learned anything new and made my way outside to my car.

Halfway across the parking lot, however, I stopped. The orange dumpster, now emptied of its contents, had been dropped back down in a slightly new position, revealing two familiar-looking items on the ground where it had previously stood. Walking towards them, I shielded my eyes from the sun to get a better look. Were those what I thought they were?

They were indeed.

I crouched down to pick one up, then stopped myself. *No. I shouldn't touch anything.* They could have important evidence on them. Instead, I pulled out my phone and punched in a number I now knew by heart.

'Detective Vargas here,' his deep voice came over the line.

'Hi. It's Sally. I just found those two Julia Child cookbooks that were stolen the night Alan Keeting was killed.' And then, as soon as the words were out of my mouth, I realized the pickle I'd now put myself into.

'And where exactly did you discover these books?' Vargas asked.

'In the Pages and Plums parking lot. They'd been tossed under the dumpster, which got moved this morning.'

'And you are at that restaurant . . . why?'

'Uh . . . for lunch?' I squeaked out.

'Right.' I could hear him exhale a slow breath, likely doing his best to not scream bloody murder into his phone. 'I'll come over ASAP. And, since you just *happen* to be there . . .' A dramatic pause. 'Could you make sure no one disturbs the scene till I arrive?'

'Will do.'

He ended the call with nary a thank-you, nor any other indication that he was at least happy the evidence had been discovered by someone who recognized its significance. But I can't say I was much surprised.

Ten minutes later, Vargas pulled into the parking lot and strode toward where I stood – now in the company of Lucinda, who'd spotted me loitering near the dumpster and had come over to investigate.

With a curt nod to the two of us, he pulled out his point-and-shoot camera and commenced taking photos of the cookbooks and the general scene. Only after the camera had been tucked back into his jacket pocket did he speak. 'So you said the dumpster had been moved this morning, revealing the books underneath?'

'Correct.' I said. 'The trash truck came to empty the container as I was heading into the restaurant, and when I came back out was when I saw the two books lying there, where the dumpster had been before it was emptied.'

'And how can you be certain they weren't in plain view the whole time, and you simply didn't notice them before?'

It occurred to me that it wasn't only me Vargas was frustrated with right about now. He had to also be supremely annoyed that his people – who'd supposedly done a thorough search of the area the night of the murder – hadn't discovered the cookbooks. But if they hadn't in fact been under the dumpster, but instead in plain view even before the trash had been emptied, then the detective had a good argument that the books had only been deposited in the parking lot *after* his cops had searched the place.

I hated to burst his bubble, almost as much as I hated to admit why I was so sure the cookbooks hadn't been in plain sight until after the dumpster had been moved. But with a glance at Lucinda, who gave me a 'ya gotta do what ya gotta do' shrug, I decided I had no choice but to come clean.

'It's 'cause, well, I was sitting for a few minutes over there' – I nodded to the white plastic chairs near the kitchen door – 'and watching a cat who was hanging out by the dumpster. If the books had been in plain sight like they are now, I'm sure I would have noticed them.'

'But you were inside for a fair amount of time after that, eating lunch, right? Which means whoever dumped the books could have done so during that time.' This newly inflated bubble of Vargas's was not long for the world, however, as my need to poke a sharp pin into its thin skin was overwhelming.

'Uh, I was actually only inside for ten, maybe fifteen minutes. So, yeah, it *could* have happened then, but it seems kind of unlikely.'

I couldn't tell if Vargas was more annoyed that he was going to have to live with the fact that his people had neglected to look under the dumpster when they'd searched the parking lot, or that I'd not only totally disregarded his order to stay off the case, but had also obviously lied to him about coming here for lunch.

Hands on hips, he glared at Lucinda and me for a few long seconds, then, with a shake of the head, crouched down to take a closer look at the books. One volume lay open on the grimy asphalt pavement, its pages fluttering in the light breeze. Pulling a pen from his shirt pocket, he used it to flip through the first few pages of the open book, one of which had clearly been ripped out.

'There's no signatures on any of these front pages, so they must have been on the one that's missing,' he said. 'I guess whoever stole them thought they'd have an easier time selling just the autographs than the whole books.'

'Any chance you can get fingerprints off them?' I asked.

'Maybe. Prints are hard to wipe off paper, but they'd be easier to wipe off these covers, so depends on where the person touched them and if they wiped 'em off – or wore gloves.'

He stood up with a grunt and headed back to his black SUV, returning a minute later with two large, plastic zip bags. After pulling on a pair of exam gloves, he carefully placed the books in the bags and sealed them up. 'Wasn't there also a box they came in?' he asked, glancing around the parking lot.

'Oh, yeah, you're right,' I said. Getting down on my hands and knees, I peered under the orange trash container. 'There it is, on the other side of the dumpster. Looks like it's been smashed flat, though.' And then I couldn't resist adding an extra dig: 'Hey, maybe you should hire me to do your crime scene searches.'

Was that a faint smile that briefly crossed his face?

NINE

Once Vargas had taken his leave, I decided to swing by my local taquería for some actual as opposed to imaginary lunch, then drove with my purchases to Eric's place to offer him some tacos *al pastor* as a peace offering. And it worked. The scowl on his face as he opened the door disappeared quickly as he inhaled the aroma of barbecued pork marinated in vinegar, achiote paste, cumin, and garlic. 'Oh, wow, you read my mind, Sal. I was so jonesing for some tacos right about now.'

'So you forgive me, then?'

His smile was sheepish. 'Yeah, I was a bit of a jerk the other night,' he said, waving me inside. 'And on the phone yesterday. Though your perpetual bull-headedness doesn't help things.'

I followed him into the kitchen and set the grease-coated paper bag on the counter. 'That's almost exactly what Vargas said the night we decided it wasn't working between us.'

'Well, he's right.' Eric grabbed two plates from the cupboard, handed one to me, then helped himself to a pair of tacos. 'The difference between him and me, though, is that I admit I can sometimes be almost as stubborn as you.'

'Almost?' I said. 'That's an understatement, coming from Mister I'm Always Right.'

'And with that, my dear, you just proved my postulation.'

With a laugh, I joined him at the dining-room table. 'I also brought you this,' I said, pulling a hardcover book from my bag and setting it on the table. 'I thought you might want something fun to read.'

He picked it up. 'Ian Fleming – cool! And it looks like an old copy.'

'Not a first edition, though,' I said, remembering Julian's snobbish remark. 'But *Casino Royale* is his first Bond book, so I thought you might get a kick out of it.'

'Thanks. I haven't read this one. I did see that old David Niven version years ago, but from my memory of how goofy it was, I'm guessing it's not an accurate rendition of the book.'

It was nice to see a genuine smile on Eric's face again – the first time he'd seemed happy since the night of the dinner at Pages and Plums. 'I take it you're feeling a little better now?'

He nodded, his mouth full of pork, marinated onion, and tortilla.

'So, what's the prognosis from Dr Singh? Have you talked to her today?'

'I have,' Eric said once he'd swallowed and wiped his mouth with a wad of paper napkins. 'She doesn't want me going back to the office yet – or anywhere, for that matter – but at least now she's talking days rather than weeks before I'm cleared for take-off.'

'Weeks?' I said. 'I had no idea that was even a possibility.'

'Yeah, well, that's one reason I've been so grouchy the past few days. And even now, knowing my house arrest shouldn't last too much longer, I'm going kind of stir-crazy. There's only so many movies and TV shows I can watch in a day, and too much reading still makes my head hurt. Which I gather is one of the reasons the good doctor doesn't deem me ready for real life yet.' He let out a sigh, then reached for his second taco.

'Dang. I can only imagine how hard this must all be for you. I wish there were something I could do.'

'How 'bout you tell me more about what's going on with that dead dining-room manager?'

I stared at him. 'Really? I thought that was the last thing you wanted to hear about.'

Eric shrugged. 'A guy's allowed to change his mind, isn't he? And besides, I'm just so damn *bored*. It'll give me something different to do, thinking about the case. And hey, maybe *I'll* be the one to solve it this time.'

I couldn't believe what I was hearing. Eric, the by-the-book prosecutor, actually wanted to get involved in a clandestine investigation of a case that would likely end up on the desk of one of his colleagues at some point in the not-too-distant future?

But then again, it also made sense. Eric was accustomed to going surfing several times a week, not to mention skateboarding and hiking and doing all sorts of other physical activities. He had to be climbing the walls with pent-up energy, confined as he was to a small condo with only a tiny balcony for outdoor space. Maybe a cerebral exercise was just the ticket for his bored and frustrated self.

'Okay, Mr Jimmy Stewart,' I said. 'I'll fill you in with all I know.'

'Huh?'

'You know, Hitchcock's *Rear Window*? Only instead of a broken leg, you've got a broken brain. And since you don't have a neighbor's apartment life to spy on,' I said, indicating the two-car garage that filled most of Eric's view from the dining-room window, 'I'll have to be your Grace Kelly and bring you news about what's going on in the case.'

'Grace Kelly, huh?' Eric shot me a suggestive look. 'So you gonna put on one of those long, silky dresses she always wears in the movies?'

'Not likely,' I said, then stood to fetch us each a glass of water. 'You'll be lucky if you ever see me even in a silk shirt.' While Eric drank from the glass I handed him, I gave him a run-down of what I'd learned so far about Alan Keeting's death, followed by the list of suspects Lucinda and I had come up with so far: Raquel, the woman who'd argued with Alan at the dinner and had also bid on the cookbooks; the bookseller, Julian; and Kamila.

'So you're certain it wasn't Lucinda?' Eric asked.

'No, I can't be *certain*. But I don't see her as being the murderer. I mean, she's the one who asked me to look into this whole thing in the first place. Would she have done that if she were the one who actually killed him?'

'Sure. She could merely be doing that to throw us all off the scent. And she definitely *could* have done it, logistically speaking, that is. Think about it: Lucinda's the one who went back inside through the kitchen door after Kamila made the announcement about finding Alan's body. She could have tampered with the evidence then, before you went inside to secure the scene.'

'True . . .' I had to admit that Eric was right. Which of course was why she was suspect number one in Detective Vargas's mind. 'But what about those stolen cookbooks?' I said. 'It doesn't make sense that she would kill Alan in order to take them when she could have done so easily without resorting to violence.'

'Same thing,' said Eric. 'To throw us all off the track and make it look like the books were the point of the killing.'

'Okay, if that's the case, then why would the person immediately jettison the books under the dumpster?'

Eric stopped chewing. 'Really? They found the books?'

'*I* found the books,' I corrected him. 'This morning, in the Pages and Plums parking lot. And get this: the pages with the signatures had been ripped out, almost as if whoever took them realized they couldn't hide the big books, but they could at least keep the autographs.'

'Weird.'

'I know.' I stared out the window at a woman walking down the sidewalk with two large grocery bags and a small child in tow. 'Anyway,' I said after a bit, 'I have other possibilities, too, though at this point I don't have any specific facts to point to any of them as being actual suspects. First, there's that guy who donated the books, an attorney named Saul—'

'Attorneys are always suspect,' said Eric with a grin.

'Yeah, and to tell you the truth, that's about all I have on him at this point. But it does occur to me that he could have had donor's remorse and decided he wanted the books back after he gave them to Lucinda. Or maybe they were insured or something . . .'

Eric was shaking his head. 'He'd already given them away, so I doubt any insurance would have still been in force once that happened. And besides, why would he then go and rip out those pages and throw the books under that dumpster?'

'Yeah, good point. But I'd still like to talk to the guy,' I said, 'if for no other reason than he had a close connection to the stolen books. Plus, I gotta admit I'd love to pick his brain more about knowing Paul and Julia Child, and talking to him about Alan's death gives me the chance to do so.'

Eric laughed. 'Gee, I wonder if Miss Marple ever used murder as a ruse to talk to someone about a famous chef.'

'Probably not. And there you have in a nutshell the key difference between the two of us.' I took a large bite of my messy taco before going on. 'Okay,' I said once I'd swallowed and wiped the grease from my face, 'there are also those people who were ogling the cookbooks with me when Lucinda took them out of the case to show to Julian. Since they clearly showed an interest in the books, I figure they should at least be on our long list, too. One's this guy named Phillip, who I actually met earlier today at Pages and Plums. And a gal I think may be his wife or girlfriend was there, and also two other women I don't know anything about. The guy, Phillip, is apparently a regular at the restaurant. And get this: he's also a medium who can communicate with the dead – at least according to him and Lucinda.'

This prompted a short laugh from Eric. 'There ya go; I bet *he's* your guy. I've never trusted those woo-woo types, taking advantage of grieving family members by pretending to be able to bring them messages from their loved ones.' With a derisive snort, he popped the last of his taco into his mouth.

'Well, I don't think they're necessarily *all* charlatans,' I said. 'I bet some of them truly believe they have some kind of psychic power. And who knows, maybe there is in fact a sixth sense that exists in some people. Like, take bats, for instance. Their ability to know where things are based on sonar or whatever it is they have, that seems like some kind of 'magical' sense to us humans who don't possess the same ability. So, what if there's another sort of sense that you and I don't have or understand, but which some people . . .' Glancing Eric's way, I noticed his gaping look and trailed off.

'Are you kidding me, Sal? You're actually *defending* those people? Maybe I'm not the only one who suffered some kind of concussion,' he said with a laugh. But when all I did was stare down at my half-eaten taco, his laughter died. 'My God,' he said, leaning forward. 'I do believe you're serious. So what the . . .?' And then he gave a slow nod of understanding. 'Ah . . . It's about Letta, isn't it?'

Embarrassed both by the tears escaping down my cheek as well as my impassioned speech just now to Eric, all I could do at that point was let out a slow stream of breath, trying to control the emotions threatening to overtake me.

He stood and walked to my side. 'Hey, it's okay,' he said, crouching down so he could look me in the eyes. 'I get it. And I'm sorry I was such an insensitive jerk just now. It *would* be great if we could communicate with our loved ones after they died. Hell, I'd sure love to have the chance to hang out with my granddad one more time and shoot the breeze.'

'I know,' I finally managed to articulate. 'And I also know it's just a fantasy. But it's such *seductive* one,' I said, wiping my tears with a sad smile. 'Because I'd really, *really* love to talk with Letta one more time and tell her how much she meant to me – and how much she still does.'

*   *   *

Javier had that night off from Gauguin, but he spent the afternoon before he left making sure everyone at work knew he was taking his girlfriend, Ana, out to eat at Le Radis Ravi, a three-star restaurant up in Los Gatos.

'Just don't order the foie gras,' said our line cook, Brian. 'It's delicious, but the portion is way too small for the money.'

'Oh, right – you used to work there. So what should we order?' asked Javier.

'The scallops with lemon-caper sauce and house-made pappardelle are pretty tasty, as are the sweetbreads. They fry them up like chicken nuggets with this amazing *glace de viande*-mustard-cream reduction. But who knows if those things are still on the menu,' Brian added. 'It's been over a year since I worked there, and I sure can't afford to eat at a place like that on this tiny salary they pay me *here*.'

'Ha, ha,' said Javier, tossing his apron onto the counter and picking up his leather messenger bag. 'And you, my friend, just talked yourself out of me sharing any of my doggie bag with you tomorrow.' Then, leaving us to it with a wave of the fingers, the chef headed out to the parking lot, whistling what sounded like the theme song from *The Love Boat*.

With Javier gone that night, Brian and I had decided to let Tomás have his first shot on the hot line during a busy weekend shift. I'd be at his side, monitoring his dishes and answering any questions he might have, with Kris at the grill station. As we had yet to find a new prep/*garde manger* cook to replace Tomás, Brian had agreed to take over those duties for the night. 'It'll be a nice break from the heat of the oven and stove,' the line cook had gallantly replied in response to Tomás's concern at this arrangement.

It was all going well until about eight o'clock, when the orders from an eight-top came in – all hot line dishes. We already had about ten tickets on the rail, and Tomás and I were methodically working through them, me trying to act cool and collected, Tomás merely trying to act collected. The perspiration coursing down his brow made very clear he was not the least bit cool.

'Two duck, one pork, three fish, and two scallops, all day!' I read from the new ticket. Then, 'We need more scallops over here!' I hollered at Brian as he skirted behind us bearing inserts of brandy-soaked apricots and chopped cilantro.

'On it!' he shouted back.

I'd just plated up two orders of coq au vin au Gauguin when the crashing of a pan onto the stove top caused me to flinch. '¡*Maldita sea!*' Tomás shouted, thrusting his left hand up in the air. The hand, I noticed, held no towel.

Damn. It was a classic rookie mistake, one I'd made more times than I wished to remember – grabbing the handle of a hot sauté pan without using your side towel as a pot holder. 'Lemme see,' I ordered the grimacing cook, who held out his hand for my inspection. The palm was red, but there was no blistering. *Good. No need for him to go to the ER.* 'Go grab some ice,' I directed, and he complied. When he returned to the line, he had a stainless-steel bowl full of ice and several cubes gripped in his burnt hand.

'I'm so sorry,' he said, embarrassment now having replaced the pain in his face.

I patted him on the shoulder. 'It's okay, dude. We've all been there. Think of it as a battle scar, a real trial by fire: the cook's badge of honor.'

'Not much honor in being a complete and total idiot,' he mumbled, dropping the ice back into the bowl and gingerly using his towel to move the offending pan back on to the front burner.

I knew how much his palm must hurt right about now, and also how the throbbing and searing pain would continue for the rest of the night. It's bad enough to simply burn yourself, but to then have to keep that burned area in close proximity to the heat of a restaurant hot line is downright misery. But I knew better than to ask him if he wanted to change stations; that would be the ultimate in shame for a line cook. For as Letta used to say, constant pain – whether from burns, cuts, an aching back, or sore feet – was indeed the line cook's badge of honor.

Luckily, after that eight-top, the tickets started to trickle down, and by eight forty-five only three remained. 'I'll take these last orders,' I said to Tomás. 'Why don't you go help Brian clean up the *garde manger*, since he's not used to working that station.' The warmth in his eyes told me how much he appreciated the face-saving request.

Once the last of the orders had been plated and sent off to the dining room, I set about cleaning the hot line – removing the grates, scraping the grime off the range top, then wiping it all down with a wet rag. As I worked, I thought about Alan's death and what Eric had said about Lucinda. *Could she be the one who'd killed Alan, after all?* It was awful convenient for her to have been the first person on the scene after Kamila had come outside to tell us all what had happened. And there certainly had been enough time for her to have done Alan in after chewing him out about that Raquel woman and before his body was discovered.

But if so, why would she take the cookbooks, and then discard them after ripping out those pages? Since Lucinda could easily have stolen the cookbooks at any time before then and blamed it on a simple theft, it didn't make sense for her to have killed Alan to get the books. But then again, as Eric had noted, it could merely have been an after-the-fact spontaneous decision, an attempt to confuse everyone about what had truly happened.

In any event, I was certainly confused.

I'd set the alarm for eight o'clock on Saturday morning, knowing there was little chance I'd awaken on my own in time to get to Alan's memorial at nine. But as I took Buster for a hurried walk around the block, I wished I'd been able to get at least a couple more hours' shut-eye. Six and a half just didn't cut it. Not when I was already running on empty in the sleep department. But such is the life of a restaurateur.

I parked the T-Bird across the street from Natural Bridges State Beach and headed down to where a cluster of people were already gathered by the water's edge. Dogs aren't allowed in state parks, and since I only tended to walk these days where I could take Buster, it had been a while since I'd been to the place. As I made my way across the sand, I admired the last remaining 'bridge' at the beach – a wide sea arch cut into a mammoth rock located just off shore. There had been two arches back when I was a kid, but the one closer to shore had collapsed during a powerful storm in the winter of 1980. Nevertheless, the one remaining arch was impressive on its own, with the ocean splashing underneath, sending dramatic plumes of water up onto the remnants of the marine terrace bluff.

The fog was just starting to lift when I arrived at the beach, but it was still chilly, and most of the folks milling about waiting before Alan's service had known to dress warmly for the occasion. It wasn't a big crowd, maybe fifteen or so, about half of whom I recognized from Pages and Plums. The others looked like your typical thirty-something Santa Cruz crowd: upscale hipsters in Merrell shoes and Patagonia puffer jackets, with a scattering of hand-knit pink hats and orange and black Giants baseball caps.

Spying Lucinda, I headed over to where she and Kamila were setting up a card table. On the sand beside them sat several boxes containing two large thermoses, a package of paper coffee cups, a box of sugar cubes, a quart of half-and-half, and a stack of what looked to be programs for the memorial service.

'Do you mind if I have a look?' I asked, indicating the stack of papers.

'Not at all,' said Kamila. 'In fact, if you could pass them out to people, that would be great.'

'Happy to help.' *More than happy*, I thought, for this gave me a perfect excuse to chat up the attendees and find out their connection to Alan. Grabbing the programs, I flipped through the top one to see what was on the agenda – if that's what you call it – for the morning's service. Kamila was going to speak, as well as several others whose names I didn't recognize. To finish off the service, someone would sing and play two songs on the guitar: Leonard Cohen's 'Hallelujah' and 'The Streets of Philadelphia' by Bruce Springsteen.

Ah, a song about homelessness. Turning to take another look at the attendees who weren't from the restaurant, I wondered if they might be people Alan had known through his advocacy for the homeless. *Could well be.* Many of those most active in our local movement had plenty of money, I knew, not to mention beautiful homes.

I walked over to where three men and a woman were sitting on a blanket spread out on the sand. 'Care for a program?' I asked.

'Thanks,' said a man with a braided beard and shaved head.

'So how did you all know Alan?' I asked as they unfolded the sheets and studied the notes and listings inside.

'Malcolm and I volunteered with him at the Santa Cruz Food Project,' the bald guy answered, with a nod toward the man across from him. 'You know, that group that hands out meals down at San Lorenzo Park?'

I nodded. 'Sure, I know about them.'

'And these other two hangers-on come along with us from time to time,' he added.

The woman by his side slapped him lightly on the shoulder. 'Hey, I help out sometimes, too.'

'I, however, choose to perform my civic duty in other ways,' said the third man, whose gaunt features suggested he could actually do with a few hearty bowls of soup, himself.

Malcolm took the man's hand with a proud smile. 'Francisco is a musician and poet,' he said, 'and he donates half of his earnings to righteous causes.'

I glanced at my program and then at the guitar case on the blanket next to Francisco. 'Ah, so you're the one who'll be performing this morning. I look forward to hearing you play.'

'And how about you?' the first guy asked me. 'How did you know Alan?'

I'd anticipated this question and had decided to go with a half-truth: 'I worked with him briefly at the restaurant. But I didn't get to know him very well, I'm sorry to say.' I gazed out at the water, where two toddlers were braving the chilly shallows, shrieking in glee as the tiny waves swept over their ankles. 'It's all just so awful.'

'Agreed,' said the man with the braided beard. 'It was so sudden, so unexpected.' Scooping up a handful of sand, he watched as it trickled through his fingers back on to the beach. Then, with a shake of the head, he looked back up at me. 'I'm Duane, by the way, and this is Monique.'

'Sally,' I said. 'Nice to meet you all. Though the circumstances could certainly be better.'

Monique opened her program and stared at it briefly, then set it in her lap. 'So I saw you talking a minute ago with that woman from the restaurant . . .'

'Right, Lucinda,' I filled in. 'She runs the bookshop part of Pages and Plums.'

'Uh-huh. I was just wondering if . . .' She glanced quickly at Duane before finishing her thought. 'If, well, maybe she said anything to you about what exactly happened to Alan? I mean, I know from the story in the newspaper that he died the night of that benefit dinner and that they're looking into what caused his death, but that's about all any of us have heard.'

'As a matter of fact,' I said in a low voice, squatting down at the edge of the blanket, 'I was working there the night Alan was killed, and I actually saw his body.' This caused an intake of breath

A Sense for Murder   87

from all four members of my now rapt audience. 'And I can tell you that it did not look like a mere accident to me. I think he was shoved into that bookcase – shoved hard, from what I could see.'

Sitting back on my heels, I studied the four faces for any signs of guilt, fear, or other suspicious reactions. But all I saw there was surprise with a healthy dose of fascination. 'So the obvious question is,' I went on, 'and maybe one of you could answer this: was there anyone who had reason to harm Alan, or to want him dead?'

My question was met with silence and frowns, and it was hard to tell whether they might have found the question to be distasteful, or whether they were merely pondering the answer to it. After a bit, Malcolm cleared his throat and looked up at me. 'Well, I can't say anything for sure, of course, but there are certain elements in our community who disapprove of what we do.'

'Yeah,' I said, 'I've read about that in the paper – that a lot of folks are upset that you don't have a permit to pass out the meals and that the Food Project causes a ruckus downtown with the big crowds they attract.'

'Big crowds of the "wrong" kind of people is what they really mean,' said Duane. 'If it was a crowd of rich dudes lining up for free power green smoothies, they'd have no problem with what we do.'

I wasn't so positive this was true, but chose not to go there. 'Speaking of that "element" who isn't so supportive of your cause,' I said instead, 'there was a woman at that Pages and Plums benefit dinner who got into an argument with Alan shortly before he was killed. Her name's Raquel Santiago, and I gather she's . . .' I stopped mid-sentence, seeing the group collectively roll their eyes. 'I take it you all know her?'

'*Do* we,' Duane said with a short laugh. 'She's at just about every city council meeting, griping about one thing or another.'

Monique was shaking her head. 'What a gadfly.'

'Totally,' agreed Duane. 'But mostly her deal is "cleaning up the streets", as she puts it.'

'Which translates to trying to force the unhoused to move out of *her* neighborhood into someone else's – preferably one she never has to set foot in.' Malcolm's sneer left no doubt as to his opinion of the woman.

'So what about her as Alan's killer?' I asked.

Malcolm frowned. 'Well, I can't say I much *like* the woman,' he said, 'but I can't see her going so far as to actually *kill* someone because they disagreed with her.' He glanced at the others, who all shook their heads in agreement.

'Huh-uh,' said Duane. 'Raquel's certainly passionate about the issue of homelessness, but then so are we all – on the other side, of course – and none of us would ever do something like that. I mean, that's what the city council meetings are for, to discuss these things in a civilized, democratic manner.'

A snort from Monique made him turn her way. 'Right,' she said. 'I've been to those meetings, and "civilized" is not the way I'd necessarily describe them.'

Duane shrugged. 'Okay, so sometimes people get a little hot under the collar, but at least they're going through official channels rather than taking things into their own hands.'

I would have loved to hear how the conversation progressed from here, but at the sound of clapping we all turned to face Kamila, who was calling us to attention. 'Okay, everyone!' she yelled out. 'We're going to begin now, so if you could all gather around so we don't have to shout, that would be great.'

I joined the others in getting to my feet, and we headed over to where the rest of the attendees now stood in a half-circle around the Pages and Plums chef. She gazed down at the sand for a moment as we all stood there in silence, then looked up and blinked several times, her jaw set.

'Right . . .' Kamila blew out a slow breath. 'We're gathered here today to say goodbye to Alan Keeting – our dear friend, our co-worker, our fellow community advocate, and one of the most generous human beings I've ever had the good fortune to know. Alan's family will be holding a service in a few weeks back in New Jersey, where they'll also be spreading his ashes, but I thought it appropriate to hold our own memorial in his honor here in Santa Cruz, in the community where he decided to make his home and where he gave so much of his time and energy helping others not so fortunate as he.

'For those who don't know much about Alan's early years, here's a little history. As a boy, he loved going to see his beloved Yankees play baseball, hanging out on the Jersey Shore, and trouncing the other neighborhood kids at back-alley games of nickle-ante poker.'

Kamila paused to allow the crowd to chuckle at this last tidbit, and I took the opportunity to scan the crowd. Lucinda was still over by the table with the coffee, and she was listening to something that a man with his back to me was telling her. As Kamila started to speak once again, I saw Lucinda put a finger to her lips, and the two quieted down and turned to face the gathering.

Was that who I thought it was? It was indeed. *Now why would Julian Bartlett-Jones be at Alan's memorial service?*

TEN

It was hard to concentrate on the rest of what Kamila said, or the other speakers who followed, given how intent I was on keeping an eye on Julian and Lucinda. While folks took turns recounting heartfelt and amusing stories about Alan Keeting, my brain was wrestling with possible reasons for the bookseller being here today.

A woman stepped to the front of the crowd and started talking about how Alan had helped her move her belongings from a campsite down by the San Lorenzo River into a tiny home that a local advocacy group had provided for her. But all during her story, I kept glancing across to where Julian still stood next to Lucinda, he apparently as intent on studying Lucinda as I was, him. Did his being here have anything to do with Alan's murder?

But then I realized, *Of course, it does – this is a memorial for the guy's death, after all.* The more relevant question was, did he come this morning for some reason other than to merely pay his respects? Because as far as I was aware, Julian didn't know Alan – he hadn't even met him prior to the night of his death.

But what did I truly know about Julian Bartlett-Jones? Could it be that *he* was the one who killed Alan and then couldn't resist showing up today? That's the way it always happened in TV shows, where the murderer would come to the funeral to watch as all the friends and family sobbed about the victim's death.

Or perhaps he was simply *afraid* that he might be a suspect, even though he had nothing to do with the death, and wanted to make a show of his concern by participating in the memorial. Or maybe he'd come for the same reason as me – for the purpose of checking out the other suspects, who he knew were likely to attend. After all, just two days earlier I'd told Julian that the police were interested in Alan's co-workers as possible perpetrators of the crime.

At that thought, I swiveled around again to check out who was on the beach. The police usually showed up, too, in novels and TV serials. And yep, sure enough, there was Martin Vargas. He was at the far back, on the opposite side of the crowd from Lucinda and Julian. *Damn.* The detective would not be happy to see me here. I should have thought to bring Allison along so I could have made the argument that I'd been asked to come help her support her good friend Lucinda.

I turned away quickly, but it was merely wishful thinking to imagine he hadn't spotted me. At close to six feet tall, I stood well above many of the people around me. Nevertheless, I did my best not to worry about Vargas's reaction to my presence at the memorial (*I have every right to be here*, I argued to myself unconvincingly), and allowed my thoughts to return to Julian Bartlett-Jones.

Okay, so if he did want to check out the other possible suspects, it made sense that he'd want to talk to both Lucinda and Kamila. And if he knew Lucinda was currently the prime suspect – *could he know that?* – then of course he'd zoom in on her as soon as he arrived. Or maybe he truly suspected her of the crime.

I turned to watch the pair once more. Francisco was now playing guitar and doing a passable imitation of the Boss's throaty voice as he sang 'The Streets of Philadelphia', and some in the crowd were taking the opportunity to whisper among themselves, Julian and Lucinda included. A glance behind me showed that Detective Vargas also had his eyes on the same two attendees.

It didn't look as if Lucinda was terribly thrilled with Julian's attentions, however, and as I watched, she shook her head and walked away. His eyes followed her as she made her way over to Kamila and Sky, and then he turned to listen to the music, a sly smile forming on his thin lips.

Francisco concluded his song with a rapid strumming of the guitar, at which point Kamila announced that unless anyone else wanted to come up and say something further, the service was over, but that we were free to stay and help ourselves to more coffee if we wanted. I was looking around to see if anyone else would step forward to speak when a hand upon my shoulder made me jump.

'Sorry, I didn't mean to startle you,' Martin said, then chuckled. 'You on edge 'cause you know how I feel about you showing up here today?'

'*No,*' I said – a little too quickly and forcefully to have much ring of truth.

'So . . . if I may ask, what exactly *are* you doing here?'

'I just felt I should come and show my support for Kamila, is all, since I was there the night Alan was . . . that he died.'

'Uh-huh.' It was clear Martin saw through my fiction, but he didn't seem terribly concerned by it, or by the fact that I was there at the memorial service. It was, after all, an event open to the public, being held at a public beach, so there wasn't really all that much he could say. But it was curious to find him unruffled by my presence.

The detective turned to watch Julian as he made his way across the sand toward the parking lot above the beach. 'I saw you staring at him,' he said with a nod toward the bookseller.

'You don't miss much, do you?'

'Not much.' He waited for me to answer his unspoken question.

'Well, don't you think it's a little odd that he showed up here today? I mean, how did he even know it was happening?'

'It was in yesterday's paper,' Martin said. 'And I don't see how it's any more odd than your being here.'

With a shiver, I shoved my hands into the pockets of my fleece jacket. The fog, which had been receding when I'd arrived at the beach, had now rolled back in, along with a nippy breeze. But it wasn't simply the weather that was giving me the chills. Only four months earlier, Martin and I had been cuddling together on his living-room couch, as easy together as a pair of puppies at a dog park. So it was supremely awkward – not to mention unpleasant – to now be treated the same as he would a mere witness or suspect in one of his cases.

Did he consider me a suspect in this case?

No, he couldn't. I shook off this thought and stamped my feet against the cold. 'Well, I think it's pretty interesting how intent Julian was on talking to Lucinda, is all. But then again, who knows – maybe they actually knew each other before the whole book auction thing came up.' And then I slapped my forehead with my palm. 'Duh! They're both in the bookselling business. Of *course* they could have known each other.'

Martin shook his head with a smile. 'You never change, do you, Sally? Can't keep a cat from its catnip.' Concluding that silence was the best response to this comment, I said nothing. 'So, I heard about Eric,' the detective went on, clearly in a chatty mood. 'How's he doing?'

Ah, safer territory, even if it was my ex asking about my current beau. 'He's going kind of stir-crazy cooped up at home with nothing to do but watch TV and read spy novels. But when I stopped by yesterday, he was in a much better mood and his headache has subsided. It looks like his doctor may release him back to normal life sometime next week.' I was about to add, 'not that he's all that eager to get back to work,' but stopped myself. It was a good bet Eric wouldn't want me telling Vargas, who surely spoke to Eric's boss on a regular basis, about his work woes.

'Glad to hear it. Head injuries like that can be scary.' At the ringing of his cell phone, Vargas held up a finger. 'Sorry, I gotta take this.' He took a few steps away and spoke briefly to whoever had called, then shoved the device back in his pocket and returned to my side. 'I have to go,' he said. 'But before I do, a word of advice. Be careful, Sally, and think before you act. I clearly can't keep you from talking to whoever you want, but know that this is damn serious. Whoever killed Alan is running scared right now, and scared people – especially those who've already committed one homicide – are the most dangerous kind.'

'Understood,' I said, returning his grave look.

'I truly hope you do.' With a quick squeeze to my upper arm, he strode off across the sand, cell phone already back up at his ear.

I glanced around to see who still remained at the gathering. Most of the Pages and Plums crew had taken off, including Lucinda, but Kamila and Sky were still here, chatting with some people I didn't know. I started towards them, but when I spied Francisco talking to Malcolm, I changed direction.

'Beautiful music,' I said, coming up to where the two stood.

'Thanks,' said Francisco with a sigh. 'It was hard keeping it together while I sang, but I guess I did okay.'

'You did great,' said Malcolm, leaning over to give him a kiss on the cheek. He then turned toward me. 'So you said you worked at the restaurant with Alan?' he asked.

'Uh . . .' I dug the toe of my shoe into the sand, wondering how honest to be with this. 'I actually only got to know him recently – the week before he died. I volunteered to help cook at that benefit dinner the night he was killed, and thought I should come today to pay my respects.'

Francisco gave me a curious look. 'Are you a big supporter of the Teens' Table organization and the work they do?'

'Well, a good friend of mine has a daughter involved in the group, and they both say wonderful things about them, so I figured I might as well lend a hand. I'm a cook by trade, so it seemed like a good cause I could contribute to.'

'If you don't mind my asking,' said Malcolm, 'I'm wondering why you really came here today. I mean, it's not as if you were a good friend of Alan's.' When I didn't answer right away, he went on. 'It's just that, given those questions you were asking earlier, I can't help but wonder if maybe you're looking into the circumstances of Alan's death?' At this point he shot me a conspiratorial look. 'You know, like you did with those other murders over the past couple years?'

Ah. He'd figured out who I was: 'the Sleuth of Santa Cruz', as the local paper had taken to calling me. Well, perhaps – given his clear interest in *my* interest – this was a good thing. I leaned forward and said in a low voice, 'Actually, I am. And anything you know about Alan might prove extremely valuable in helping me figure out what really happened to the poor guy.'

Malcolm glanced at Francisco, who raised his eyebrows and then nodded. 'Go on. I think we can tell her.'

'Tell me what?'

'Well, Alan didn't want this to get around, but now that he's dead, I guess it wouldn't hurt for us to tell you. The thing is, he'd been living in his van for a couple months before he died.'

'Alan had been living in his *van?*' This was news to me. *Did Kamila and Lucinda know?* If not, the fact that Alan had kept it from them was telling . . . of something; I just wasn't sure what. And if they had known, it might be equally telling that they'd chosen to keep the information from me. And then I wondered, *Did Vargas know?* He had to, I figured. And it certainly wasn't the sort of information the detective would share with me if he did have it.

'Yeah,' said Malcolm. 'It's weird, I know. I gather he had to vacate his house for some reason or other. He was pretty vague about exactly why, but people in his situation often are. He didn't tell anyone but me and Francisco, as far as I know, and the only reason we found out is because we happened to see him hanging out next to his van late one night and asked him about it.'

'Where'd you see him?' I asked.

Malcolm pointed in the direction of the parking lot above us.

'Right near here,' he said. 'You know the street that runs into Delaware where all those RVs have been parking lately?'

I did indeed. My father had been complaining for months about 'all those transients' taking over our streets, even though he lived almost two miles away from the area.

'But he made us promise not to tell anyone,' Francisco said. 'Which is also pretty typical. It's the whole shame thing of losing your housing. And not only that, but apparently one of the home-owners on the street had been harassing the people parking there – pounding on their windows and screaming at them at night when they were trying to sleep. Alan was pretty upset by that. So sad.'

'And ironic, too,' I commented, 'given his work as a homeless advocate. I wonder what happened to him. I know he and Kamila – the head chef and co-owner of Pages and Plums – were living together up until they broke up a couple months ago, so maybe he'd been relying on her paying him rent or something. But he had recently gotten a decent-paying job as dining-room manager at the restaurant.'

'Having a good job doesn't mean you can afford housing in Santa Cruz,' Francisco said with a shake of the head. 'Rents here are astronomical, as I'm sure you know. And who knows? Maybe he had a financial breakdown of some kind.'

'Or an emotional one caused by his breakup,' added Malcolm. 'That's what I suspect.'

I was about to ask whether they'd noticed anything else unusual about Alan in the days leading up to his death, when Malcolm pulled his phone from his pocket and checked the time.

'Oh, shoot,' he said. 'I have to be somewhere in twenty minutes. Gotta get going.' Planting another kiss on Francisco's cheek, he trotted over to where Duane and Monique stood talking with several people I didn't recognize. After a quick word with them, Malcolm made his way across the beach toward the parking lot.

'I should head out, too,' said Francisco, picking up his guitar case. 'Nice meeting you. Good luck with your quest. He didn't deserve to die like that.'

Alone once more, I considered my options. I could go chat up Duane and Monique and ask them more about Alan, but decided now was not the time when I saw that they seemed involved in a rather intense conversation. Kamila, however, was currently off by

herself, repacking the coffee supplies into the cardboard box. I
headed her way.

'Hi,' I said to the chef. 'Need any help?'

'Oh, thanks. Can you grab those cups and hand them to me?'

I grabbed the two stacks of coffee cups and passed them over.
'Looks like some have a bit of sand in them,' I said.

'A little extra mineral supplement never hurt anyone,' she
responded with a laugh, and set the cups in the box next to
the carton of half-and-half. 'Here, you wanna help with this
table?'

As we collapsed the legs on the folding table, I pondered how
to raise the question I wanted to ask. But then Kamila herself gave
me the opening I needed. 'I'm sorry if I came across as rude
yesterday when I cut you off like that. This whole thing has just
been so . . . difficult.'

'No, you were absolutely fine. You've been going through a lot
this past week.'

Kamila leaned the card table against the stacked boxes and
stared out to sea. 'True, and you don't know the half of it.'

I followed her gaze, where a trio of brown pelicans appeared to
be hanging motionless in the air, held aloft and almost stationary
by the strong onshore wind. 'Well, I think I may have heard a key
piece of that "half" just now,' I said with a glance in her
direction.

'Oh, really?' The way she cocked her head reminded me of
Buster, when asked if he wanted to go for a walk. 'Do tell.'

'Those guys I was talking to a minute ago, who worked with
Alan on his homelessness issues . . . they just told me that he'd
been living on the street in his van for the past two months.'

Kamila's jaw dropped – a literal sagging of several inches – and
she stared at me in open-mouthed disbelief. Either she had the
acting abilities of a Meryl Streep or she hadn't known this about
Alan. And my guess was she was no Meryl Streep.

After several seconds she managed to close her mouth and
swallow, then blinked several times in quick succession. 'What?'
she said in a soft voice. 'I don't understand.'

'Nor do I. It doesn't seem to make any sense. Didn't you say
that Alan owned the house you two lived in? Or at least that he
was doing some remodeling there, which certainly implies owner-
ship . . .' And then I remembered that it had been Lucinda who

had told me this, not Kamila. *Oops.* It was so hard keeping all this sleuthing intel straight in my head.

But the chef didn't appear to notice my slip-up. 'He did own it,' she said. 'Though I don't know how much he still owed on the mortgage. Alan didn't like to discuss money with me – probably because he was not as, shall we say, "cautious" with it as I am. And he was considering remodeling the kitchen, which I thought would be a frivolous waste of money, since it was perfectly good as it was.'

'And if anyone would know kitchens, it would be you,' I said, hoping to encourage this sudden willingness of hers to talk.

She nodded absently, then turned to stare once more at the flock of pelicans, which had moved only slightly farther out to sea. 'I knew he bought a van after we broke up, 'cause he'd drive it to work. But it just doesn't make any sense for him to all of a sudden be living in it.'

'Well, you did just say he wasn't very cautious about his money. So maybe he had some kind of financial crisis you didn't know about?'

'Maybe. But it would have had to have been awful fast. Or something he'd hidden from me,' she added, a hint of bitterness creeping into her voice.

'Plus, the timing is also intriguing, when you think about it.' At Kamila's frown, which I took to mean she wasn't following my train of thought, I elaborated. 'You know, so soon after your breakup?'

She turned to face me, hands on hips. 'You think *that* caused him to spiral into financial ruin?'

'No, no, I'm not saying that at all.' (Though I suppose I kind of was, when I thought about it.) 'I guess I just find it kind of interesting.'

Hoping she wouldn't clam up given the uncomfortable turn the conversation had now taken, I switched tracks. 'So, to change the subject a bit, you said during your remarks today that Alan had family back East?'

'Uh, huh.'

'Is that who's going to inherit his estate, do you know? That is, if there's any estate to inherit . . .'

'Yeah, I gather anything there is will go to his brother in New Jersey,' she said. 'I only met him once, when he came out to visit right after Alan and I got together, but he seems like an okay guy. Not that it looks like there'll be much for him to inherit, as you point out, if it's true Alan's been forced to live in his van for the past two months.'

And then she put her hands to her face and burst into tears.

ELEVEN

Sunday dinner the next day was a small affair: just Dad and his girlfriend Abby, my cousin Evelyn, Nonna, and me. Evie and I tore lettuce and sliced tomatoes and cucumbers for the salad, while Nonna arranged the salami, prosciutto, marinated vegetables, and provolone cheese on a platter. As we carried the food into the dining room, Dad and Abby jumped up and trotted into the kitchen, returning with the rest of the feast.

'*Salut, cent'anni!*' said Abby, once we'd all settled into our seats, raising her glass in the Solari family's traditional toast. With a grin, my dad clinked glasses with her, drank down half his wine, then reached for the antipasto plate.

Evie had just received the course list for her upcoming first quarter as a transfer student at UCSC, and was full of news about 'discrete mathematics', 'programming abstractions', and other computer science classes whose names I didn't even begin to understand. And she'd also 'met someone', she whispered into my ear.

'Really? A boy?' I asked, and she laughed.

'Well, I think he'd prefer to be called a "man", but yeah, he is of the male persuasion. I met him at work a few weeks ago, and we really hit it off.'

Evie worked several days a week at the Vista Center for the Blind and Visually Impaired, where she ran technology workshops for other people who were blind like she was. 'Is he one of your students?' I asked, 'or one of your fellow teachers?'

'If you're wondering if he's blind, the answer is sort of. He's got a severe case of juvenile macular dystrophy, which is called that 'cause it starts when you're young. Anyway, he's unfortunately losing his eyesight at a pretty rapid rate, so he's in my Wednesday workshop, where I work with people at imminent risk of blindness.'

'Oh, dear. That must be scary for him. But at least he's got a master instructor to help him navigate it all. So what's his name?'

'Evan. Evan and Evie – pretty cute, huh?' she added with a

giggle. 'And he'll be a junior up at the university this year, too; he's a physics major.'

My dad had now tuned into the conversation and smiled at this last bit of information. 'Ah, glad to hear he's a science nerd. I was worried he might be one of those green-haired liberal arts types.'

'He actually has blue hair and a pair of nose rings, and he plays bass in a grunge band,' Evie said. Then, after allowing enough time for Dad's eyes to grow wide, she grinned. 'Okay, so maybe the first two aren't true, but the last one is. And the band's really good. Lucy and I went to hear them last night.'

'Speaking of boyfriends,' Abby piped up, 'where's Eric? Has he got a big trial to prepare for?'

Right. I hadn't told any of them about his concussion. But I didn't want to go into detail about it right now. It would only serve to make everyone – including me – worried, when there was nothing we could do about his plight. 'He's at home resting,' I said. 'He had a little surfing accident, but should be fine in a day or two.'

I could tell Abby wanted to press me further, but at a subtle shake of the head from Dad, she let it go. He knew me well enough to realize that if I wanted to talk about it more, I would, in my own time. Nevertheless, at least I now had a good reason for leaving early. Once we'd finished the main course, I excused myself, loaded down with containers of antipasto, salad, Sunday gravy, pasta, and tiramisu, which Nonna insisted on packing up for 'poor Eric'.

And 'poor Eric' was glad she did. 'Oh, baby! I was hoping you'd bring me an early dinner,' he said when I appeared at his door a half-hour later.

I set the multiple packages down on his dining-room table. 'I gotta get to work, so I can't stay long. But before I go, I do want to let you know what I learned at Alan's memorial. I tried calling yesterday, but you didn't pick up – which I have to say, got me a little worried . . .'

'Yeah, sorry about that. I'd turned off the ringer to take a nap and spaced out turning it back on.'

As Eric piled a plate with Nonna's delicacies and commenced to chow down with great enthusiasm, his appetite having apparently now returned to normal, I told him about meeting the group of homeless advocates, and about Julian the bookseller being there and how he'd seemed so intent on talking to Lucinda.

'Mmmmm,' was Eric's response, though it wasn't clear if he was commenting on my story or on the food. Perhaps both.

'And Vargas was there, too,' I added. This caused Eric to momentarily stop his chewing and look up at me. 'But the funny thing was, he didn't seem surprised – or even all that upset – that I'd come to the service.'

'Probably because he knows you pretty well by now,' Eric said with a grin, then speared a chunk of sausage and popped it into his mouth.

'But here's the biggest news. It turns out Alan was living in his van for a couple months before he was killed.'

Eric set down his fork. 'Whoa. Do the cops know? Did you tell that to Vargas?'

'I only learned about it after he'd left, but I gotta assume they know.'

'Don't ever *assume* anything,' said Eric, licking red sauce off his fingers. 'It just makes an "ass" of "u" and "me".'

'What, you think I should call and tell him? I'm not sure that would be such a good idea . . .' Eric merely shrugged, the easy answer to everything. 'So anyway, the two guys I talked to,' I went on, 'the ones who'd volunteered with Alan at the Santa Cruz Food Project, they said they didn't know exactly why Alan had been living in his van, just that he'd apparently had to move out of his house for some reason. But they also said that people who end up homeless are often cagey about how they lose their housing. One of them also told me he thinks it might have been the result of some sort of emotional breakdown after Kamila split up with him.'

'Sounds possible,' Eric said.

'Yeah, I guess. So anyway, after I heard that, I talked to Kamila and asked if she knew about his living in his van, and she seemed completely surprised at the news. She told me he owned the house they'd been living in together, but that she has no idea how much of a mortgage he might have on it. And also, she said, he'd never been all that great with money. Oh, and speaking of money, she told me that Alan's brother in New Jersey is the sole heir, and he hasn't been on the West Coast for years, so . . .'

'So a murder committed in order to inherit his estate is not a likely scenario,' Eric finished for me.

'Right.'

Pushing back his chair, Eric stood and carried his now-empty plate to the sink. 'I say we take a look at this house of Alan's,' he said.

'Huh?'

Eric grabbed his laptop, typed something into the search bar, then leaned forward to peer at the screen. 'Looks like someone named Alan Keeting owns a property at 205 Juniper Street, downtown. Here, let's check it out.' I came around to his side of the table to watch him type the address into Google Maps, then click on the photo that appeared below the search bar.

A two-story Victorian-style house appeared on the screen. Its wood siding was painted a pale blue with dark blue trim. The landscaping out front was simple but tidy, the box hedges trimmed and the rose bushes pruned and bare. 'Looks like this photo was taken in winter,' I observed. 'And it could be years old, so who knows what the place looks like now.'

Eric turned to me with a glint in his eye. 'Which means you need to go down there and investigate. And then report back to me what you find.'

'Agreed. Sounds like a plan,' I said.

However, eager as I was to take Eric's advice and immediately go snooping around Alan's house, I had no time to do so that day. I'd been scheduled to show up at work at three thirty, and by the time I made it back to Santa Cruz from Capitola, it was almost four. Javier had already set out the *mise en place* for the hot line and was stirring the pot of béarnaise sauce atop the stove when I rushed into the kitchen.

'Sorry I'm late,' I said, washing my hands, then pulling on my chef's jacket and joining him at the Wolf stove. 'I stopped by to see how Eric was doing after Sunday dinner and, well . . .'

Javier waved his hand. 'No worries. And how is he?'

'Better. Much better, in fact. I wouldn't be surprised if they released him from his confinement in the next couple days.'

'Glad to hear it. So, you wanna give Tomás a hand prepping the squid for tonight's special?'

Ah, so that was to be my punishment for being late. 'Yeah, sure,' I said with a laugh. 'My pleasure.'

I'd just returned home from Buster's walk the next morning and was brewing a much-needed pot of coffee to both wake me up and take the chill off the cold, damp day, when the strains of a surf guitar rang out from my phone.

Now, why would Eric be calling so early? 'Hey, what's up.'

'Guess where I am,' he said, his voice glum.

Oh, no, the hospital, was my immediate thought.

But before I could come up with a response that wasn't quite so scary as that, he answered his own question. 'I'm at work.'

'Oh, wow. That's great!'

'Yeah, maybe.' A pause. 'I mean, it's great that Dr Singh released me from my home prison, but I gotta say: now that I'm back here, I'm remembering all the reasons I used to fantasize about being anywhere except the office.'

'I'm sorry, Eric. That sucks. But maybe they'll let you ease back into work? You know, take a half-day today?'

'I suppose that's true. But the more I play that card, the more likely they'll continue to give me these podunk cases, like the stupid hit-and-run that was on my desk when I came in this morning.'

I had no good answer to that. I'd been in the same place not too long ago as an associate attorney, dreading going to work each morning only to spend my days poring over tedious medical malpractice depositions, drafting interrogatories, and responding to motions to compel discovery. 'Well, at least as a county employee you don't have to worry about making those damn billable hours,' was all I could come up with.

Needless to say, this didn't improve Eric's mood.

'Anyway,' he said, 'I just wanted to call and let you know the good – and bad – news. And also to see if you wanna hang out tonight after I get off work.'

'Absolutely. How 'bout you come over to my place and I'll cook dinner for us?'

'Now *that* is something I will most definitely look forward to.'

After ending the call, I poured myself a cup of coffee and pondered what to do with the day. Although Gauguin was closed on Mondays, most weeks I stopped by there anyway to check the stock and order supplies from our vendors. Javier, however, had said he'd take those tasks today, as he wanted to go in anyway and test out a recipe for Asian-inflected pork ribs he'd been considering for a new main course. Which left me with an unusual and glorious full day off work. What to do?

Some sleuthing, that's what.

Pouring my coffee into a to-go mug, I grabbed my wallet and keys, tossed Buster a dog biscuit, and headed out to the garage. The fog had lifted, so I put the top down on the T-Bird and cruised downtown, enjoying the combination of the cool breeze and hot sun on my face.

Alan's house was only a few blocks from Gauguin, on a small street lined with Victorian-era homes painted in a variety of bright colors. A row of sycamore trees, with their psychedelic, multi-colored bark, lined both sidewalks, adding shade as well as lending the area a quiet, residential feel. A host of newer model cars lined the street: from where I sat, I could see two Priuses, a Suburu, a Mini Cooper, and a cherry red Tesla.

Pulling up in front of a house with pale yellow siding that nearly matched my car, I turned off the engine and gazed across the street at the property that had belonged to the Pages and Plums dining-room manager. It was very similar to the rest of the homes in the neighborhood, with a nice paint job and well-kept yard.

Remembering Kamila's comments about Alan discussing a kitchen remodel, I studied the building for any indication of active construction, but saw nothing. No contractor's trucks were parked on the street, nor was there a work permit posted in the window or any sign of lumber, appliances, or pipes waiting to be installed. Maybe the materials were in the side yard?

I climbed out of the T-Bird, crossed the street, and – checking first to make sure no dog walkers or nosy neighbors were coming my way – headed to the side of the house and looked over the gate. Nothing but a neatly coiled hose atop a brick path and a row of redwood planters containing roses with the last of the season's blooms.

Well, no reason not to see if anyone was in the house right now. Mounting the steps to the front porch, I rang the doorbell, waited a few seconds, then knocked sharply on the door. No response. With another quick look around me, I lifted the front door's mail flap and peered inside. All I could see was a pile of letters, magazines, and junk mail flyers scattered across the hardwood floor.

Apparently no one had been collecting Alan's mail in the week since his death. If that was in fact Alan's mail. *Could someone else be living here now?* I squinted down at the letters on the floor once more, trying to read the addresses. At least one looked like it had Alan's name on it, but I couldn't make out any of the others. Dropping the flap, I stood back up and returned to my car. *What on earth could have made Alan move out of this lovely home and start living in his van? And where was the van, anyway?* I thought, glancing down the street. Probably with the police, I figured. Alan had likely driven it to work the night he was killed, after which the cops would surely have taken it into custody as evidence.

But even though I couldn't check out the van, at least I could see where he'd been parking it. Or at least where he'd parked it on the occasion that Malcolm and Francisco had seen him. After taking a few photos for Eric of Alan's house, I jammed the stick into first and headed over to the far west side of town.

The street they'd likely been talking about was right off Delaware Avenue, near Swift Street. For some reason, it had become the go-to place for folks to park their RVs and vans over the past several months, and I'd read numerous letters to the editor from neighbors complaining about the noise and trash that they claimed had arrived along with the new residents.

Pulling up to the curb behind an RV with the name 'Minnie Winnie' blazed across its side (though it sure didn't seem all that 'minnie' to me), I shut off the engine and climbed out. The wide street was part of a subdivision I guessed to have been built sometime in the 1970s. The single-story ranch-style homes all had two-car garages, which made for more available street parking than downtown, where most garages – if there were any at all – had been converted into extra living spaces. And this neighborhood was far enough away from the university that there was no restricted parking, which was probably one of the reasons it had become popular with the street-living crowd.

Only a few vans and RVs were there now, but I guessed that come evening the population would grow. Walking down the street, I was struck by how neat and clean the area was. No trash littered the sidewalk or road, and the few large vehicles that were there seemed well cared-for and in good shape. So much for those letters I'd read. *Or perhaps one of the neighbors had taken on the job of cleaning up any trash that was left?*

No people were about, this being mid-morning on a weekday. Which was too bad, as I'd been hoping to ask anyone I ran into whether they'd noticed Alan living there and if they'd ever spoken to him. But not even a dog walker appeared to be around. Definitely a different feel from my older and closer-to-downtown neighborhood, which seemed to always be teeming with people.

After taking a few photos of the street and the vehicles parked on it, I climbed back into the T-Bird and started the engine. As I was releasing the parking brake, however, I saw a car in my rearview mirror coming down the street towards me. Watching it drive past and then pull into a driveway two houses down from where I was parked, I switched off the engine. Perhaps this person would know something about Alan. But as I was about to climb once more out of the car to go talk to him, I stopped.

Wait. I know that guy. He slammed the door of his older model red Corolla, and I watched as he strode up the pathway to his front door. It was Phillip, the Pages and Plums customer who claimed to be a medium..

He lives on the street where Alan had been parking his van?

Too surprised to do anything but sit there and stare as he let himself into his house, I shook my head in confusion. *Could* Phillip *be the one who's been harassing the homeless on the street?* I couldn't wait to talk to Eric about this new development.

Next on my list for the morning was a visit to the law offices of Saul Abrams. Based on what I'd learned from his website, which proclaimed the firm to be 'the premier appellate counsel' in the state of California, I expected his digs to be rather grand. Or at least similar to those of my old law firm, with a fancy lobby, large conference room, and private offices for all the attorneys. After all, the website had boasted of over forty million dollars in affirmed judgments in the areas of First Amendment, real estate, tax fraud, and insider trading cases.

So I was surprised to discover that his office was, in fact, right upstairs from a shop on Pacific Avenue specializing in cookies and ice cream. But then again, I mused, his was just a two-attorney practice, so it wouldn't make sense to have more than a small office. And given what I knew of Santa Cruz real estate, even this place couldn't have been cheap.

Ignoring the enticing aroma of chocolate that set my stomach rumbling in a plea for one of the chocolate-chunk-peanut-butter brownies advertised on a placard outside the store, I took the stairway to the right of the cookie shop, where a brass plate affixed to the door at the top proclaimed 'Saul Abrams, Esq. & Assoc.'

Not sure whether I should knock or simply let myself in, I did both, tapping first on the door, then trying the handle. It was unlocked, so I stepped inside and found myself in a cramped waiting area with a small metal reception desk, currently unoccupied. To the right of the desk was an open door, through which I could see another much larger, wooden desk, piled high with accordion folders and fat binders, which I recognized to be deposition and trial transcripts.

'Hello?' I called out, seeing no one about.

A head popped around the door. 'Oh, hello,' the young man said. 'Sorry, I didn't hear you come in.' Walking behind the reception desk, he flashed a 'be nice to the client' smile, then frowned as he flipped through the calendar sitting open on the desk. 'Uh, do you have an appointment? I don't see anything here.'

'No, I don't. I was just passing by and hoped that Mr Abrams might be free to speak with me for a few moments. I won't take up much of his time. That is, if he's here?'

'I'm here!' a voice boomed out from the other room. 'Who is it?' Abrams said, then stepped through the door to see for himself. As he stared at me, likely trying to place my face, his gray brows moved up and down several times, reminding me of a pair of fat caterpillars perched atop his wire-rimmed glasses.

'Hi, I'm Sally Solari,' I said, extending a hand. 'We met briefly at that ill-fated benefit dinner last week at Pages and Plums.'

He shook his head as he took my hand. 'So very sad what happened to that poor man. But yes, I remember you, now. You're the attorney-turned-chef who was asking about Paul Child, as I recall.'

'Guilty as charged. And I have to say I'm a bit jealous of your being lucky enough to get to know him.'

'Well, I can't say I knew him all that well, as I was only ten when we moved away from New England. But my dad owned an art gallery in Boston that Paul used to visit, and I believe he even showed some of his paintings and photographs there on one occasion.'

Waving me into his inner sanctum, Abrams motioned for me to take a seat on a leather-upholstered chair that had seen better days. 'So, Ms Solari,' he said, settling himself down at the paper-covered desk, 'any chance you're looking to get back into the hallowed legal profession again any time soon? Because I seem to find myself suddenly in the market for a new legal associate.'

'Oh?'

He let out a harsh laugh. 'It's why you find us in a bit of a state this morning. My former associate suddenly decided over the weekend that he'd be happier drinking beer on the beach with his new girlfriend, who happens to live in Puerto Vallarta, than fighting the good fight with those of us protecting the rights of the unfairly accused.'

'Wow. That's harsh. He gave no notice whatsoever?'

'Nope.' The attorney gazed out the window which looked down upon the shopping district below, and from his tight jaw, I could tell that the joviality he was putting on was merely an act. He was indeed mighty angry at his former colleague. With good reason, it seemed.

'Well, thank goodness I've gone inactive with the bar,' I said, 'so I'm not tempted to return to the fold and help you out. But if you're serious, I actually know someone who might be interested.'

It was his turn to say, 'Oh?'

I told him about Eric and his years with the district attorney, during much of which tenure he'd prosecuted white-collar crime cases like those taken up on appeal by the Abrams law firm. 'But he's become dissatisfied of late with his job. Ever since the new DA came into office, he's been assigning all the important, high-profile cases to this other guy who sucks up to the new DA like some disgusting leech.'

Abrams nodded. 'Well, we're just a small, boutique firm here, so the benefits wouldn't be the same as for a government job, but the work would definitely be far more interesting. Does he have appellate experience?'

'Absolutely. And I can assure you Eric's a talented writer – he even won the first-year writing award in law school for his moot court appellate brief.'

The lawyer leaned back in his chair with a smile. 'Mr Byrne sounds very promising. Here.' Reaching into the desk drawer, he pulled out a business card and leaned forward to hand it to me. 'Why don't you have him contact me if he is in fact interested, and we can talk. It could prove very fortuitous your stopping by this morning. Which brings us to the question: why in fact *did* you stop by?'

'It's about those cookbooks you donated for the Teens' Table benefit auction. I'm wondering if they somehow could have been related to Alan's death. You know, since they were stolen at the same time he was killed.'

He pursed his lips. 'I suppose that's possible, given the timing of the two events. But I can't see why anyone would kill someone for them – they weren't *that* valuable. Have they turned up, by any chance?'

'They have. It appears that whoever took the books jettisoned them in the Pages and Plums parking lot that same night, but not before ripping out the pages with the signatures on them.'

Saul Abrams's face blanched, something I doubt he could have very easily faked. 'That's awful,' he said, then flashed an embarrassed smile. 'Not to discount that poor man's death or anything, which was of course far more awful. But those books, they held a sentimental place in my heart, and to have them . . . *vandalized* like that . . .' He shook his head with a sigh.

'So what do you know about Julian Bartlett-Jones, the fellow who was the high bidder on them?' I asked. 'Any chance he could be involved with what happened?'

A look of distaste passed over the attorney's face. 'I have to say, part of me is actually relieved he didn't end up with the books.'

'How come?'

He held my gaze for a moment without speaking, then leaned back in his chair. 'I suppose there's no reason not to tell you, as it's all in the public record. I was opposing counsel on an appeal in which Mr Bartlett-Jones was a party. He was suing another bookseller for defamation, and after it was all over, I swore to have as little contact with the man as possible. I've not patronized his bookstore since.'

'What were the specific issues in the case?' I asked.

'I'd rather not go into detail, but I will tell you it was an action I felt to be purely a nuisance lawsuit. Let's just say the man's sense of entitlement – and his questionable ethics – do not match my own.'

'I take it you prevailed on the appeal?'

His smile was coy. 'I did indeed.'

'So it sounds like he could have a pretty big chip on his shoulder regarding you. Any chance he could have killed Alan and then stolen the books and ripped out those pages as some sort of payback to you? Are his ethics that low?'

'To actually *kill* someone?' Abrams seemed taken aback by the question. 'Look, I may not like the guy, but to accuse him of murder is another thing altogether.' With a frown, he tapped his index finger atop a stack of manila folders. 'And besides,' he said, 'knowing the gentleman's taste for bringing defamation lawsuits, no doubt it's best if I hold my tongue.'

TWELVE

The August weather in Santa Cruz can fall anywhere between a drizzly cold to baking hot from the dry Diablo winds blowing down from the inland desert. I'm no fan of those scorchingly warm days, not least because they have the potential to bring dangerous wildfires with them, but I get awfully tired of the persistent marine layer that can settle over our town for days on end. So I was happy that today ended up being sunny and warm after its cool, foggy start.

I'd decided to make steak for dinner, since it was one of Eric's favorite dishes, and I thought it would be fun to pull out the Weber and hang out in the backyard. And even if Eric hadn't yet been cleared for cocktails after his head injury, I could enjoy one while I tended the grill. In addition to the rib-eyes I'd bought, I was also preparing the veg and potatoes outdoors, and Eric stood by kibbitzing as I basted everything with a lime and garlic vinaigrette. Buster sat at attention next to the barbecue, ready to pounce should an errant piece of food find its way onto the ground.

Eric had not been happy to learn I'd told Saul Abrams about his being disgruntled at work and had suggested Eric as a replacement for his AWOL associate. 'What if it gets back to the DA's office?' he'd said, his voice rising almost a full octave in response to my account of the conversation I'd had with the appellate attorney. 'If my boss hears about this, I'm *toast*. I'll never get a good case again.'

'Don't worry, he's not going to talk, least of all tell anyone in the prosecutor's office. The guy's an attorney; he's used to keeping sensitive information to himself. But what do you think about the idea of checking out the possibility?'

'I dunno . . .' Eric picked up the tongs and started to lift one of the steaks from the grill, but I grabbed his arm.

'Let them sit longer, so they get a nice crust.'

'Fine.' Setting down the tongs, he reached for his lemonade instead. 'I mean, it is kind of enticing. I know about Saul's firm, and they do good work. They have an excellent reputation, and it would be great to be involved in something meaty and interesting like an appellate practice for a change. But . . .'

'But what? I mean, I get that the idea of making such a big life change is kind of scary, but what could it hurt to simply talk to the guy?'

Eric shrugged. 'Yeah, maybe. But let's change the subject for now. Did you learn anything from Saul that might be relevant to the case?'

Ha! I thought with a smile. *So Eric has indeed gotten the sleuthing bug.* I recounted what Abrams had said about being opposing counsel in a lawsuit brought by Julian, and how he considered the other's ethics to be questionable. 'But he wasn't willing to discuss any details – or the possibility that Julian could have had anything to do with Alan's death. He implied that his reluctance to talk was from fear of a defamation lawsuit by the guy, but I'm thinking it could have been something else.'

'Like fear of the guy himself?' Eric said with the raise of an eyebrow.

'Who knows?' Lifting the steaks to take a peek at their under-sides, I deemed them ready to flip, then brushed the perfectly browned surfaces with marinade. 'But I'm definitely going to ask Lucinda about Julian next time I see her. I'm dying to know what he was bending her ear about at the memorial.'

'So what about the other suspects?' Eric asked.

'Ah. I have some very interesting news on that front. Guess who I discovered lives on the same street where Alan had been parking his RV?'

Eric frowned. 'That woman who argued with him at the dinner?'

'Nope. Though I will get to her in a second. It's Phillip, that guy I met at Pages and Plums who claims to be a medium.'

'No way,' he said, eyes wide.

Pleased at the reaction this information had prompted, I grinned. 'I know – so bizarre. Or maybe not. I'm thinking he might be the one Alan told those guys about, who'd been harassing the home-less on the street where Alan was parking. I mean, it's too much of a coincidence otherwise, don't you think?'

'Sometimes coincidences are just that,' said Eric, raising his glass to his lips. But then he stopped and set it back down. 'Wait. Didn't you say this Phillip character is a regular at Pages and Plums?'

'Uh-huh . . . Oh, right. So he would have known Alan, and vice versa.' It was my turn to frown as I tried to remember exactly what Malcolm and Francisco had said about the person harassing the homeless on Phillip's street. 'They said the guy would yell and pound on the RV and van windows at night, which means that, whoever it was, Alan probably wouldn't have actually seen him doing it.'

'Are they positive it was a man?' asked Eric.

'I'm not sure. I guess that's what Alan must have told them. Though they could have merely been assuming it was a guy. And some women do have deep voices, so even if Alan thought it was a guy, that doesn't mean it necessarily had to have been.'

Eric nodded. 'True. But the question is, if it *was* in fact Phillip, did he know that it was *Alan* inside the van?'

'Yup, that's the question, all right. I'm thinking maybe I need to head over to Pages and Plums for lunch again tomorrow and see if he's there.'

'You're not gonna just come out and ask him about it, are you?' Eric said, and I shot him a *duh* look.

'Of course not. You think I'd be that obvious? I'll get him talking about other things and then somehow lead the conversation to the issue of homelessness. Maybe ask him about that Raquel woman who got in the argument with Alan. Speaking of which, I Googled her name – it's Raquel Santiago – and came up completely empty. She's apparently not on social media, and I couldn't find an address or job or anything to do with her online.'

'Huh. Maybe the name you have is her married one – or her maiden name – and she generally goes by the other? It's sometimes hard to find women online 'cause of the different names.' Eric watched as I pulled the steaks off the grill, then flipped the corn on the cob and slices of zucchini and potatoes. 'So, what else do you know about her besides her name?' he asked.

'All I know about her, besides the fact that she made a bid on those Julia Child cookbooks, is that she's apparently a gadfly at city council meetings, going on about "cleaning up the streets" and the like. Wait – when do those meetings happen?'

'On Tuesdays,' said Eric, 'but they're at different times, and not every week. Here, lemme look it up.' He tapped out a search on his phone, scrolled through a few pages, then smiled. 'You're in luck: there's one tomorrow at eleven a.m.'

'Cool. I'll definitely go down there. And then afterwards I can head over to Pages and Plums for lunch. Here,' I said, handing him the platter with the steaks. 'Take this over to the table, would ya? We're about ready for the main event.'

Eric complied, followed closely by Buster, nose held high, tracking the delicious scent of grilled meat. Heading inside, I fetched my sauce – a blend of sour cream, mayonnaise, Cotija cheese, garlic, chili powder, and lime juice – and brought it out to the picnic table. As I pulled the squash, corn, and taters off the grill, Eric poured me a glass of the Côtes du Rhône I'd selected to go with the meal, and we sat down to eat.

I could worry some more about Lucinda, Kamila, Julian, Phillip, and Raquel tomorrow. Right now it was time to enjoy our feast.

The Santa Cruz City Hall is a 1930s-era structure built in the Monterey Colonial Revival style, and with its Spanish gardens, bricked courtyard, blue-tiled fountain, and elegant colonnades, it's one of the more historic and lovely properties downtown.

It had been many years since I'd attended a city council meeting, but I'd read enough about them in the paper recently to know to get there early, as the seats tended to fill up fast. At a quarter to eleven, I strolled through the stone archway leading to the council room, outside of which at least thirty people were milling about, waiting to be let inside. Perching myself on the edge of the fountain, empty because of our ongoing drought conditions, I studied the crowd. Several I recognized as Gauguin customers, but the rest were unfamiliar to me.

After about five minutes, the door to the chambers finally opened and we all streamed indoors. The long wooden benches reminded me of pews. Adding to the sanctuary-like impression, a low railing, similar to the one between the nave and altar at Nonna's parish church, separated the benches from the front of the chambers. On the other side of the partition stood two tables on either side of a wooden podium. Seven of our esteemed city council members sat at the long, raised podium, leaning forward to talk amongst themselves while various city employees took their seats at the tables and flipped through sheets of paper.

I grabbed a spot on the aisle near the back, so I could make an easy getaway – I'd heard these things could go on for hours – and then looked about me to see if Raquel was in attendance. No such luck.

Promptly at eleven, the rap of a gavel called us all to attention and, after a quick roll call, the meeting was opened up to public comments. Each person who'd lined up to have a turn speaking was granted three minutes, which turned out to be a blessing, as a good number of the comments consisted merely of rants and diatribes. Most seemed intended far more for the gratification of the person speaking than any possible edification of those of us in attendance. But the council members did a commendable job of appearing interested, nodding where appropriate and thanking each individual for their input.

Other than one person deeply concerned about the color of the new trash cans that had been placed along the Pacific Avenue shopping mall, all the comments that morning related to the proposed ban on sleeping outdoors. This edict was set to be voted on in a few weeks, and every comment was strongly opposed to the ban.

Several people voiced concern that by prohibiting outdoor sleeping, the ordinance would in effect criminalize homelessness, a condition over which most of the unhoused had no true control. Moreover, they argued, the camping bans don't actually reduce the number of those living outdoors. They merely drive them out of sight and into more dangerous locations, where it's also far more difficult to access the public services they so dearly need.

Valid points, I thought, studying the faces of the council members as they listened to these arguments.

But then I turned back to the mic as a new voice piped up: 'I'd like to state a contrary view, which is unlikely to be popular among those in attendance today, but which I know to be shared by many concerned residents of this city.'

Swiveling around on the bench to get a better look, I saw that it was Raquel who was speaking. So she had shown up, after all. And I could see that my memory of her being a big woman was correct. She had a stocky build, and was as tall as all but one of the men standing in line waiting to speak after her.

'I have nothing against the homeless,' Raquel said, prompting several audible groans and 'yeah, sures' from the audience. 'However, encouraging them to camp out on our sidewalks helps no one – not those sleeping outdoors in the cold and the rain, nor the residents whose neighborhoods they fill with discarded needles, rotting food, and other garbage too unpleasant to even discuss.'

Her voice was deep and melodious, and under other circumstances, I might have been tempted to ask if she was interested in joining Eric's chorus, which I knew was always in need of new singers. 'So I support the ban,' she went on, 'but I also support increasing the services to help these people find *real* housing – not tents or vehicles, but apartments, or at least temporary shelters, where they can live with a toilet and shower.

'What you people need to understand,' she said, shaking a finger at the room at large, 'is that those of us in favor of this ordinance have just as much a right to use the city's public spaces as anyone else does. When we can't even navigate the sidewalks in front of our own homes because they're blocked by people passed out in cardboard shelters, then something is severely wrong with our local government.'

There was a brief silence after she finished speaking, followed quickly by several choice insults directed her way. The bang of the gavel quieted everybody down, and I watched as Raquel glared at the two men who'd shouted at her, then strode from the room.

Jumping up, I followed her outside. 'Wait,' I called out as she started across the brick courtyard. She turned around with a scowl on her face, no doubt expecting further abuse. 'I just wanted to say I really appreciated your comments.'

'You agree with me?'

'Well, let's just say I'm still undecided on the issue. But I thought you made some very salient points, and those guys in there reacted completely unfairly to what you said. It's a really complicated issue.'

'Yeah, it is.' She studied me a moment, as if trying to place my face. 'Do I know you?'

'Well, we haven't actually met, but I was at that benefit dinner last week at Pages and Plums, you know, where—'

'Where that man was killed. Right.' The scowl had now returned. 'Is that why you're here? Are you a cop or something? Because I already told them everything I know.'

'No, no, I'm not with the police. I was one of the cooks that night, and since I spent a bit of time outside mingling with the crowd, I thought you might recognize me. I also couldn't help noticing that you made a bid on those Julia Child cookbooks, so

I'm thinking we might be kindred spirits of a sort. I'm Sally Solari, by the way,' I said, extending a hand.

She glanced down but did not take my hand. 'I have to say I find it peculiar that you showed up here today and then followed after me just now. What exactly is it that you want from me?'

I decided to come clean. Partially, at least. 'Okay, you're right. I did come down here today for a specific reason. But it's not really about you. The cops suspect Lucinda, the gal who runs the bookshop part of Pages and Plums, of killing Alan Keeting, and she asked me to help prove her innocence.'

'By implicating me,' said Raquel.

'No, no,' I repeated with a vehement shake of the head, hoping she couldn't read my true thoughts. 'I just figured that, since Alan was so involved in the homeless issue, I might be able to meet some other folks in that crowd. You know, learn more about him from people who knew him.'

'Well, I can't say I "knew" the guy, that's for sure. My only contact with him was that night at the dinner, when he started railing at me out of the blue. I mean, I've certainly seen him at these meetings on occasion and heard his holier-than-thou tone about—'

'Wait,' I said, the import of what she'd just said sinking in. 'You mean to say that *he* started that argument between you two at the dinner?'

'Yes, absolutely. Which is what I told the detective that night. I was just sitting there minding my own business, when all of a sudden this guy comes up and starts hollering at me – calling me a "fascist" and "heartless" in front of my wife, the couple we'd come with to the dinner, and everyone else at our table. It was incredibly embarrassing, not to mention rude and obnoxious on his part. So I let him know exactly what I thought of him and his ilk.'

Ah. So that was why Vargas didn't suspect Raquel of Alan's murder. She hadn't had some pent-up anger at him which had finally exploded that night. She'd merely been responding to *his* anger when they argued.

Assuming, of course, that she was telling the truth.

And there was something about that last phrase she'd used that reminded me of . . . *Right.* It had been my father, when yelling at that homeless man in front of Solari's about 'you and your kind.' No matter how much she protested otherwise, it seemed clear that Raquel did indeed harbor ill feelings against Alan and the other homeless advocates.

'So I'm guessing your wife and friends vouched for you between the time you argued with Alan and when his body was discovered in the bookstore?'

Raquel made a *huffing* sound. 'Look, I've already told all this to the police. But if you must know, the answer is no. By that point of the evening, we were all kind of table-hopping, so I wasn't in my original seat for that entire time. But the people I was talking to can vouch that I was in fact with them, and I gave all their names to that detective who interviewed me.'

Not that that proved anything, I mused, for she could have simply slipped inside and walloped Alan in between her table-hopping, and no one would have been the wiser. 'So can I ask you something else?' I said.

I wasn't sure she was going to respond, given the sour expression on her face. But after a moment, she let out an exaggerated sigh. 'Whatever,' she said in a tone of disgust. 'Is it about those cookbooks? 'Cause I already told the police all about that, too. I was hoping to buy them for my mom, who's a huge Julia Child fan, but then that guy kept bumping up the bid and it got way too steep for me. But I would never in a million years have stolen them. I just bid on them as a whim; no big deal at all.'

'No, it's not about that,' I said. Though, I couldn't help thinking, it was mighty interesting how her brain had immediately gone there when I'd said I had a question for her. *Could her having bid on the books in fact be somehow relevant?* 'It's something else entirely,' I continued. 'I was just wondering: Have you heard anything about someone harassing the people who are living in their vehicles over on the Westside? Because apparently some guy's been yelling at them and pounding on their windows in the middle of the night.'

A man and a woman emerged from the city council chambers at this point, and Raquel waited until they'd made their way through the colonnade and under the stone archway before answering. 'I think I know who you mean,' she said, lowering her voice. 'He's often at the meetings, and he's *very* anti-homeless, virulently so. He wants them all to simply disappear off the face of the earth and doesn't give a damn how that happens. I mean, as you know,

I totally get it – they're a real problem here. But I'm not like that guy. I simply want the city to do a better job policing them, dealing with the needles and garbage all along the levee and downtown. And they shouldn't be living in front of our homes. I agree with the guy on that front. But I'd never pound on their windows or scream at them.'

'What's he look like, this guy?'

'Uh, medium build, longish dark hair. Probably in his forties?'

'Was he here today at the meeting?'

'I didn't see him, but then again I came in late, so who knows? But he's pretty noticeable, 'cause he tends to wear these really loud Hawaiian shirts all the time.'

Phillip. Could it in fact be him?

THIRTEEN

I spotted Phillip as soon as I walked into Pages and Plums a half-hour later. He was seated with the same woman who'd joined him for lunch the Friday before and who'd been with him the night of the benefit dinner. And yes, once again he sported a brightly colored Hawaiian shirt, this one decorated with flying fish and outrigger canoes.

Lucinda was in the bookstore, ringing up a purchase. I waited till they'd finished their transaction, then headed her way. 'Oh, hi,' she said, shutting the till. 'You here for lunch? Or,' she added in a low voice, 'do you have any news about . . .?'

'Both,' I said. 'You have a minute to talk?'

'Absolutely. What'd you hear?'

Coming to stand next to her, I recounted what I'd learned about Alan sleeping in his van for the past two months.

'Whoa,' said Lucinda. 'I had no idea he'd lost his house. You have any idea what happened?'

'Not much. All I know is what Kamila told me about him never having been particularly good with money. Oh, and one of the guys I talked to at the memorial volunteered with Alan at the food bank. He thinks it might have something to do with Alan having some sort of emotional breakdown after he and Kamila split up.'

'How bizarre.' Lucinda stared toward the kitchen, where Kamila could be seen through the pass window, standing at the hot line cranking out the lunch tickets.

'And get this,' I continued. 'I went over to take a look at the street where the guys I met at the memorial said Alan had been parking his van at night, only to see Phillip pull into a driveway on the same block and let himself into the house.'

'You mean he lives on the exact same street where Alan was sleeping at night?' Lucinda's voice had now increased to that of a loud stage whisper, and I motioned with my hands for her to keep it down. Glancing about the bookstore, however, I saw that no one appeared to be taking any notice of us. Phillip and his companion over in the restaurant were deep in conversation, and too far away, in any case, to have heard anything we were saying.

'Sorry,' said Lucinda, her voice soft once again. 'But that is just *so* weird.'

'I know. And there's even more.' I told her about the city council meeting and speaking with Raquel Santiago that morning, and what she'd said about Alan starting the argument at the dinner that night. 'She could, of course, be lying,' I said, 'but she actually seemed like a pretty reasonable person to me, so I'm guessing it's likely true. Especially since the other people around her at the table that night would know if it wasn't what had really happened. Though she did admit that she was table-hopping after the argument, so logistically speaking, she could have killed Alan.'

Lucinda shrugged. 'She and pretty much everybody else there were switching seats around about then. It always happens at events like that, once the main course is finished.'

'I also asked if Raquel knew anything about a guy harassing people who sleep in their vehicles at night, and she said there's this man who's really anti-homeless at a lot of the city council meetings who she thinks could be doing it. And . . .' I paused for dramatic effect, then inclined my head in Phillip's direction. 'He's known for wearing loud, Hawaiian shirts.'

Lucinda stared across the room at the twosome as they ate their meal. 'But it's not as if he's the only one in town who dresses like that,' she said after a bit. 'Like, check him out.' She nodded at a man in a blue and yellow shirt festooned with ukuleles and grass huts currently perusing the travel section of the bookstore.

'True. And come to think of it, Eric is pretty fond of Hawaiian shirts, too. But, still . . .'

'I know,' said Lucinda. 'It is an interesting coincidence in this case.'

Watching Phillip twirl a ball of pasta in white sauce on to his fork, I had an idea. 'I think we should take him up on his offer to do our readings,' I said. 'It might be a good way to gain his confidence and get him talking. And who knows? Maybe in the heat of the moment – as he's predicting our future love life, or communicating with my dead Aunt Letta, or whatever it is he professes to do – he'll let something important slip.'

Lucinda grinned. 'Okay, I'm game. Shall we go over there right now and ask him?'

'No wait.' I grabbed her arm. 'There's something else I want to ask you about.'

'Oh?'

'It's about Julian, the bookseller who was bending your ear so much at the memorial service.'

'Ah, him.' She rolled her eyes. 'What a blowhard.'

'So what was he talking to you about all that time?'

'Himself, mostly.' Based on my own short meeting with the bookseller, this didn't much surprise me. 'But I actually suspect he has some sort of romantic notion about us,' she went on, 'and that was simply his way of flirting. Maybe he thinks that since we're both in the same business, that makes us the perfect match. He kept asking if I was interested in going out for coffee with him. Oy.' Lucinda blew out a breath, then laughed.

'I think you should take him up on it,' I said.

'What? No way.'

'No, hear me out.' I recounted what Saul Abrams had said about the defamation suit Julian had brought and how the attorney believed Julian's ethical code to be woefully lacking. 'So I'm thinking we need to at least consider him as a possible suspect,' I said. 'And maybe if you take him up on his offer for coffee – in a public place, of course – and get him talking about Saul and stuff, he might drop an important piece of information. Something that could help clear your own name.'

Lucinda frowned as she thought a moment. 'He did email me this morning, as a matter of fact, suggesting we meet tomorrow. Here, lemme see exactly what he said.' Reaching under the register, she pulled out a soft, brown leather briefcase, removed her cell phone and punched it to life. 'Here it is,' she said after a minute. 'He wants to meet at Cruzin' Coffee tomorrow at nine a.m. But I dunno. It seems kind of scary, going by myself to hang out with someone who you suspect might be a murderer? I mean, even in a public place . . .'

'How about if I "just happen" to show up at the same time, and you invite me to join the two of you?'

'I can imagine how well that will go over with him,' she said with a snort, 'but sure, it sounds kind of fun, actually. As long as you *promise* to be there.'

'Scout's honor,' I said, flashing my three-finger Girl Scouts salute. 'I wouldn't miss it for the world.'

With a gleam in her eye, Lucinda typed a quick message, hit send, then stowed the cell phone and briefcase back away. 'Right, that's done. Now let's go chat up Phillip.'

He looked up at our approach and smiled. 'Howdy, Lucinda,' he said, then turned to me. 'And you're . . . Sally, right?'

'Good memory.'

'Nah. It's my sister's name, so it was easy to remember. And this is my partner, Meg.'

Meg extended a hand. 'Glad to meet you. We're almost done eating,' she said, indicating what remained of their lunches: a few strands of fettuccine Alfredo with what looked like zucchini and red peppers for Phillip and a quarter of a club sandwich for her. 'But if you're here to eat, you're welcome to join us.'

'Sure. Don't mind if I do.' Pulling out a chair, I took a seat at the table.

Phillip looked up at Lucinda. 'So how's it going? Are the cops still harassing you about Alan's death?'

She studied him a moment, mouth tight. 'Actually, I have a question for you related to that.'

No, don't let him think we want our readings because of Alan! Fixing Lucinda with an intent stare, I willed her not to go there, not to let him know what we were up to. But what she ended up saying was far worse:

'I just found out that Alan had been living in his van for the past two months here on the Westside and that someone had been harassing him in the middle of the night by shouting and pounding on his windows. Someone who apparently likes to wear Hawaiian shirts,' she added, turning her gaze to the bright shirt hanging loosely from Phillip's wiry frame. I reached out a hand to touch her arm, but she shook it off. 'And now I find out that you live on the same street where he was parking.' Refocusing on his face, she raised her hands in a question. 'So was that *you*, Phillip?'

He pushed back his chair and stood. 'No way,' he said, palms out. 'You have me so completely wrong. I would never in a million years do anything like that. I totally support the rights of the unhoused and have no issue whatsoever with them parking on our street. In fact, *I'm* the one who invited Alan to park in front of our house – with Meg's approval, of course,' he added with a quick look her way.

What? I glanced at Lucinda. *Could this be true?* If so, it sure put to rest one of my prime theories about the case.

But Meg was nodding agreement. 'It's true,' she said, as if reading my thoughts. 'And we'd let him come in and shower every few days if he wanted to. There's absolutely no way Phillip would harass him – or anyone else – like that.'

Lucinda's body deflated like a soufflé that had been poked with a fork. 'Really?' she asked, sinking into the empty chair.

'Really,' said Phillip. 'I was outraged when I learned he'd lost his home, and immediately asked what I could do to help. Letting him live in his van in front of our house seemed like the least I could do.'

'But why did he . . .?'

'Why did he have to move out?' Phillip sat back down and took a sip of water. 'I'm not sure; he never said, exactly. But I got the feeling it was some kind of financial mess he got into after he and Kamila broke up. He was pretty secretive about the whole thing, probably from shame.'

'I gather that's pretty common,' I said. 'Especially with people who've always had a home and then suddenly find themselves on the street.'

Phillip gave a sad shake of the head. So true. The only way I even knew what was going on with Alan is that I happened to drive by him as he was getting ready to bed down for the night in his van. When I pulled over to ask what was going on, he just kinda broke down in sobs. But he made me and Meg promise not to tell anyone else what had happened.'

This sounded a lot like the story Francisco and Malcolm had told me, minus the sobbing part. *How vulnerable it must make you feel, to be living on the streets of a small town while trying to hide that fact from those you know.*

As Phillip swirled the last of his pasta on to his fork, I considered my options at this point. On the one hand, given what he and Meg had just told me about their inviting Alan to park in front of their house, Phillip had now dropped well down on my list of suspects. But I was still interested in getting him to talk. If nothing else, he clearly knew more about Alan's last days than most anyone else.

My thoughts were interrupted by Sky approaching the table with Phillip and Meg's check. 'Would you care for anything to eat?' the server asked me. After ordering the creamy mushroom omelet I'd enjoyed so much on my first visit to the restaurant, I turned to Phillip. 'Do you remember when we talked the other day – when you offered to do Lucinda's reading about Alan's death – and then you asked if I'd recently lost a loved one?'

He cocked his head. 'I do,' he said. 'It seemed as if the loss had affected you deeply. Are you interested in communicating with this person? I'd be happy to do a session with you.'

I glanced over at Lucinda, who – although she had now put on an air of casual indifference – I could tell was waiting to follow my lead. But even though I was interested in what Phillip would have to say at such a reading, I had no desire to be the victim of some kind of a scam. 'How much do you charge?' I asked.

'Nothing. I never charge for my readings. It's a gift I was born with, which I'm happy to share freely with those not so lucky as me.'

'Okay,' said Lucinda, startling me by slapping her hand atop the wooden table. 'I'm game. Would you still do one for me, too?'

'I'd be honored. Are you free now?'

'I think so. Why don't you finish your lunch while I go make sure Ellen's all right with handling the bookshop for a bit. We can use the bookstore office, if that works for you.'

'That'll be fine,' he said, then turned to Meg. 'Assuming it's okay with you if I hang out here for a while?'

'Sure, no problem. I'll just browse in the bookstore, and if I get bored, I'll shoot you a text and walk home without you.' Standing up, she headed for the cash register to pay the bill, leaving the two of us alone.

'So how about you?' asked Phillip, using a slice of French bread to soak up the remaining sauce on his plate. 'Would you like me to do a psychic reading for you, too?'

'Uh . . . okay, I guess so. Why not? You can do Lucinda's while I eat my lunch, and then I'll go afterwards.'

'Great,' he said, then popped the bread into his mouth.

Lucinda's reading took about a half-hour, and I was just finishing up my omelet and salad when they emerged from the Pages and Plums office. 'I'm gonna head to the men's room before our session,' Phillip said to me. 'Be right back.'

'How'd it go?' I asked Lucinda when he'd gone.

'Interesting, I guess is the best word for it. Though he did say something pretty melodramatic about a guy in a black coat.' Then, glancing up at the clock on the wall, she said, 'Oh, shoot; it's later than I thought. Ellen's only on till one, so I gotta get back to work. But we can talk about both our sessions tomorrow after coffee with Julian. Don't forget, okay?'

'I won't. See you then.'

I paid my bill, then Phillip returned and led me into the bookstore office. A large metal desk was covered with papers as well as a pair of open cardboard boxes filled with books, and more boxes of books sat on the floor. A poster advertising Michael Pollan's *In Defense of Food* was tacked on one wall, while another showcased a framed print of a Wayne Thiebaud painting of slices of cake. Gesturing for me to take a seat at one of the two folding chairs in the space, Phillip pulled his phone out of his shorts pocket and switched it to mute before settling down onto the other seat.

'Oh, good idea. Lemme turn mine off, too,' I said.

Our phones now both silenced, he leaned back and studied my face. 'So, who is it that you're interested in communicating with?'

'Uh, my Aunt Letta,' I said. 'But it's not like I think I can actually communicate with her. I just . . . I don't know . . .'

The hint of a smile peeked out from the corners of his mouth, as if he were in on a secret to which I was not privy. 'Look,' he said, leaning forward, 'let's see if you can just forget any preconceptions and we'll see where this little talk takes us, okay?'

'Sure. Whatever.' Sitting up straight, I set my hands on my knees, ready for him to start chanting or intoning some ancient mantra.

Instead, he laughed.

'What?'

'The first thing is for you to try to relax,' said Phillip, mimicking my stiff posture, then shaking out his arms. 'This isn't a psych test or an oral examination. We're simply going to talk. I'm going to see if I can make a connection with your inner being and, hopefully, with those in the spiritual realm who were once close to you, such as your Aunt Letta. Here.' He held out a hand. 'Actual physical contact helps greatly with making the connection.'

'Should I close my eyes?'

'Only if you want to.'

I held out my hand, which he took in a soft but firm grip. 'I invite you to imagine a place in your mind similar to a dream state,' he said, 'but accessible right now, while you are awake. A place where anything is possible, like a waking dream, where you can free your body to soar high above windswept meadows as you gaze down at the fields of purple lupin and yellow mustard below.'

As Phillip spoke, I watched his eyes, which remained focused on a point to my right and behind me – not at my own eyes, as I would have expected. His voice was smooth and soft, and it struck me that he was attempting to hypnotize me through the power of suggestion.

'A place where you can glide through the crystal-clear waters of a white sand beach,' he went on, 'or splash through the shallows astride a magnificent horse with a gait so smooth it feels as if you're being rocked in your mother's arms. Or a place where you can go back in time to when your Aunt Letta was still with us, here in the physical world.

'Now I invite you to imagine that your aunt is sitting here with us right now. She's smiling at you, proud of all you've done, of who you've become. Imagine her loving face as you allow your body to relax: your fingers, your hands, your arms and legs, the base of your neck.'

His voice seemed now to be incrementally slowing down. And as I continued to hold my gaze upon his, my eyes became tired, no doubt from concentrating so intently on his face. I shook my head to regain my focus.

Phillip stopped speaking.

'Well?' I said.

'Well, what?'

'Did you make contact with Letta?'

He let go of my hand. 'I'm afraid not. You're a tough subject, not terribly susceptible to sharing your innermost feelings.'

A surge of pride swelled through me – at my ability to resist being hypnotized by some hack pretending to have psychic powers. Though at the same time I felt a tinge of disappointment, as well.

Had I really hoped he could communicate with my dead aunt?

'Let's try something else,' said Phillip, leaning back in his chair and closing his eyes. 'This time, I invite you to simply allow yourself to be open to the possibility that, even if she isn't here right now as a spirit visiting us from the afterlife, your Aunt Letta is here as a vital presence in your *mind*. That she's been with you all along.'

He stopped speaking, and I could hear as he took several long breaths and then let them out in a slow stream. As I listened, I realized that my breathing was matching his.

'Because,' he went on in a soft voice after a bit, 'as long as you hold her memory in your thoughts and in your heart, she can never leave you. She will always be a part of what makes you *you*. It's as if her soul has joined with yours, and the two of you are now one.'

A strange tickling made me reach up to touch my cheek, and I was surprised to find moisture there. Phillip opened his eyes and looked into mine, but both of us were quiet.

It was as if Letta *were* there with me right now. But not via clairvoyance or a psychic reading or any other woo-woo kind of thing. I could feel a sudden warmth inside my chest that arose from the memory of all the times we'd hung out in her kitchen together cooking, or gone hiking up at the Pogonip, or simply sat in her living room watching old black-and-white movies while munching popcorn and sipping Champagne.

With a smile, I realized that I felt like Dorothy, returned home from Oz. Letta had been here all along, in my heart and in my mind. I simply needed a nudge to recognize the feelings I had for what they were. 'Thank you,' I said.

Phillip smiled. 'Sometimes a person is so very dear to you that there is no need for a visit from the spirit world – because they've never truly departed your world.'

FOURTEEN

D ropping my keys on the counter, I knelt on the floor to greet Buster, whose frantic kisses seemed more appropriate for an absence of days than the three and a half hours I'd been away from the house. Once our little love fest had run its course, I let him out the back door, took a seat at the red Formica table, and surveyed the kitchen: the vintage O'Keefe and Merritt stove; the green and yellow tile countertop crowded with an old mixer, blender, and ceramic cookie jar in the shape of a fat pig; the framed photo next to the fridge of my aunt at the hot line at Chez Panisse, blowing a kiss to whoever held the camera.

It wasn't hard to conjure Letta when I was in this room. I'd always thought of this as 'our place' – where we'd hang out together on her nights off, she whipping up a platter of spaghetti puttanesca, me sitting at this same red table, the two of us sipping Chianti or Sangiovese and exchanging stories and wisecracks about our respective jobs.

Closing my eyes, I spread my palms out on the table. *I know you're gone*, I said to myself. *That there's no 'essence of Letta' out there, able to discern my thoughts. But at the same time, I also know that I will never ever let you go – that you will always be here with me. No matter where I am, but especially here in this beautiful kitchen, in this beautiful home.*

I opened my eyes and turned to look at the photo on the wall. 'I love you,' I mouthed to the young woman in chef's whites and raven-black braids. Then, with a sigh, I stood and let Buster back inside. Walking through the living room, I removed his leash from its hook by the front door and called out his name. 'Time for a walk before I have to go to work!'

We headed the two blocks down to West Cliff Drive, where a line of people stood gazing out to sea. Joining them at the railing, I was amazed to see that the water just beyond Its Beach was positively teeming with sea life. Hundreds – perhaps thousands – of seagulls, cormorants, brown pelicans, and other birds floated in the water, virtually covering its surface, with a host of others soaring overhead. A shadow briefly blocked the sun, and I looked up to see a large V of pelicans break formation as several dive-bombed the water, narrowly missing a flock of squawking seagulls bobbing just past the waves.

'Whoa,' I said to the woman standing next to me. 'Must be the anchovies running. Check out all the fishing boats so close by.' I nodded toward the dozen or so seiners and trawlers floating offshore, their outriggers and winches sticking out at all angles like some kind of deranged spider.

'I know. Amazing, right? And check out the sea otters.' She indicated a spot near the rocky base of the point, where a pair of the sleek, brown-coated creatures were diving in and out of the surf. 'Feeding frenzy for all,' she said.

'All except the poor anchovies,' I responded with a laugh.

After standing for a few more minutes to watch the sea-life spectacle, I felt a tug on the leash as Buster grew impatient with my dawdling. We continued on our walk, the dog stopping to sniff at the various gopher holes lining the path, until we reached Woodrow Avenue, where I turned right to head back home.

I would have liked to call Eric and tell him all that had happened since we'd last seen each other this morning, but a glance at the time on my phone told me I had to hustle over to Gauguin. Instead, I shot him a text: 'Interesting development on the case. Talk after I get off work?'

He wrote right back: 'Better yet, I'll come by G around 10. Save me something yummy for dessert.' Smiling, I shoved the phone back in my pocket. It was good to have the old Eric back.

Once I was at work, the evening passed quickly. A party of twelve had come in for a birthday celebration, which kept Javier, Tomás, and me busy for much of the shift. It hadn't taken long for Tomás to get comfortable on the line, and now that his burned hand had improved, he was proving to be a valuable asset as we cranked out plates of spot prawns with citrus and harissa, duck two ways, and our special for the night, seared salmon with roasted corn, tomatillo, and red pepper sauce.

Finally, at about a quarter to ten, after the staff had sung 'Happy Birthday' to the honored guest and the big party were all enjoying their various desserts, I leaned against the long table running down the middle of the kitchen. 'Good job,' I said to Tomás after drinking down a glass of ice-cold water. 'Your first big rush, and you handled it like a trooper.'

'Thanks. And I gotta say, it kinda felt like that – a big rush. You know, like when you're in the zone playing soccer or something, and time just flies by 'cause you're way too distracted to notice?'

'Yeah, that can certainly happen, all right.' Spying Eric's blond head through the pass, I waved as he was seated at table six, under the woodblock print of sugar cane that Letta had brought back from a trip to Hawai'i. 'But right now, my dogs are barking. What this gal needs is to sit down for a minute and say hey to my honey. You and Javier okay to hold the fort for a few minutes?'

'No worries,' said Tomás. 'There's only a couple tickets left, so we got you covered.' Javier just grinned and shooed me off as he would a stray dog who'd wandered into the kitchen.

'What'd ya save me for dessert?' Eric asked as I walked up to him.

'Nice to see you, too,' I said, leaning down to give him a kiss before taking a seat. 'And I had saved a slice of the chocolate ganache tart for you, but then I got so hungry I ate it myself.'

'Very funny.' Brandon approached the table with a menu, which Eric waved off. 'I'll just have a slice of the chocolate ganache tart,' he said.

'Uh . . . there isn't any chocolate tart . . .' The server shot a nervous glance my way.

And then I laughed. 'Because there never was any to begin with. Give him that piece of chocolate cake with dulce de leche icing. I saved it out for him on the counter in the *garde manger*. And could you bring me a slice of the peach pie?'

'You got it.'

'Oh, and a double espresso decaf, too,' Eric called out to Brandon's retreating figure. 'Thanks!'

'So,' I said, stretching out my legs and wriggling my toes. 'Have you thought any more about maybe contacting Saul Abrams about that job?'

'I have. I thought about it a lot today, as a matter of fact.'

'And?'

He shook his head. 'I dunno. It's scary, thinking about changing jobs. I mean, it's true I've been really unhappy at work, and I know I've been bending your ear constantly bitching about it, but it's been my job for what, almost ten years now? What if I left and then hated the new job even more? At least I know what to expect at the DA's office.'

'Like more bar fight and shoplifting cases?'

He shrugged.

'Look. It's not as if you'd actually be risking anything at this point. What could it hurt to just call the guy and set up a meeting with him? 'Cause I'm guessing that if you don't, you're gonna spend the next few months kicking yourself for not at least checking out the possibility of a new job.'

Eric frowned as Brandon set down his espresso and our desserts. 'Maybe I'll call him tomorrow,' he said, unwrapping the sugar cubes and dropping both into his cup.

'Atta boy.'

'So what happened today with regard to the case; you said there were "interesting" developments.'

'There were, indeed. First off, I went to the city council meeting this morning and talked to that Raquel woman, who told me that it was *Alan* who started that argument at the dinner, not her.'

'Huh. Did she say why he started it?'

'She figured that Alan had heard her speak at the city council meetings and got angry about her anti-homeless stance, and then when he saw her there that night he just started right in, shouting at her and calling her a fascist and stuff.'

Eric snorted. 'If I could have five dollars for all the times that word's been thrown about inappropriately, I'd be the richest man in America. So you think he could have pissed her off enough for her to go and whack him in the head?'

'Who knows? She's definitely got the build for it – she's a tall, strong gal. And I also learned that she didn't spend the whole time after the argument at her table, so she could have gone inside the bookstore without anyone being the wiser. But I'm thinking that if Alan started the argument, it actually demonstrates the opposite of my original thought. It seems that Raquel *didn't* have much reason to go after him, hence the reason Vargas doesn't consider her much of a suspect.'

I took a bite of my peach pie, then let out a moan of pleasure. The buttery crust was tender and flaky, and the filling – a mix of roasted peaches, brown sugar, and a hint of bourbon and salt – was a true flavor bomb. Dipping my next fork-full into the dollop of sweetened crème fraîche nestled next to the pie, I popped it into my mouth and savored the exquisite dessert. Amy had outdone herself with this one.

'But the other thing that Raquel told me,' I went on, 'may be even more important. When I asked if she'd heard anything about some guy harassing the homeless at night by shouting and pounding on their windows, she said she had. And then she told me there's this guy who sometimes comes to the city council meetings who's super anti-homeless, way more than her, she said, who she thinks could be the culprit. And get this: he wears a lot of Hawaiian shirts, just like that Phillip character.'

Eric's chocolate-cake-laden fork stopped in mid-air. 'Ah-ha!' he said. 'Great find!'

'Yeah, well, maybe not so great. Turns out Phillip and Alan were friends, and Phillip was the one who invited Alan to park in front of his house at night. So it doesn't make a whole lot of sense for him to later be harassing the guy.'

'Unless maybe they got in some kind of argument after he'd started parking there?' Eric said, mouth full of cake.

'But if that were the case, wouldn't Phillip just ask Alan to move on? It doesn't make any sense for him to go and torment the guy. Oh, and also, Lucinda and I had Phillip do our psychic readings today.'

This got Eric's full attention. He pushed aside his plate, now scraped clean of all signs of cake and ganache icing, and leaned forward across the table. 'Do tell.'

I recounted how I thought Phillip may have been trying to hypnotize me. 'But when that didn't work,' I said with a smirk, 'he simply had me think about the fact that Letta is still with me, as a memory and as a part of who I now am. It was kind of sweet, actually. And as he was talking, I realized that he was right. I'll never truly lose her, because she *is* a part of me and always will be.'

'Truth,' said Eric, taking my hand.

'So, anyway,' I said, blinking rapidly, 'in other news, Lucinda is meeting Julian the bookseller tomorrow morning for coffee. Remember how I told you he was being so attentive to her at Alan's memorial? Well, Lucinda thinks he has a crush on her. So I'm going to "just happen to show up", and then join them at her invitation. Who knows? Maybe he'll drop a clue about those Julia Child books or something.

'And as for that mystery man who'd been hounding Alan at night, I'm at a loss right now. Lots of people like Hawaiian shirts,' I said with a nod toward the palm-tree-decorated gem Eric was sporting that night. 'And I can't help thinking maybe Raquel was lying to me – that she wants to pin it on Phillip for some reason. I just can't figure out *why*.'

Now that Tomás was officially on the hot line two nights a week, we needed to readjust our kitchen schedule at Gauguin. I'd put out the word – via Craigslist, the Santa Cruz Restaurant Owners Association, and several other industry outlets – that we were on the lookout for a new prep cook, but no likely prospects had yet emerged. The one guy who'd stopped by to talk about the job had reeked of stale beer and weed, and I'd sent him on his way with a polite, 'No thank you.'

Wednesday morning therefore found me up early, scheduling sheets and a strong cup of joe before me on the kitchen table. Both Kris and Brian had offered to help out with the prep work and *garde manger* as needed, and I was also training one of our dishwashers the art of filleting a fish, deboning a chicken, and various dice cuts for vegetables. But how to juggle all the different kitchen stations with everyone's individual abilities and avail-ability? Not an easy task.

Eric had opted to sleep at his own place last night, which turned out to be a blessing, as it made my rising early the next day that much easier. Nevertheless, I'd still only managed to roll out of bed a little after nine, and I was supposed to meet Lucinda at ten fifteen. A glance at my phone told me it was already ten o'clock. Time to get a move-on. Maybe after my coffee date I could finish up the scheduling over at Gauguin.

Tucking the work sheets into a manila folder, I walked out to the garage and tossed them on to the passenger seat. It was already warm out, so I lowered the T-Bird's canvas top, fired the old girl up, and headed over to Cruzin' Coffee. As soon as I walked inside the shop, I heard my name called out by Lucinda. 'Sally!'

'Oh, hi,' I said, crossing over to where she and Julian sat at one of the tall booths that ran along one side of the room. 'Fancy meeting you here. I just came in for a quick jolt before heading over to the restaurant to work on my dreaded scheduling.'

'Care to join us?' she asked, prompting a fleeting scowl from her companion which I pretended not to notice.

'Sure. But I can't stay long.'

'Neither can I,' said Lucinda. 'I have to be at the bookstore at eleven.'

'As do I.' Julian graced me with a thin smile as I took a seat next to Lucinda. 'So, how did your friend like his gift?'

Ah. He remembered me. Not surprising, though. He likely didn't have a lot of customers coming into his store to ask about a recent murder. 'He was absolutely *thrilled* with it,' I said. Although the bookseller chuckled at my lame joke about the James Bond novel, he didn't attempt to hide his eye roll, either.

Having already consumed one very strong cup of coffee that morning, I opted for an Americano – a watered-down espresso – from the burly server who came to take my order. There was a moment's silence after he left, and then Lucinda cleared her throat. 'So Julian was just telling me about his son in Oxford. He's doing his undergraduate degree there, at . . . which college was it?'

'He's reading history at New College which, despite its name, is actually one of the oldest of the colleges at the university, having been founded in the late fourteenth century.'

'Is your family from England, then?' I asked, glad to finally have an excuse to pose my question about the bookseller's origins.

'Oh, no. We're from the Bay Area – and Ohio, before that. Though I, too, studied at Oxford as an undergraduate. Balliol College,' Julian added with a smug smile.

Well, la di da. I knew from my pal Allison that Balliol was considered one of the most elite of the Oxford colleges – not to mention the alma mater of Lord Peter Wimsey, the fictional sleuth known equally well for his collection of fine books and manuscripts as his keen intelligence.

'Oh, so that's where you picked up your accent,' I couldn't help letting slip.

A look of what might have been embarrassment passed over his face before he quickly changed the subject. 'And how about you – where did you study?'

'UCLA undergrad in poli-sci,' I said, 'and then I came back up here to do my law degree at Monterey College of Law. My mom was being treated for cancer at the time, so I wanted to be near the family.'

Lucinda frowned. 'Oh, I didn't know. Is she . . .?'

'She died about five years after I graduated. Which is how I ended up back at Solari's – to help out my dad after she was gone.'

'I'm so sorry,' said Lucinda. Julian bit his lip and was silent. *Great. Way to put a damper on the conversation, Sally.*

'It's okay,' I said. 'It's been quite a while now.'

'Did you ask Phillip about your mother as well as your aunt?' Lucinda asked, then turned to Julian. 'Sally and I both had psychic readings yesterday – from one of my customers at work.'

'Uh . . .' My first thought was, *Why on earth is she bringing Phillip up in front of Julian?* But then I realized it was probably a good idea – turn the discussion to the case without his knowing we were interested in *his* part in it all. 'No, we only talked about Aunt Letta. I've had years to process Mom's death, and had quite a while to prepare for it before it happened, too. But with Letta . . . I dunno. It was much more sudden and so *violent*. And it's still recent and . . . raw.'

Lucinda set her hand on mine. 'Was it helpful, the session?'

'Surprisingly, yes,' I said. 'How about yours?'

'So who exactly is this guy?' asked Julian, clearly not happy about being left out of the conversation. Lucinda's strategy was working.

'Phillip's a regular at Pages and Plums who claims to be psychic, so we thought it would be interesting to have him do our readings,' she said. 'He thinks he can figure out who killed Alan Keeting, and thereby help me, who the police apparently consider a suspect in the case.'

'Really?' His eyes grew wide. 'That's horrible. And did he? Come up with anyone?'

I studied Julian's face for any suggestion of nervousness at the direction our conversation had turned. But all I could discern was what appeared to be honest concern that the object of his affections could be a suspect in a murder investigation.

'No one specific,' she said, lifting her cappuccino to her lips.

The waiter set down my coffee, and I reached for the pitcher of cream. 'So what exactly did Phillip say?' I asked. 'Did he try to hypnotize you?'

'Huh-huh, nothing like that. Why? Were you hypnotized?'

'No, but I think he might have been trying to. Anyway, go on with your story.'

'Well, he just had me close my eyes while he held my hand,' said Lucinda. 'We sat there like that for few minutes with him mostly quiet, but occasionally saying things like, "Yes, I can feel you." After a bit, he let go of my hand and told me he knew it wasn't me who killed Alan. He'd had a vision of a man in a dark coat who snuck into the building after Alan that night, knocked him in the head with something – he wasn't clear on that point – and then stole the boxed set of cookbooks. That's the melodramatic part I mentioned to you yesterday. It all sounds pretty hokey to me.'

'Wait. How did Phillip know the books had been stolen?' I asked.

'I told him,' said Lucinda, 'when we were talking about helping prove my innocence.'

'Ah.' I'd continued to watch Julian as she recounted her tale and, at the word 'cookbooks', saw his eyes narrow. 'They found the books, you know,' I said to him. 'Or rather, I did, and then called the cops. Someone had thrown them under the dumpster in the Pages and Plums parking lot.'

'Oh, dear. Were they much damaged?' Julian asked.

Deciding that it would be best not to provide too many details, and knowing that Vargas certainly wouldn't appreciate it, I opted for a noncommittal reply. And it seemed best, in any case, to see if Julian let slip anything about the missing pages. 'Well, being tossed under a dumpster and then being left there out in the elements for several days isn't great for any book, so . . .'

He nodded, his brows furrowed. 'Because, not to seem too unfeeling about that poor man's death, but I'd still be interested in making an offer on them if they're still in decent shape.' Was he simply pretending to not know what had happened to the books, or did he in fact have no idea? I couldn't tell.

'Maybe after this is all over, you can take a look at them and decide if you want to or not,' said Lucinda. 'But for now I'm sure the police will want to hold on to them for evidence.'

'Understandable.' Julian stood up and shook out the silky fabric of his black slacks. 'Please excuse me, but I'm off to the gents' room. Back in a flash.'

I swiveled around to watch his retreating form, then turned back to face Lucinda. 'So what about this man in the dark coat?' I asked. 'Did Phillip have anything else to say about him? Like, what kind of coat? A jacket, sports coat? It wasn't a particularly cold evening, so I'm guessing it wouldn't have been one of those long, winter types.'

She shook her head. 'He didn't say. And he couldn't describe the man himself, either. He said he'd need something the man himself had touched in order to get a better picture of him.'

I tried to imagine Detective Vargas allowing Phillip to come down to the station and hold the cookbooks in his hands while attempting to 'channel' the person who'd stolen them. Not likely.

After Julian returned, we talked a little longer about clairvoyants and mediums and whether any of them had any actual 'powers'. I opined that the best 'true' psychics were merely those with an incredibly strong sense of empathy and intuition – people expert at reading others' faces, body language and emotions. But Julian pooh-poohed even this.

'All utter nonsense,' he said with a wave of the hand, then glanced at the elaborate gold watch on his wrist. 'Oh, I should be going. I've got someone coming in at eleven to show me his collection of first edition Durrells. Lawrence, that is, not Gerald,' he added, not attempting to keep the snobbery from his voice.

Lucinda grabbed her briefcase and stood, as well. 'I'll walk you out,' she said to Julian, then turned to me. 'Any chance you could give me a ride to work? I'm on foot. I was planning to walk to the restaurant, but it would be nice to get there that much earlier.'

'No problem,' I said, instantly reading her meaning: that it would be good for us to debrief about Phillip and Julian on the ride over to Pages and Plums.

After paying for our drinks, which Julian insisted on doing for the entire table, we walked outdoors to my car. His eyes lit up at the sight of the creamy yellow classic. 'They simply don't make cars like this anymore,' he said as he ran his finger over the shiny chrome of its rear fin. 'A pity.'

'Go ahead and climb in,' I said to Lucinda as I walked around to the back to stow my bag inside the small trunk.

She settled down into the bucket seat. 'Believe it or not, I've never ridden in a convertible before. Do I need to tie my hair back?'

'Nah. We're not going far or fast, and the windshield does its job pretty well.' I slammed the trunk shut, came around to the driver's side, and opened the door. 'Oh, sorry,' I said, seeing her holding the file with my scheduling sheets. 'Let me throw that in the trunk, too.'

But Lucinda didn't answer. She was staring down at the folder and, as I watched, she carefully removed two pages that had been sticking out from the top. Looking up at me with wide eyes, she held the pieces of paper out for Julian's and my inspection. 'What the hell?'

They were the missing pages from the Julia Child cookbooks, the blue ink of the two authors' signatures standing out on the page, bright as a neon sign.

FIFTEEN

Slack-jawed, I tried to come up with something to say, but all I could manage to croak out was a repeat of Lucinda's question: 'Wha . . . what the hell?'

She and Julian were both staring at me, and when I finally yanked my gaze from the papers to their faces, what I saw there was not pretty. The confusion in Julian's eyes I could understand, since I myself was dumbfounded. But the look of anger – no, betrayal – that Lucinda wore was heartbreaking.

'I have no idea how those got there,' I pleaded. 'Truly, I swear I'm as baffled about this as you are.' I reached for the papers, but Lucinda held them away from me.

'We need to call the cops,' she said. 'They might have fingerprints on them.'

'Yeah, you're right.'

And then, when I went to pull my phone from my pocket, Lucinda shook her head. 'No, I'll do it.'

Whoa. She thinks I might fake the call? This was bad.

I listened as she spoke to the dispatcher, explaining that she'd just found the missing pages from the cookbooks which had been stolen the night of Alan Keeting's death. Lucinda gave few details, only that they'd turned up in a folder belonging to 'someone else'.

'No, I have to get to work right now,' she said to the person on the other end of the line, 'but I'll have them there for the detective. It's Pages and Plums, on the Westside. Right, of course.'

Ending the call, she slid the papers back into my scheduling folder, being careful to touch them as little as possible. 'She told me to keep them where I found them, so I guess I'll have to hold on to this file for a while till the cops can take a look at it. Detective Vargas is gonna meet me at Pages and Plums.'

Julian, who'd been listening, rapt, to the conversation, cleared his throat. 'Well, I don't believe I'm needed right this instant, so I'm going to hurry on to my appointment right now. But if anyone needs to talk to me, they know where to find me.'

Lucinda turned to face me after he'd left.

'You can't possibly think . . .' I stopped, unable to complete the sentence.

'I don't know what to think. But you gotta admit it's pretty weird, having them show up here like this.' She nodded at the manila folder in her lap.

'Agreed, but we'll get to the bottom of it,' I said, sliding into the driver's seat. 'Let's head on over there, and I'll talk to the detective when he arrives.'

Which I was *so* not looking forward to.

'What is it about you, Sally, that attracts trouble wherever you go?' Vargas was shaking his head as he studied the two title pages from *Mastering the Art of French Cooking*, volumes one and two. I was fairly certain he didn't suspect me of stealing the pages, nor of Alan's murder, but the detective was clearly not at all happy with me right about now. He held one of the papers in his gloved hands up to the light and squinted.

'Do you see any fingerprints?' Lucinda asked. 'Because mine are for sure there – at the very top, where I pulled them out of the folder.'

He set the paper back down. 'Hard to tell, but I'll get the lab techs on it. Paper actually takes prints pretty well – sucks up the oil from your fingers like a sponge.'

'Good,' I said, 'since that will prove I never touched them. Oh, wait. But I did, come to think of it. That night at the dinner, at least volume one.'

'Mmmm,' was Vargas's noncommittal response to this. 'Why don't you tell me everything you can about the chain of custody of this file.' He tapped an index finger on my scheduling folder.

'I was working on the papers this morning at my kitchen table, then stuck them in this folder to take to Gauguin to work on later.'

'And the folder was empty when you put your papers in there?' he asked.

'Yes, definitely. And I took the folder out to the car and then left it on the front seat when I went into Cruzin' Coffee to meet Lucinda and Julian.' This prompted a raised eyebrow. 'Julian Bartlett-Jones was there?'

'Uh, yeah. He had asked Lucinda out for coffee, but she didn't want to meet him alone, so we decided it would be good if I were there, too.'

'Right. Of course . . .' Vargas let out a long and weary sigh. 'Okay, so what happened next?'

'I went into the coffee shop, and the three of us drank our coffee and talked for about a half an hour. When we came out to the car, Lucinda found those ripped pages in my file.'

'Was the car unlocked?'

'Yeah, the top was down, so it would have been easy for anyone to have just stuck them into the file, real quick.'

'But if this was indeed a set-up, the person with the pages would've had to have known you were going to be there at the coffee shop,' Vargas observed. 'So who knew that?'

'No one except Lucinda. Who was with me the whole time I was gone from the car,' I hastened to add with a glance her way.

'Did you tell anyone about your coffee date with Sally?' the detective asked Lucinda, and she shook her head.

'No, no one.'

I thought for a moment. 'Oh, and Eric knew, too, though I seriously doubt he would have mentioned it to anyone. But the thing is, my car's pretty recognizable. Even if you don't know me personally, I post lots of pictures of it on the Gauguin social media pages. So it's possible the person just saw it sitting there and took the opportunity to put the papers in my file.'

But even I knew this was an unlikely scenario.

'Look,' said Lucinda, glancing over at the cashier's desk, 'I should really go open the till. Do you still need me, or is it okay if I leave?'

Vargas waved her off with his fingers. 'No, that's fine. We're done here for now. I'll let you know if I have any more questions.' He pulled an evidence bag from the valise he'd brought with him, then picked up the file folder.

'Can I keep the scheduling forms I was working on?' I asked. 'I don't want to lose the work I've already done on them.'

'I need to keep them for now, in case they have prints on them. But it wouldn't hurt for you to take some pictures of them.' Still using his gloves, he spread the Gauguin forms out on the table for me to photograph.

'So, it occurs to me,' I said as he replaced the forms into the folder and slid it into the evidence bag, 'what if it was Julian who put those pages in my file?'

'Julian?'

'I just remembered that he was gone for a few minutes this morning – said he was going to the men's room. But I was facing the other way, so he could easily have dashed outside to slip those pages into my car.'

Vargas frowned. 'Was he carrying a bag or briefcase when he left? 'Cause these pages don't look like they've been folded, so he couldn't have had them in a pocket.'

'No, I don't remember him having anything like that. Oh, but . . .' I turned to watch Lucinda as she counted out the cash in the register.

'What?' His eyes followed my gaze.

'Lucinda had a briefcase.'

'But you said she was with you the entire time.'

'She was . . .' I thought back, trying to remember the exact events after we'd finishing our coffee that morning. 'The three of us walked out to my car, and Lucinda got into the passenger seat while I went to put my bag in the trunk. So she definitely would have had time to pull the pages from her briefcase and slip them into that folder without me seeing.'

I was keeping my voice low as I monitored Lucinda's movements. She was still at the register, talking to her assistant Ellen, and didn't appear to be paying any attention to the two of us. And then I put my hand to my mouth. 'Oh, wow. Here I've been so sure it couldn't have been her. But Lucinda *was* the one who was inside the bookstore right after Kamila found Alan's body.' I turned to face Vargas. 'And she was the one who asked me for a ride to work after coffee this morning. Maybe she planned this whole thing – to set me up by asking for my help, then stashing those pages in my car. When she saw that folder there on the front seat, it would have seemed like she'd struck gold.'

Vargas was shaking his head. 'But what about Julian? Wouldn't he have seen her do that and said something?'

'Not if they were in on it together,' I said.

After Vargas headed back to the police station, I stood for a moment in the bookstore, trying to decide what next to do. I'd originally been planning to go over to Gauguin to work on the scheduling, but given what had happened that morning, I wasn't sure a sedentary task was what I needed right now in my agitated state.

The idea that someone was trying to set me up was unsettling enough. But in addition, Martin Vargas – though not as angry as I'd feared he might be – was clearly not happy with me poking my nose into Alan Keeting's murder. He'd let me know in no uncertain terms that he wouldn't be nearly so forgiving should he discover I'd continued to meddle.

Not that I truly wanted to, in any event. Now that it seemed Lucinda might have been taking me for a ride all this time, my heart was no longer much in the case. *Has she been lying to me about this whole thing? Should I tell Kamila?*

I turned a thoughtful gaze on the cook as she stood at the hot line stirring something with a wire whisk. We'd been together the entire time during which Alan could possibly have been killed, true. But although I'd originally thought that she could have gotten someone else to do the dirty deed on her behalf, now – when I really thought about it – this theory seemed pretty far-fetched. Sure, I could imagine almost anyone striking out in anger at an ex-lover in the heat of the moment, but would Kamila plan it ahead of time and actually convince someone to do it for her? No, it just didn't fly.

Nevertheless, I mused as I watched Kamila through the pass, it wouldn't be a good idea to confide in her that I now suspected her business partner and good friend of Alan's murder. Not only would she not believe me, but there was a good chance she'd go immediately to Lucinda to tell her what I'd said.

With a sigh, I turned away from the kitchen and started across the bookshop. But then, at the sight of a familiar form sitting at one of the tables in the dining room, I stopped. It was Phillip, apparently alone today for lunch. As I watched, Sky placed a glass of iced tea in front of him, then pulled out his tablet and took his order. As the server headed to the kitchen to turn in the new ticket, Phillip looked up and caught my eye. With a smile, he gestured to the chair across from him, but I shook my head 'no', pointing my thumb in the direction of the parking lot. No way did I want to talk with him right now.

I was halfway across the room when Eric's surf guitar ringtone chimed out from my pocket. 'Hey,' I said, stepping outside into the sun. There was a chair set up next to the door, so I took a seat. 'What's up?'

'Mnnnnhhh,' he intoned, chewing and swallowing what I guessed to be a bite of tuna fish sandwich with mayo, chopped celery, and Tabasco sauce – his favorite midday meal. 'Sorry. I didn't expect you to pick up so quickly. I just wanted to let you know that I talked to Saul Abrams on the phone this morning, and I have to say we really hit it off. I like the guy. He's smart, has a snarky sense of humor, and the kind of cases he takes on seem really interesting. So, long story short, I'm going down to his office tomorrow morning before court to discuss the details of what exactly it would mean if I were to join his law practice.'

'Wow. That's great, Eric!'

'Nothing's definite yet, of course,' he hastened to add. 'We only danced around the subject of money, and I'd want full say over any cases I work on, so we'll see what happens. But it's definitely a start.'

'Indeed it is. And you already sound way happier than you usually do when I talk to you at work.' Which was true. The glee bubbling over in his voice reminded me of a kid on the last day before summer vacation. 'Here's hoping you two can come to a mutually beneficial agreement.'

'Thanks. So, hey, did you learn anything interesting at your coffee date with the two booksellers this morning?'

'Other than the fact that Vargas may now consider *me* to be a suspect in the case?' I answered with a snort.

'What?'

I described Lucinda discovering the ripped pages from the cookbooks in my scheduling folder, and how – although I didn't truly think the detective suspected me of Alan's murder – the event did throw an industrial-sized wrench in the works regarding my theories about the case. 'Not that I'm even all that motivated anymore to figure out who the hell killed Alan.'

'Sounds like what you need right about now is some R&R,' said Eric.

'Yeah, you're right. I think I'll take Buster up to the Pogonip for a walk in the redwoods before I go to work. It should be nice and cool up there, and maybe if I just let my mind rest for a bit, the clues will somehow magically fall into place and I'll figure it all out. Or I'll decide to drop the matter entirely.'

We chatted a bit more about Eric's interview with Saul Abrams the next morning, and after wishing him good luck, I ended the call. Then, deciding it would be best to try to at least pretend things were normal between Lucinda and me, I stepped back inside the bookstore to say goodbye. She was over in the cookbook section of the store talking to a customer, and I was about to head her way when I realized that the man she was talking to was Julian. What was he doing here? He must have finished up his fancy book meeting. But still, I didn't think he had any employees, so he'd have had to close shop to come all the way across town to Pages and Plums. *What could be so important for him to discuss with Lucinda in person rather than just over the phone?*

Well, I sure didn't want to talk to the two of them together right now. Hoping they hadn't spotted me, I hurried back outside and across the parking lot to my car. As I drove home, I kept clenching my hands and shaking them out in an attempt to release some of the nervous tension that had once more built up inside me. I definitely needed that walk, now.

Buster was waiting at the door when I let myself in, tail wagging and anticipation in his eyes. 'You're in luck, good buddy,' I said. 'Wanna go for a walk up in the redwoods?' This, of course, only set him off further, barking and spinning around in circles at the magic word, 'walk'.

'But ya gotta wait a bit. I need to eat something, first.' His ears lowered on hearing the not-so-magic word 'wait', and he sank to the floor. But as soon as he heard me open a jar of peanut butter, the dog was back in business, sitting expectantly at my feet as I prepared my lunch. After scrolling through my messages as I ate my PB&J, I changed into my walking shoes, grabbed Buster's leash, and we headed out the door and into the car. Then, once at the trailhead at the end of Spring Street, I raised the T-Bird's top and locked the car, and we set off down the trail.

The Pogonip – named for the creek that runs through the land – is a 640-acre parcel owned by the City of Santa Cruz that abuts UCSC. Once host to a polo field, golf course, and clubhouse patronized by the likes of Spencer Tracy, Walt Disney, and Mary Pickford, this panoramic land is now a protected green space of live oak-dotted meadows, woodlands, and redwood forest, home to myriad critters that inhabit its varied terrain.

And we'd gone no more than a few hundred feet before Buster spotted one of those very critters, a dusty-brown lizard scurrying across the dirt fire road. 'No,' I told the dog as he strained against the nylon strap, 'dogs have to be on leash here. And besides, there's way too much poison oak for you to be allowed off the trail, kiddo.'

It was hot as we made our way along the fire road, originally used for hauling logs, cattle, and limestone from the ranches and quarries owned by Henry Cowell, one of the largest landowners at the time in all of California. But once we turned right, downhill, we soon entered a cool canopy of coastal redwoods, bay laurel and Douglas fir. Birds flitted in and out of the trees, and I could hear the splashing of water from the nearby creek. *Ah . . . heaven.*

I was lost in a daze, recalling the times I'd joined Letta and Buster on these same trails, when the dog suddenly stopped. A rustling noise had put his eyes and ears on alert. I knew what he was thinking: *squirrel?*

'Leave it,' I said, and we continued down the narrow trail. A sassy jay scolded me from atop the rust-red branch of a stately madrone, and a cool breeze tickled my sweaty arms. At the bottom of the gully the path flattened out, with stands of young conifers bordering the trail on either side. Stooping to admire a tiny pink flower, I was struck by all the sounds I could hear: insects buzzing, birds chattering, water tinkling, scurrying coming from the underbrush . . .

And then Buster was gone, the leash yanked abruptly from my hand.

'Buster!' I called out. 'You get back here *now!*'

No response. *Damn.*

He'd darted into the forest, out of my view. And if he'd gotten wind of a cottontail or ground squirrel, there was no way he'd come back simply to please me. There was nothing for it but to go after the errant dog.

Picking my way through the brush, I did my best to avoid the poison oak – which, fortunately, was now in its prime, its vibrant red hue a clear warning to not brush up against the oak-shaped leaves. I made my way through a stand of young Douglas firs, then emerged into a small clearing. A wadded-up blanket next to a pile of trash suggested this was, or had recently been, someone's campsite. But where was Buster?

I stood still to listen to the sounds of the forest. *Yes*, that sounded like an animal moving through the undergrowth. Turning towards the noise, I spotted the dog at the edge of the clearing, head down and jaw working. *Oh, no.* He'd found something to eat. Hoping it was nothing too disgusting like coyote poop or a decomposed rodent, I dashed over to him. I was just in time to see the last of

whatever he'd been wolfing down – something dark red and cylin-
drical – before it disappeared into his mouth.

Thank goodness. It was just a hotdog. Probably something
whoever was camping here had left behind. Exhaling in relief, I
leaned down to grab his collar.

And then, in a flash, it was as if someone had *me* by the collar
– a collar that was getting tighter by the second.

SIXTEEN

Releasing Buster, I reached up quickly and managed to wedge two fingers between my skin and whatever it was around my neck. At the same time, the dog backed up and started barking like crazy, the high pitch of his yelps indicating more fear than aggression.

I tried to turn around to see who my aggressor was, but the further tightening of the leather strap around my neck – *a belt?* I managed to wonder – made any such movement impossible. Instead, I concentrated on using my hand to keep the pressure off my windpipe as much as I could. But I was unsuccessful, and slumped forward as dizziness started to come on. The tension further increased around my neck. Somewhere in my brain I still heard Buster's hysterical barking, but it seemed distant and surreal, as if in a dream.

And then the pressure suddenly ceased.

I fell to the ground, gasping and grabbing my neck, gradually becoming aware of a pair of bodies grappling together next to me. I rolled over on to my back and watched dimly as one of the two – clad in a dark hooded sweatshirt and dark shorts – pushed up and away from the other, then darted off into the forest, the offending belt swinging from his right hand.

The other reached out to touch my shoulder. 'Are you all right? You're bleeding.' A male voice, deep and husky. I looked up at the bearded face bending over me, a weathered face that could have been anywhere between thirty and sixty years old.

'I . . . I think so,' I managed to cough out. Examining my hand, I saw there was indeed a tiny amount of blood on my fingers. The belt must have broken the surface of my skin. Reaching up to touch my neck once again, I could tell it was only a small cut. The bruising would be far worse.

Buster came over and began licking my face with a ferocity that surpassed his previous barking. 'Hey, buddy,' I said. 'It's okay now.'

'You can thank him for making all that racket, 'cause it's what made me come see what the heck was going on,' the man said. 'Do you know who that was?'

'No idea.' I coughed again, then collected Buster into my arms as I tried to calm the shaking that was now fast overtaking me. After watching me for a moment in silence, the man stood, as if about to leave. 'Wait,' I said. 'Did you get a good look at the guy? What'd he look like?'

'Who knows? He had that hoodie pulled tight around his head and a bandana over his face, so no. I couldn't even swear that it was a guy, to tell you the truth. Though he was pretty strong, so . . .' The man shrugged. 'It coulda been one of the dudes that's been camping around here lately. There's one who's kinda nuts – goes off on folks sometimes for no reason at all – and he has the same build as that guy just now. I do my best to stay away from him.'

'Well, I sure appreciate that you didn't stay away this time and came to my aid,' I said. Then, nodding toward the wadded-up blanket, 'So are you camping here?'

'No, I stay farther off the trail. And I don't leave my trash around like that,' he added in a disgusted tone.

'I take it, then, that you wouldn't have left any hotdogs lying around?'

'*Blech.*' His face screwed up into a grimace. 'I'm vegan, so no way would I even touch one of those things.'

'Got it.' I slowly rose to my feet and stood there a moment, taking a few deep breaths. 'Well, thanks again. I'm Sally, by the way.'

'Robbie,' said the man, extending his hand. 'Glad to be of service. You think you're okay to walk back by yourself?'

'Yeah, I'm okay.' Without thinking, my hand went up to my throat and I coughed once more. 'I'll probably have bruises here tomorrow, but my legs are fine.' Picking up Buster's leash, I was about to start back down the trail, but then turned back. 'By the way,' I said, 'is there any way for me to contact you if I need to?'

Robbie gazed into my eyes for a few seconds before shaking his head. 'I'm pretty much off the grid, as they say. But folks around here know me, so . . .'

'Right. Okay. Well, thanks again.'

With a wave, Robbie turned to head off into the forest and was gone.

I made my way back to the trail, then started uphill toward my car. I'd only gone a few steps, however, before I had a sickening realization: *What if my attacker tries again?* And then I tried to reassure myself that I was perfectly safe. *He wouldn't be so brazen as to do it on a public trail, surely?* I'd passed several other hikers on my way down here, and there were bound to be more people on such a lovely afternoon as this, *right?* Nevertheless, as Buster and I made our way along the narrow trail, I started at the sound of every cracking twig and nearly jumped out of my skin when a young woman suddenly appeared from around a bend in the path.

By the time we finally emerged from the forested area onto the fire road traversing the meadow at the top of the hill, my heart was thudding and I was soaked in sweat. But I'd seen no sign of my attacker, and Buster seemed completely calm, though he was likely tired and thirsty, as was I. Luckily I had water in the car and, after letting the dog drink from my cupped hands until he was satiated, I downed the rest of the bottle. Then, lowering myself into the car, I leaned back in the seat. I felt boneless, exhausted, the adrenaline drained from my system.

What on earth had just happened? Was it merely a random act of violence by a deranged soul, or could it have something to do with Alan's death?

That night at work, I kept the high collar of my chef's jacket buttoned all the way up, to hide as much as I could of the ugly red abrasion around my neck. Although I'd called Detective Vargas to report the incident, I didn't care to spend the whole evening explaining what had happened to the Gauguin kitchen staff.

Not surprisingly, Vargas's first reaction had been as much exasperation with me as concern. But when I explained that I'd only been taking a hike and not investigating anything to do with Alan's death, he calmed down. He told me, however, that there wasn't much the police could do at this point. I had no way to ID my assailant or even contact the guy who'd come to my assistance, and the department didn't have the resources to send someone up to the Pogonip on what would likely amount to a wild-goose chase for footprints or other evidence at the campsite where the attack had occurred. And he was probably right. The only clue that could possibly have provided any information was now sitting in Buster's stomach. So it was with a combination of frustration and unease that I headed off to my shift at Gauguin.

One of our specials that evening was abalone-style calamari, made by pounding locally caught squid into thin steaks, dipping them in seasoned flour, then pan-frying them quickly in butter so the outsides become crispy but the steaks remain nice and tender. Served with a squeeze of lemon and a scattering of chopped chives, the squid dish – with its buttery, slightly salty flavor – is surprisingly similar to the far more expensive abalone, and never fails to sell out whenever we offer it.

But the suckers are a pain to clean, so as soon as I got to work that afternoon, I found myself in the *garde manger* helping Tomás remove the tentacles (which we'd deep-fry for an appetizer dish), the ink sac (used in our black risotto special), the long piece of cartilage running down the body, and the skin from each of the slippery cephalopods. It was also farmers' market day downtown, which meant we'd be getting an early rush, so Tomás and I worked quickly, not speaking much. Which was fine by me, since my voice was hoarse and I still coughed easily after my near-strangulation.

Plus, I had a lot to process. Because if nothing else, what had happened today up at the Pogonip had served to rekindle my interest in the case.

It was now personal.

The attack had to be related to the case. It seemed like far too much of a coincidence to be anything but. Especially considering the timing, just hours after those pages from the Julia Child book had been found in my car. *But who could it have been?* I'd told Eric I was going to take a hike up in the Pogonip, but who else could possibly have known that I'd be up there this afternoon?

I thought back to my phone conversation with Eric. I'd been sitting on that chair right outside the Pages and Plums door, and although I hadn't noticed anyone lurking about at the time, I supposed that someone standing around the corner inside the bookshop could have overheard me. Or even been listening on purpose.

Someone like Lucinda or Julian.

I must have let out a little gasp, because Tomás looked up at me, concern in his eyes. 'Are you okay? Did you cut yourself?'

'No, I'm fine. I just thought of something, is all.'

'Ah.' His frown told me he would have liked to know more, but he didn't push it.

Of course, Phillip had also been at the restaurant today, I mused, reaching for another squid from the bucket. But he'd only just ordered his lunch when that call came from Eric. So even if he had eavesdropped on our conversation, how could he have had time to pay for his drink, cancel his lunch order, and then follow me as I left Pages and Plums? Because, I realized, if someone had specifically targeted me, they'd have had to follow me all the way up to the Pogonip. There were a lot of different trailheads into the park, and I hadn't told Eric which one I was going to use.

And more importantly, the only motivation I could imagine for the attack was my interest in Alan's death. But Phillip had been Alan's friend and had actually been helping him out at the time he was killed. So it made no sense that he would have anything against me. If anything, Phillip should be supportive of my investigation.

Which meant it had to be either Lucinda or Julian.

Yanking the head off my next squid with far more force than necessary, I tried to remember who'd been working today at the Pages and Plums bookstore. I didn't recall seeing anyone besides Lucinda there, and none of her helpers had come in while I'd been talking to Eric. So it couldn't have been Lucinda who'd followed me up to the Pogonip, unless she left the bookstore unattended. Unlikely.

But it could have been Julian. He'd obviously closed up his own shop to come see Lucinda, so he could have simply kept his store closed a little longer while he tailed me from Pages and Plums.

I shook out my hands, then reached for another squid. *But why follow and attack me today?* I wondered. *What could have triggered such an action?* It had to be related to those cookbook pages . . . or the aftermath of their discovery . . .

Ah! Maybe the reason Julian had rushed over to Pages and Plums was because Lucinda had called to tell him about Vargas's reaction to her finding those ripped pages in my scheduling folder. The detective had made it pretty obvious that he didn't think I was the culprit, so perhaps Lucinda had been frustrated that their plan was foiled. And maybe she'd even realized that the scheme had in fact made her *more* of a suspect than before.

Still, what was the sense in strangling me? An attempt to scare me off the case? Or just an angry impulse? Neither explanation seemed likely.

Okay, so what if the goal was once again to deflect suspicion to someone else? The fact that the attack had occurred at a campsite likely wasn't a coincidence. But how would blaming a homeless person for the attack on me – and, by logical conclusion, also for Alan's death – fit into this whole thing? Alan had been an *advocate* for their rights.

With a sigh, I tossed the last cleaned squid body into the hotel pan and went to wash my hands. None of it made any sense at all.

I asked Eric to come stay with me that night. Partly, it was because I wanted to tell him in person what had happened to me that day and let him see for himself that I was, at least physically, okay. But also, I really needed someone to hug.

He was already at the house when I got home from work and greeted me at the front door with a cocktail and a kiss. I'd texted him only that 'something' had happened in the case, as I hadn't wanted him to spend the night worrying about me. But as soon as Eric saw the bruising around my neck, he set down the drink, grabbed me by the hand, and led me to the couch.

'Ohmygod!' he said, sitting down next to me. 'What the hell happened? Are you all right?'

I reached up to touch the tender area, looked him in the eye, and then started shaking all over, tears in my eyes.

'Oh, Sally,' he said, taking me into his arms. 'This is just too much. Tell me whoever did this, and I'll . . .' His arms tightened around my body. 'I dunno what, but it won't be pretty.'

The image of the slender, boyish Eric facing off against my aggressor in some sort of testosterone-fueled mega battle was enough to momentarily take my mind off that leather strap tightening around my windpipe, and I let out a small chuckle.

Eric released his hold on me and sat back with a tight smile. 'Well, I can't say as I'm terribly flattered by your reaction to my offer to kick that guy's butt, but I guess I'm happy it made you laugh.' He handed me my bourbon-rocks. 'Here, I think you could use this. So you wanna tell me what happened?'

He listened without interrupting – which proved how serious

he thought this all was – as I explained everything that had happened since meeting Lucinda and Julian for coffee that morning. I also went through the theories I'd come up with at work regarding who might have been involved in both the planting of the cookbook pages and the attack on me, and why.

Biting his lip, Eric stared at Buster asleep on the floor. 'My money's on that Julian character,' he said. 'I got a bad hit off him when we met at the benefit dinner; he seemed like a real creep. And from what you say, he's the one who had the best opportunity. Does he have the same build as the person who attacked you?'

'Close enough,' I said with a shrug. 'I didn't get much of a look, other than to know that whoever it was was relatively tall with an average build. Which could describe Julian as well as both Lucinda and Phillip. But not Raquel, come to think of it. She's got a sturdier build than whoever attacked me. Or Kamila, who's pretty short. So, hey, at least we can finally rule those two people out. But with a bulky hoodie on, it's hard to really tell what someone looks like. And the guy who came to my rescue, Robbie, he said the person had on a bandana, so he couldn't see their face.'

'What's Vargas think?'

'Not much. Or at least nothing he was willing to share with me. I'm pretty sure he thinks it was some mentally ill person who's camping up there, like that guy Robbie told me about.' Leaning back, I took a long drink of my Maker's Mark, then curled my legs up onto the couch. 'Look, could we change the subject and talk about something else? I think I need to get my mind off all this for a while. Like, how are you feeling about your interview tomorrow morning?'

'Not bad. I did a little research this evening about some of the cases Saul's taken on over the past few years – you know, so I can sound like I actually know something about the subject when we meet. And they're really pretty interesting: a lot of white-collar defense work like real-estate fraud and insider trading, but also some more exciting stuff like section 1983 civil rights and First Amendment cases. And hey, I figure if we don't hit it off, I wouldn't want to work there anyway. So it's a no-lose situation, right?'

'Right,' I said, though I knew that this was pre-emptive, defensive posturing on Eric's part. If the meeting didn't go well, he'd be absolutely crushed.

'Anyway, there's something else I'd like to talk about, too,' said Eric, turning to face me.

'Oh, yeah?' From the earnest look in his eyes, I started to get uncomfortable about where this might be going.

'Yeah. It's about our living situation.'

'Oh . . .'

He swallowed before going on. 'So, I did a lot of thinking while I was holed up all those days at my place, and I get now how you wouldn't want to live there. Even I started going pretty stir-crazy in that small, one-bedroom condo with its tiny kitchen and living room and no yard to hang out in.'

'So you want to move in here with me? That would be great!'

'Yeah, it would be, except for the fact that – like I said before – I'd have to give up the equity I've accrued in the condo. Being a renter just doesn't cut it if you want to stay permanently in this town.'

'Well, why not just lease your condo to someone else?'

He shook his head. 'The CC&Rs don't permit it.'

'Oh, right. Of course.'

'But here's the thing: if I sold the condo and used the money for a down-payment on another place – a single-family house with a yard and stuff – then we could move in there together.'

'No way could you afford a down-payment on a house anywhere near town,' I said. 'We'd have to live up in the hills or all the way down in Watsonville – if you could even afford that, given the price of real estate these days. Huh, uh.' I crossed my arms over my chest, as if protecting my very being from such an idea. 'I need to be close to Gauguin – and near Nonna and Dad. And besides,' I added, doing my best to control the tremble in my voice. 'I couldn't possibly leave this house. Not Letta's home.'

SEVENTEEN

I didn't sleep well that night. Each time I started to drift off, a vision of that leather belt tightening around my neck would shake me awake, gasping for air. And the fact that Eric fell almost immediately into a deep slumber didn't help. There's nothing like lying next to someone who's snoozing restfully to increase your own insomnia.

A little before eight the next morning, Eric crept into the bedroom to see if I was awake. He'd been up for an hour, he said, anxious about his meeting with Saul, and was hoping I could wish him good luck before he left.

'Good luck,' I said as he leaned over to give me a kiss. 'Call me later to let me know how it went.'

'Will do. Oh, and I walked Buster and gave him his breakfast, so hopefully he won't bug you and you can get a bit more rest.'

'Thanks – you're the best!' I lay back on the pillow and closed my eyes, but try as I might, I couldn't fall back asleep. Although my body was exhausted, my brain was running on overdrive. After a half-hour, I finally gave up and headed downstairs for a hit of caffeine.

I'd just opened up the newspaper – Eric had thoughtfully left it on the counter next to the pot of coffee he'd brewed – when my phone buzzed. It was a text from my law school pal, Nichole, up in San Francisco: 'Is tomorrow your day off work? Mei and I are thinking of spending the day in Santa Cruz on Saturday, and we'd love to make it an overnight trip if you're up for houseguests.'

'Absolutely!' I wrote back. 'It's been way too long, girl!'

I watched as the dots floated on my screen, waiting for her reply: 'Great! We should be at your place tomorrow around five.'

'Perfect,' I tapped back, then set the phone on the kitchen table, only to have it immediately buzz once more. This time, it was a text from my cousin, Evie: 'meet 4 coffee this am? Evan will be there.'

I smiled. So she was serious enough about her new boyfriend that she wanted me to meet him already? 'Yes!' I responded. 'But why don't you come to my place? I have some peach pie I brought home from work to go with the coffee.'

'gr8! C U soon!'

I took the pie from the fridge and put it in the oven to heat, then went to take a shower. After pulling on a pair of jeans and a 'nice' T-shirt (a yellow V-neck with no stains on it), so as to not look too much the slob for Evie's beau, I headed back downstairs. I was just setting out some plates and forks when the doorbell rang.

Buster charged for the door, slipping and sliding on the hardwood floor while barking furiously at the ax murderer – or worse yet, the mailman – who was no doubt on the other side. Holding him by the collar, I let the two youngsters inside, and as soon as Buster realized it was Evie, his barks turned to urgent whines as he jumped up and tried desperately to lick her face.

'Where's Coco?' I asked.

'We took the bus here, and dogs aren't allowed. Though I guess I could have pretended she was a service animal,' Evie said with a grin, tapping her white-tipped cane on the floor.

As my cousin knelt down to return Buster's love, I extended a hand to Evan. 'Hi. I'm Sally. So great to meet you.'

'Likewise,' he said. 'Evie's always talking about how awesome you are.'

'Well, I don't know about that. But I do have pie.'

'Good enough for me!' Evan grinned, but then the smile froze on his face. It took a second as I wondered what I could possibly have done to offend him before realizing what it was he was reacting to.

'Oh, right,' I said, reaching up to touch my throat. It must have been pretty bad if Evan, with his poor eyesight, could spot it so easily.

Evie stood back up. 'Oh right, what?' she asked.

'Evan just noticed some bruises that I have on my neck,' I answered with a sigh. 'Come sit down and I'll tell you all about it, 'cause it's kind of a long story.'

They followed me into the kitchen, where I directed them to take a seat at the red Formica table as I fetched coffee, half-and-half, sugar, and slices of peach pie. Once we were all digging into our breakfast, I told them the entire story: Alan being found dead at the benefit dinner I'd cooked for, Lucinda asking me to investigate, Eric helping, the various suspects we'd come up with, Lucinda finding the ripped pages in my scheduling folder the day before, and finally, the attack up at the Pogonip.

'I can't believe you didn't tell me any of this before,' said Evie, poking morosely at her pie. 'But I guess it's really my fault. I've been so preoccupied with work and . . .' She turned toward Evan, and if I hadn't known better, I'd think she was actually gazing into his eyes.

I reached out to lay my hand on hers. 'No, it's not you at all. I haven't even told my father what's going on. Though I suppose I should.' I knew, however, that Dad would be more than disappointed to hear that I'd gotten myself into trouble by once more investigating a murder. Resisting the urge to touch my neck once again, I cleared my throat. 'But I gotta say it does feel good to get it all off my chest to you. So what do you think? Am I crazy? Was it just some mentally deranged stranger who attacked me yesterday, or does it sound like it could be related to my investigation of Alan's death?'

Evie tapped a finger on the table as she considered her answer, then shook her head. 'No, I think it has to be related. It seems just too much of a coincidence, otherwise. But as to *who* it was who followed you up there, who knows? What do you think, Evan?'

'Uh, I'm not sure it's really my place to offer an opinion.' Glancing my way, he licked his lips. 'I mean, I only just met you . . .'

Evie laughed. 'You can tell Sally anything, Ev. She's no shrinking violet or anything.'

'Huh?' he said, which caused her to laugh once more.

'I read it in a book. I think it means she's not a wuss, right, Sally?'

'Correct. On both counts. Feel free to tell me what you think, Evan, if you have any ideas. I could use all the help I could get at this point.'

'Okay,' he said, letting out a breath. 'To me it seems that maybe you all have it wrong about that Alan dude's death. What if it wasn't a planned murder, but instead self-defense? Like, you know, he was coming on to that woman who works there . . . What's her name?'

'Lucinda?'

'Yeah, Lucinda. And he gets really aggressive, so she just lashes out at him. She sure wouldn't want to tell anyone 'cause, even if it was self-defense, she could still be in hella trouble since he actually dropped dead.'

'Huh. The only problem I see with that theory,' I said slowly, 'is that given what had just happened right beforehand, since Lucinda chewed Alan out over the argument he had with the dinner guest, Raquel, I doubt very much he'd be inclined to view her, you know, in a sexual way. He would have been far more angry than aroused, I'd imagine.'

'Those two aren't mutually exclusive,' observed Evan.

I nodded. 'True. And you do raise an interesting point: what if it *was* self-defense? 'Cause after how he railed at Raquel in public, I could certainly see Alan being super aggressive and maybe even physically threatening to Lucinda when she took him down a notch for his behavior. The question is, how can I find out if he was the kind of guy to do such a thing?'

They had no answer to that, and the conversation turned to more pleasant topics, such as the best way to make a peach pie and the young couple's upcoming year at UCSC.

After they left, and after Evie made me pinkie-swear that I wouldn't go for any more walks out in the country alone until this had all been cleared up, I sat for a while longer in the kitchen, pondering her boyfriend's contribution. I knew Alan had at least a bit of a temper, given how he'd verbally accosted Raquel that night at the dinner. Though this information, I mused, was only as trustworthy as its source. And although I'd concluded she wasn't the one who'd tried to strangle me the day before, that didn't necessarily mean she'd been telling the truth about who'd initiated their argument that evening.

But, assuming *arguendo* (as my ex-lawyer brain couldn't help phrasing it) that Alan did have a hot temper, how could I learn if it had ever escalated from verbal to physical?

Kamila would know.

So what excuse could I use to go see the Pages and Plums cook this time? And as soon as I asked myself this, I had the answer.

'Dad.' My father turned around on hearing his name and smiled as I walked across the Solari's kitchen to where he stood monitoring a pot of bolognese sauce on the stove. I leaned in to give him a peck on the cheek, then grimaced. 'You thinking of growing a beard?'

'No way,' he said with a laugh, rubbing a hand across the salt-and-pepper stubble. 'Abby swears she'll break up with me if I ever do. But since she's out of town for a few days, I'm just being lazy. So what brings you down here this morning?'

'What, I have to have a reason to visit my loving and generous father?'

He gave the pot a swift stir, then set the wooden spoon on the counter. 'Uh, huh. I figured it had to be something you wanted.' But the smile that accompanied this comment told me he was happy I'd come to visit, even if there was an ulterior motive.

'Okay, guilty as charged.' I tugged at the turtleneck collar I'd chosen for this visit, which was rather stifling in the hot kitchen. Luckily it was a foggy morning, so Dad had no reason to suspect that the style choice was solely to prevent his seeing the black and blue marks decorating my neck. 'But it's no big deal. I was just wondering if I could pick some of the plums on your tree. I have a friend who'd love to make some jam, and I happen to know you have a ton of 'em right about now.'

'Sure, take all you want. I'm happy to give them to a good home. Any news on Eric? I haven't heard from you since Sunday.'

'Yeah, sorry about that,' I said, staring down at the scuffed wooden floor. How was it that parents were so very good at playing the guilt card? 'I've just been busy. But Eric's doing much better. He went back to work on Monday. Though I have to say, even though he's happy to be cleared for normal life again, he's not too thrilled about being back at the DA's office.' I told Dad about Eric's interview with Saul that morning, then glanced at my phone. 'I bet he's finished by now. I wonder why he hasn't texted.'

'Something probably came up,' said Dad. 'I'm sure he'll get back to you soon.'

'Yeah, probably right.' Nevertheless, I couldn't help worrying that maybe the interview hadn't gone well. 'And also,' I said, jamming the phone back in my pocket, 'he's been talking about us moving in together.'

'That would be great, hon! Would he move into Letta's – I mean, your house – with you?' It was funny how, even though Dad owned the place and I lived in it, the two of us still thought of the home as 'Letta's'. I wondered if we'd ever think of it in any other way.

'Ay, there's the rub,' I said. 'Neither of us really wants us to live together in his condo, but Eric doesn't want to lose the equity he's accrued in the property, so he's thinking of trying to sell it and buy a bigger place we could live in. But given the crazy real-estate market in Santa Cruz these days, who knows where he'd be able to buy.'

Dad frowned. 'Yeah, that'd be no good if you ended up all the way down in Watsonville or Salinas. The commute would be tough.'

'Yep.' I slapped my thighs. 'Anyway, I should get going. Thanks for the plums. And I'll call you later to let you know how Eric's meeting went.'

A half-hour later, after swinging by Dad's backyard to harvest his fruit, I poked my head into the Pages and Plums kitchen. Since it was only eleven thirty, the lunch rush had yet to begin, and Kamila was standing at the cutting board next to the yellow KitchenAid mixer, slicing a loaf of crusty sourdough bread.

The cook looked up as I came through the door. 'Sally,' she said in a tone that managed to simultaneously express cordiality and wariness.

I held up the paper bag in my hand. 'Hi, Kamila, I just stopped by to give you a present. My dad's tree is absolutely loaded down with these plums, and when he asked if I knew anyone who might want to take some off his hands, I of course thought of Pages and Plums. They're Satsumas.'

'Oh, wow. Thank you!' She accepted the gift with a grin. Opening the bag, she pulled out one of the green-and-maroon-skinned plums, inhaled its aroma, then bit into the fruit. 'Delicious!' she proclaimed, wiping the red juice from her chin. 'I can use them for a clafouti for tomorrow's dessert special. Though I think I'll save a few out for myself just to eat. Do tell your father thank you from me.'

'I sure will.'

Kamila set down the bag and returned to her bread slicing. 'So I heard from Sky that a policeman was here yesterday talking to you and Lucinda,' she said with a glance my way. 'What was that about?'

'Oh, Lucinda didn't tell you?'

'Huh, uh. But then again, she left so early that we didn't really have much chance to talk. And she's not due in till noon today. I'm guessing it had something to do with Alan's death?'

Lucinda left the store early yesterday? I would have loved to know exactly what time she'd left, but didn't want to make Kamila any more suspicious about my showing up at the restaurant again. 'Yeah, it did,' I said. 'The pages that had been ripped out of those cookbooks turned up in my car, and we were trying to figure out how that could have happened – who put them there.'

Kamila stopped her slicing. 'Any ideas?' she asked.

'The detective couldn't say,' I parried, not wanting to directly respond to the question. 'But the whole thing does raise another question you might be able to answer. About Alan, that is.'

'Oh?'

'Well, we've all been working under the assumption that he was attacked by someone, but I'm wondering if maybe . . .'

'If what?'

I had her full attention now. 'If it's possible that the opposite happened – that *he* actually attacked someone else, someone who ended up killing him in self-defense.'

She shook her head slowly, as if trying to make sense of what I'd just said.

'I guess what I'm asking,' I went on, 'is if that scenario seems possible to you. Was Alan the kind of guy who might physically . . .' I searched for the right word. 'Threaten someone? Maybe especially if he'd been provoked first?'

'No. I've never seen him get physically aggressive. He could be a hot-head verbally, yeah, for sure. But he never laid a hand on me – or even came close to it, if that's what you're asking. But then again . . .' Kamila shook her head once more. 'I do imagine he felt publicly shamed, with Lucinda chewing him out like she did, and right in front of all those people at the dinner. Who knows how he might have responded to that. Wait,' she said with a sharp intake of breath. 'You don't think *Lucinda* could have done it, do you?'

'I have no idea who did it, or even if my self-defense theory is completely off the wall. I'm just trying to think of all the possibilities.'

'Well,' said Kamila, 'I hope the police figure it out soon, so we can all work on leaving this horror in the past. And so that Alan's family can finally have some sort of closure. Oh, speaking of his

family, I got a call from Alan's brother this morning. He's flying
out to deal with the house Alan left him. It turns out it's worth a
pretty penny, and with very little mortgage outstanding.'

'Huh. Seems even weirder that Alan would have been living in
his van, then, don't you think?'

She shrugged. 'Maybe he cleared out to do that remodel he'd
been talking about. Though it would have to be a pretty extensive
project for him to want to vacate the place completely. Matt – the
brother – told me the property was ready to go on the market right
now. He didn't mention anything about unfinished work on the
place. So the whole thing is kind of bizarre. Do you think I ought
to tell the police what Matt told me?'

'Wouldn't hurt. Though I'm guessing they're already in contact
with the guy.'

'Yeah, I suppose so.' She turned back to her bread, but at the
call of 'Order up!' from the pass, set down her knife and started
across the kitchen toward the hot line.

'Well, I should let you get to work,' I said. 'Enjoy the plums.'

'I will – and thanks again to you and your father.'

Driving home, I pondered what Kamila had told me about Alan's
house. 'A pretty penny' in Santa Cruz likely meant a property
worth well over a million bucks. *Why on earth would someone
move out of a place like that to live on the streets in their van?*

The only person I could think of who might know the answer
to that was Phillip. But I was leery of talking to the guy again.
Even though he'd been friends with Alan, and even though it also
seemed unlikely he was the one who'd followed me up to the
Pogonip, the guy had been at Pages and Plums right before
the attack had happened. So I wasn't willing to scratch him
completely off my list of suspects just yet.

But his partner, Meg – she was another matter. Maybe I could
somehow get her alone to ask what she thought of Alan.

EIGHTEEN

I was preparing a lunch of cottage cheese with roasted beets and mayonnaise when Eric finally texted me: 'Call when U have time.' Setting down the mayo jar, I punched in his number, and he picked up immediately.

'Hey, Sal. Sorry it took so long for me to get back to you, but I had to rush right to court from Saul's office. Janice is down with the flu, and I had to cover her pretrial motions this morning at the last minute.'

'No worries,' I lied, since I had in fact been worried about not having heard from him. 'So how'd it go with Saul?'

'Well, he offered me the job.'

'No way! That's awesome!'

'Yeah, it is . . .' Eric didn't sound all that enthusiastic.

'Wait, what's the problem? You didn't like him – or the work?'

'No, it's not that. We got along great, and the cases sound super interesting. And I'd get to argue them myself, some even in the Ninth District Court of Appeal. So, heck yeah? I'd *love* to come work for him.'

'But . . .?'

He let out a sigh. 'But the pay would be significantly less than what I make now. Also, there's the fact that I'd no longer get the benefits I have as a government employee. Those would be pretty big hits, financially. And now that we're talking about me selling the condo and buying something else, I'm thinking I'll need that money more than ever.'

'Yeah, I get it. Lots to think about. But that sucks.'

'Tell me about it.' Another sigh. 'Anyway, I asked for a few days to consider it, and Saul said there was no big hurry – as long as I let him know within a week or so, it's fine. So at least I don't have to make any hard decisions right this second.'

'Sounds like he really wants you, to give you that much time.'

'Uh, huh,' he answered morosely, making me wish my last comment back. 'So how are you doing?' Eric asked. 'How's your neck?'

'About the same. It doesn't hurt too much, and my cough is gone, but it's pretty ugly. I'm wearing a turtleneck to hide the marks. Kinda like in high school when we'd wears scarves so our parents and teachers couldn't see our hickeys,' I added with a chuckle.

'I wouldn't know,' said Eric. 'I never engaged in such prurient conduct – at least not in high school.'

'Yeah, like I believe that.' I could well imagine that he'd been a pretty hot item back in his teens. I'd seen Eric's high school yearbook photo, and he definitely would've been considered one of 'the cute boys'.

'So, any new developments on the case? Have you heard from Vargas whether they have any suspects for your attack?'

'No, and I don't think I ever will. I doubt he's done anything other than file a report and then send it off to some cyber no man's land, from what he said yesterday. But I do have some other news.'

I told Eric about Evan's idea that Alan might have been killed in self-defense, which prompted a side discussion about the fact that yes, Evie now had a boyfriend, who seemed pretty cool, as far as I could tell. Once we got back on to the subject of Alan Keeting, I explained how I'd used the ruse of my dad's Satsuma plums to visit Kamila, and how she'd totally taken the bait.

'Or rather, the *plums*,' Eric couldn't resist interjecting.

'Right. And although she pretty much pooh-poohed the idea of Alan's being the instigator of the fight since, according to her, he's much more of a yeller than a physical aggressor, she did tell me something quite interesting.'

'Oh yeah?'

'Yeah. She said that Alan's brother recently told her that Alan's house is worth a ton of money, and that it's ready to be put on the market *right now*.'

'Sorry to be dense,' said Eric, 'but why the emphasis on "right now"?'

I explained Kamila's theory that Alan had moved into his van because of an extensive remodeling project he'd planned for his home. 'But if the property is ready for sale right this instant – and from what it looked like when I was nosing around the place, there was no construction going on at all – then that can't have been the reason he moved out.'

'Which begs the question, then,' said Eric, 'why *did* he?'

'Correctamundo. And the only people I can think to ask about that are Phillip and his partner, Meg, since they let him park in front of their house.'

Eric took a drink of something which, from the *clunk* I heard immediately afterwards, I concluded was coffee in a sturdy ceramic mug. 'You could always ask Phillip for another psychic reading,' he suggested.

'Yeah, but I don't really want to talk to him about the case. I mean, I'm pretty sure he's just this smarmy guy who happened to be at both that benefit dinner and at Pages and Plums right before I was attacked, but I can't be *positive* he's not the one. So I'm thinking I'd rather get Meg alone to talk to her.'

'But wouldn't she just go and tell him afterwards all about your conversation?'

'True. But then it would be *after* our conversation, so at least I'd get her opinion before Phillip had a chance to talk to her about it.'

'And how do you plan on getting her to open up?' Eric asked.

'Good question. Obviously, I don't want to just go knock on her door, since Phillip might be there. Plus they don't even know that I know where they live, so it would definitely raise an eyebrow if I suddenly showed up there. But I've seen her several times at Pages and Plums with him – twice in the past week.' I thought a moment while Eric drank more of his coffee. 'I know,' I said. 'I can see if Kamila would be willing to let me know if Meg shows up at the restaurant with Phillip.'

'You think she'd do that? And would you even want Kamila to know what you're planning?'

I poked impatiently at my roasted beets with the paring knife. 'Well, I certainly don't want to ask *Lucinda* to do it at this point, since she and Julian are now two of my prime suspects. And I'm guessing Kamila would be willing to go along with the plan, especially if I tell her that I think Phillip and Meg might have information that could help clear Lucinda.'

'In other words, you'll lie to her.'

'Yup. Though that still doesn't solve the problem of getting Meg alone, away from Phillip.'

'Aha! Here's where I come in,' said Eric. 'How about if I show up at the restaurant with you, and you suggest that Phillip do *my* reading? We rarely have court between noon and one thirty, so I bet I could get over there and have time for a quick session with the guy. And besides, it sounds kind of fun. I've never had a psychic reading before.'

'Ohmygod, Eric, that's brilliant! Phillip is so in love with himself and his "gift", he'll never suspect a thing. And hey, maybe you can ask him whether you should change jobs. He did help me with my feelings about Letta, after all.'

'Oy. I suppose it would be a good excuse to ask for a reading, but that's all I need right now – some woo-woo nutjob advising me on my career path.' Eric barked out a short laugh. 'Anyway, speaking of my career path, I'd best get back to work. I've got a scintillating opposition to a motion to suppress that's due tomorrow. The fun never stops.'

'Nope, guess not. Talk to ya later.'

I ended the call, then finished preparing lunch and took it out to the backyard to eat. The fog had burned off, so I changed from my turtleneck to a tank top and sat at the redwood picnic table as Buster sprawled in the sun on the brick patio, waiting for me to finish and set down the empty bowl.

After my meal, I moved to the living room to finish up the Gauguin scheduling. At about two o'clock I called Kamila, figuring she'd be done with all the lunch tickets by then. 'Sally?' she said. Her voice sounded a tad testy, but at least she'd picked up.

'Hi, Kamila. So sorry to bother you at work, but I have a small request.'

'Uh, huh . . .?'

'Um, well, it has to do with our discussion earlier today, you know, about why Alan was living in his van? It occurred to me that those people who were letting him park at their house – Phillip and Meg – they might know the answer to that question, or at least have some intel that might help explain it, in any event. I know they often eat lunch there, so I was wondering if maybe you'd be willing to call or text me if they come into the restaurant? That way, I could come down there and talk to them about it.'

Kamila was silent for a few seconds. 'I dunno . . .' she finally said.

'I'm just thinking it might really help Lucinda's case to find out if there was something fishy going on with Alan and his van life,' I went on. 'Since, you know, like we talked about, she was the one who basically publicly humiliated him right before he was killed. So the cops are probably still focusing on her . . .'

I let that last sentence dangle, like a juicy hunk of squid at the end of a forty-pound test line, hoping she wouldn't latch on to the flaw in my logic: why wouldn't I ask *Lucinda* to let me know when the pair came into the restaurant?

'Well, I guess I could do that,' Kamila said after a bit. 'If it's not too busy in the kitchen, of course.'

'Of course,' I agreed. 'I totally understand how crazy it can get when you're in the weeds. So, for sure, only if you get the chance. But if that happens, it would be great – thanks so much. Oh,' I added as if it were an afterthought, 'and let me know if you'd like some more plums. My dad's tree still has a ton.'

Utterly shameless, I know. But a little bribery couldn't hurt, right?

That night at Gauguin, Javier and I let Tomás take on full hot line duties again, with only one other cook by his side at the Wolf stove. Since tomorrow was my Friday off, I told Javier he could have the grill station if he preferred, since he'd be handling the line the following night. 'That'd be great,' the chef said, happy to have a change of pace from the frenetic sautéing, sauce-stirring, pan-frying, and oven-tending that the hot line required.

I'd been a tad worried that our typical Thursday night rush – which could often be as crazy as a busy weekend – would fluster the young cook, but Tomás handled himself like a pro, even when we ended up with over a dozen tickets on the rail all at once. And he experienced no slip-ups like he had the previous week when he'd burned his hand grabbing that hot pan.

'I gotta tell you, Tomás,' I said when we had a breather between orders, 'I'm super impressed. It usually takes newbies a lot longer to get the rhythm and pacing of the line down, but you're already as confident – and competent – as someone who's been doing it for months. What's your secret?'

He grinned like a proud schoolboy. 'I dunno. I guess it's just watching you and Javier all this time. You're good examples to learn by.'

'Flattery will get you everywhere,' I responded with a laugh, then drank down half the glass of ice water I held in my hand. 'But truly, I think it might be time to make your promotion official

– and permanent. You think you're ready to leave the prep work behind?'

'*¡Claro que sí!* I am *totally* ready!'

'Good,' I said. At the sound of Brandon's call of 'Fire table seven!' from the pass, I reached for the ticket. 'Now I just need to find someone to fill your old job.'

Tomás glanced over my shoulder at the order and, without being asked, ladled clarified butter into a sauté pan and set it over the flame to fire the second item on the ticket, an order of pan-fried sanddabs. 'You know,' he said, swirling the butter around the pan, 'I have a cousin who might be interested. She's a prep cook at this Mexican place down in Watsonville, but she's been talking for a long time about trying to get a job at a more high-end restaurant.' He stopped, then frowned. 'I'm sorry. I don't mean to be pushy. I mean, just 'cause she's my cousin . . .'

'Is she like you?' I asked. 'A hard worker who's smart, reliable, and a pleasure to work with?'

'Oh man, you're really embarrassing me, now,' said Tomás, the flush on his face backing up the comment. 'But, yeah, for sure. Rosa is all those things. We cook together sometimes for family gatherings, and she's great. We've even talked about opening our own restaurant together some day.'

'Okay, then, tell her to contact me if she's interested. I'd love to get someone hired as soon as possible.'

Tomás pumped his fist. 'You're awesome, Sally. Thanks. I'll text her tonight.'

'And if I do hire Rosa,' I said as he reached into the cooler for a pair of sanddabs, 'don't you two be leaving anytime too soon to start that new restaurant, promise?'

'Promise.' With a grin, he dusted the fish with flour and laid them gently in the sizzling butter.

Eric had gone out that night with some college friends who were in town and texted me afterwards to say he was heading home to do some soul-searching about his career path. Which I took to mean he wanted to be alone.

Fair enough. I had some thinking of my own to do. So after work, I settled down on the living-room couch with Buster beside me, a bourbon-rocks in my hand, and Stan Getz playing on Letta's 1980s-era stereo. I'd considered putting on *Tosca*, but decided that some smooth jazz saxophone would better suit my contemplations than Puccini's plaintive arias of jealousy, regret, and death.

My plan was to see if I could try to make some sense of all the apparently disparate information I had regarding the various suspects in Alan's death. Best write it down, I concluded, and grabbed a piece of scratch paper from the recycling and a pen. I started with the names Lucinda, Julian, and Phillip across the top of the page. Then, after a moment's thought, I grabbed a second sheet of paper and added Kamila, Raquel, and Meg to my list.

After drawing lines between the six names, I divided the pages into three sections from top to bottom: '1. Alan's Death,' '2. Planting Pages in My Car,' and '3. Attack at Pogonip.' Then, for each of the three incidents, I jotted down thoughts about how the people might be involved.

First, Alan's death. It seemed clear that all six of them had the 'opportunity'. The murder had occurred after most people had finished their main course and were therefore roaming around the tables in the parking lot, so any of them could have been in the bookstore at the time of the murder. As a result, I didn't bother with making any notes about that particular element of the 'holy trinity' of crime solving.

And, when I thought about it, I realized the same went for 'means', since it seemed apparent that the culprit had merely shoved Alan into the sharp corner of the bookcase. So no special talent or tool required there.

That left only 'motive' with regard to incident 1. For Lucinda, I wrote: 'self-defense? anger at something A said when they argued? old power struggle with b/c dining-room manager? or anger for something else entirely?'

Not much to go on there, I thought with a shrug.

I moved on to Julian's possible motive for killing Alan: 'Cookbooks?' I wrote. But given his obvious desire for them, why would he then rip out those pages and throw the books under a dumpster? I added another note: 'Or simply an accomplice to Lucinda? (Q – are they involved?)' But that was all I could come up with. Again, not very much.

Any motive for Phillip was even murkier. What would he have had against Alan? I could think of nothing, aside from the possibility that Alan hadn't seated him in a timely manner for lunch one day or that he'd failed to properly squeegee the shower at Phillip's house. And ditto for Meg.

That left Kamila and Raquel. As for Kamila, an ex-lover was always a suspect. Charlie Rich was right when he sang 'Behind Closed Doors'. Who knew what sort of issues Alan and Kamila might have had, or even why they had truly broken up, for that matter? After chewing on my pen for a bit, I wrote: 'bad breakup? abuse? money issue?'

Raquel at least had a clear motive, as their animosity toward each other had been on view for the whole world to see. But could Alan's stance on assisting the homeless, or the fact that he'd called Raquel out that night at the dinner really have been enough cause for her to *kill* the guy?

Staring at my scribblings, I tapped out an impatient cadence on the paper with my pen, then stood to make another drink. Writing it down wasn't helping at all. If anything, it was only serving to show me how very opaque the whole thing was. I was still on the wrong side of the curtain to understand how this show worked.

I changed the music to a more upbeat Talking Heads CD and forged on to section 2 of my notes: 'Planting Pages in My Car'. Lucinda absolutely had both the means and opportunity to stick those ripped cookbook pages into my scheduling folder, since she'd been sitting in the car holding the folder right before she'd supposedly 'discovered' them. And the same went for Julian – though only if he was in on it with Lucinda, as she would have seen anyone do it.

But the question was, *why?* The only possible reason – for any of the suspects, for that matter – had to be to place suspicion on me for Alan's murder, or at least for the theft of the cookbooks. But again, this only begged the same question: *why?* I had no answer for that, other than perhaps that it was merely to throw another spatula in the works and further confuse things. Which it certainly had succeeded in doing.

As for Phillip, I couldn't see how he'd have done it. He had no way of knowing I'd be at Cruzin' Coffee that morning, so it could only have been him if he'd just happened to spot my car sitting there with the top down.

But then I had a chilling thought: *Unless he'd been following me.*

And the same was true for Meg, Kamila, and Raquel. Anyone

would have been able to put those pages in my car if I'd been followed wherever I went that morning. A shiver ran up my spine. *Could I still be under surveillance now?*

Even though I was snuggled safely in my own home next to a dog who'd bark at the sound of anyone who got within thirty feet of the front door, I couldn't help glancing quickly around me. I got up to check that the front and back doors were both locked, then paced back and forth in time to David Byrne's frantic singing. Then, realizing what song was on, I laughed out loud. 'Psycho Killer'. Perfect.

With a wry smile, I plopped back on to the sofa and moved on to question 3. Who had tried to strangle me up at the Pogonip the day before? Running a finger lightly over my neck, I considered who had the means and opportunity to have followed me up to the park. The fact that Lucinda had left work early yesterday weighed heavily – both on my analysis of the case and on my heart. I truly didn't want to believe she could have done such a thing. I'd felt like we were becoming *friends*.

But the fact was, she had both the opportunity and the means. Lucinda could simply have tailed me from Pages and Plums to my house, and then up to the Pogonip. She was certainly tall and strong enough to have grabbed me, and her body type matched that of my attacker, as well.

But what about that hotdog? Assuming it hadn't simply been something on the ground that Buster happened to sniff out, it must have been a trap. Whoever followed me had heard me tell Eric I'd be taking the dog with me to the park, and the tasty treat was intended to distract Buster during the attack. *Do they sell hotdogs at Pages and Plums?* I didn't think so.

And then I remembered a menu item that had tickled my taste-bud imagination the first time I'd eaten at the restaurant. The sandwich with merguez – a skinny sausage with a dark red color, just like the meat I'd seen Buster gobbling down right before that belt had been whipped around my throat. I drew a heavy circle around the words I'd written next to Lucinda's name: 'means AND opp'.

As for motive, again, it would be the same for all the suspects: either to scare me off my investigation or, worse, to ensure I had no ability to continue snooping. Which could only mean there was something serious to hide – such as Alan's murder.

Next up was Julian. He'd also been at the bookstore when I'd told Eric I was going walking with Buster up at the Pogonip. But even if he hadn't overheard our conversation, Lucinda could have told him about it. And she could have given him a piece of sausage, too, if they truly were in on all this together.

What about Phillip? He had only just ordered his lunch when I'd left Pages and Plums. So while he could conceivably have overheard my phone conversation with Eric and then rushed to follow me, it didn't seem likely he could have hustled out of there quickly enough to tail me – unless he'd done a dine-and-dash at his favorite eating establishment. Plus, since I couldn't imagine any good reason for him to have killed Alan, it made no sense for him to try to scare me off the case. 'Poss but not likely means & opp; unknown motive', I wrote under his name.

As for the other three, as far as I knew, only Kamila had been at Pages and Plums yesterday, and there was no way the cook would have left her job to follow me up to the Pogonip. Moreover, none of those women had the build of my attacker. After writing 'no opp; wrong build' under Kamila, Raquel, and Meg's names, I set my notes on the coffee table and sipped from my Maker's Mark. At the sudden movement, Buster woke up, turned around twice, then settled back down in the exact same position as before.

It was of course possible, I mused, that my assailant yesterday had in fact been that guy Robbie had talked about – a mentally unbalanced man whose attack had simply been a random act of violence.

But I didn't think so.

NINETEEN

The very next day, Friday, I got a text from Kamila: 'those 2 people here now'.

'Thx!' I wrote back, then immediately called Eric. 'I'm so glad you picked up,' I said when he got on the line. 'Phillip and Meg are at Pages and Plums right now. Can you meet me there for lunch?'

'Absolutely!' he said. 'Be there in about fifteen minutes.'

I arrived first and waited in the parking lot for Eric to pull up. Then, after quickly reviewing our plan, we headed inside. As I'd hoped, Phillip saw us as we were standing at the host stand and waved in greeting. Taking this as an invitation to join the two of them, who were luckily seated at a table for four, I nudged Eric forward and we walked across the room to where they sat. Meg was still working on a salade Niçoise, but Phillip had only a few bites left of his steak sandwich.

'Fancy meeting you here, Phillip,' I said. 'Eric and I were just talking about you.'

'Ah, so that's why my ears were burning just now.' With a smile, he held out his hand. 'Glad to meet you, Eric. This is my partner, Meg. Would you care to join us?'

'Sure, why not? And I'll fill you in on why your name came up.'

'I'm all ears,' said Phillip, 'red as they might be.'

'So . . .' I glanced at Eric. 'Maybe you should tell the story?'

'Okay.' He let out a sigh worthy of a great Shakespearian player. 'It's about my job. I'm trying to decide whether I want to quit to go work for someone else, and I'm having a hard time with whether it's worth it to forgo a higher salary for a more satisfying position elsewhere. And, well, Sally told me how helpful you were about her aunt, so I just thought you might be willing to do a session with me.'

Phillip laughed. 'I'm not a licensed counselor or therapist, you know. What I do is sense the types of energies people are experiencing, and I use those vibrations to open them up to considering where different paths might take them – how their future might unfold, depending on the choices they make.'

'Uh . . .' Eric's tight expression told me he was doing his best to restrain himself, skeptic that he was, from rolling his eyes at the whole 'vibrations and energies' thing. 'Yeah, that sounds like it could be really helpful. Would you be interested in doing a reading for me? And not to presume, but soonish? 'Cause I have to let the person know about the job pretty quick.'

'I'm nearly done eating,' Phillip said, 'so we could do it right now before your food comes out, if you want. That is, if we can use the office again.' Phillip cast his eyes about the bookstore, where Lucinda's salesclerk, Ellen, stood at the register. 'But I don't see Lucinda around anywhere to ask her.'

I jumped up from my chair. 'I'll ask Kamila,' I said, and hurried over to the kitchen, where I could see the cook as she stood monitoring a breast of chicken sizzling in a pan. Catching her attention, I leaned over the pass and asked, 'Would it be okay if Phillip used the office for one of his readings with Eric? It won't take too long, I don't think.'

She arched an eyebrow and shot a look over to the table where Eric, Phillip, and Meg sat. 'Fine by me, as long as no one else needs it right now.'

'I'll check with the staff in the bookstore to make sure. Thanks.'

Once she learned that Kamila had given the okay, Ellen said she had no problem with the plan. So after Eric and I ordered (a bowl of cream of broccoli soup with toasted baguette slices for me, and a steak sandwich with fries 'extra crispy' for him), Eric and Phillip retired to the bookstore office.

'Sorry Eric stole away your date,' I said to Meg after they'd left.

She waved a hand. 'That's all right, I'm used to it. He absolutely loves doing his readings, so I'm happy for him, actually.'

'Yeah, he does seem to have quite the knack for it. Did he tell you about the session he had with me?'

'No, Phillip never talks about what happens in his clients' readings. He takes his readings very seriously, like the doctor–patient privilege, I guess.'

'Right, I suppose that makes sense.' I took a sip of water as I pondered how to turn the conversation to Alan. 'So, does that mean he doesn't even mention *whose* readings he's done? 'Cause I'm really curious if he ever did one with Alan.'

Meg gave me a quizzical look. 'Why would you wonder that?'

'Well, I get the impression that he – Alan, that is – might have had some personal issues he needed to deal with. And I'm just wondering if they could have had anything to do with the reason he was killed.'

'Oh, right. I guess the local paper calls you the Sleuth of Santa Cruz for good reason.' Meg chuckled as she poked at the lone green bean still on her plate, then set down the fork. 'I truly have no idea if Phillip ever did Alan's reading, but I'd say there's a good chance he did, since he tends to corral all his friends into doing so if he can.' Meg smiled, then leaned forward, elbows on the table. 'You know, now that I think about it, there was something a little odd that happened . . .'

When her voice trailed off and her eyes moved to the distance, I was afraid she might change her mind about telling me whatever it was she'd remembered. 'Oh yeah?' I prompted. 'Do tell.'

'I don't recall exactly what it was that prompted it, but for some reason, Phillip started to get a bit suspicious of Alan. Was it maybe that he always had clean clothes for work, even though he rarely asked to use our washer and dryer?' She shook her head. 'I'm not sure, to tell you the truth. But it was something like that. Anyway, so Phillip got it in his head to follow Alan when he left his spot in front of our house one morning, and when he got back home, he just mumbled something about how Alan had found somewhere else to live. Phillip didn't give any details, and I didn't ask, but Alan never parked at our house again after that day.'

'Huh, interesting,' I said. 'So how long ago was this?'

Meg cocked her head and stared blankly toward the kitchen as she thought. 'A couple weeks back, maybe? Right, it would have been exactly two weeks ago, because I remember Phillip and I met at Pages and Plums for lunch later that day. We have a standing date here every week, 'cause I work a half-day on Fridays and finish at eleven thirty.'

'Which means it was only three days before Alan was killed,' I said. 'Weird. I wonder if his death is somehow connected to that change in circumstances.'

Meg shrugged. 'Who knows? But you're right, it does make you wonder.'

At the appearance of Sky bearing Eric's and my lunches, I leaned back to let him set down my soup and pondered this revelatory information I'd just received while buttering my toasted baguette. 'Do you know if Phillip talked to Alan at all the night of that benefit dinner?' I asked. 'Maybe to find out more about this new place where he was living?'

'Not in my presence he didn't, but once we'd finished the main course, Phillip and I split up to go visit with different people who were there that night. So I guess he could have, but if so, he didn't mention it to me.' She took a sip of iced tea, then frowned. 'Do you think I should tell Phillip to contact the police to let them know that Alan had found new housing right before he was killed? It does seem like it could be important. Phillip didn't have a chance to tell them about it the night of the dinner, because they sent us all home, saying they'd be in touch if they needed to interview anyone. But since they never contacted me, I bet they never reached out to Phillip, either. I'm sure he'd be happy to talk to them, though, if you think it would help.'

Oh, boy. I had no desire for Phillip to know I'd been interrogating his girlfriend about his relationship with Alan. But then again, she was bound to tell him about our conversation, no matter what. 'Well, it certainly might help for him to offer to talk to the cops,' I said. 'But they're probably already aware of all this. I'm sure Phillip's not the only one who knew about Alan's housing situation.'

'Yeah, probably true.' Meg glanced at her phone and set it back on the table. 'I wonder how much longer they'll be,' she said, pushing back her chair. 'Knowing Phillip, it could be a while, so, if you don't mind, I'm gonna go check out the bookstore for a little bit.'

'No, no, that's fine,' I said. 'I'll sit here and savor the last of this delicious soup.'

I'd scraped my bowl clean – the creamy broccoli purée was indeed quite tasty – by the time the two men finally emerged from the bookstore office. Eric thanked Phillip and sat down across from me, and I watched as Phillip and Meg headed out after paying their check. Meanwhile, Eric switched on his phone, which he'd silenced during his psychic reading, and checked back in with the cyber-world.

'Oh, shoot,' he said, scrolling through his texts. 'They needed me ten minutes ago. Gotta deal with an emergency protective order for one of my witnesses, so I guess I'll have to get this to go.' Eric trotted over to the host stand and returned with a cardboard container for his steak sandwich. 'I'll try to call you later. Otherwise, we can debrief tonight at dinner with Nichole and Mei. And the doc says I'm now cleared for adult beverages again, so it'll be a celebration of sorts.' Leaning over to give me a quick kiss goodbye, he grabbed his box and headed for the door.

And I guess I'm paying for lunch.

Eric did not call, and I spent the afternoon at Gauguin doing our produce and seafood orders, paying invoices, and helping Javier fix a broken faucet in the women's bathroom. When Kris and Tomás showed up for their shifts around four, I headed home. I'd have just enough time to walk Buster and change my clothes before the evening's activities.

Nichole and Mei didn't arrive till after five o'clock. 'Sorry we're late,' Nichole said as she climbed out of her Prius, 'but there was a wreck on Highway 17.' Since our dinner reservations were for five thirty, we had little time for chitchat as they dumped their bags in the guest bedroom and 'refreshed' themselves quickly before we had to head out.

'So where are we going for dinner?' asked Mei.

'Downtown, to Kalo's.'

She clapped her hands. 'Oh, goodie – I adore their mac nut-encrusted mahi mahi!'

Eric had not yet arrived at the restaurant, even though we were close to ten minutes late, but no one in our little group was surprised. Much as I loved other aspects of his personality, Eric's lack of punctuality for things other than court appearances was a frequent source of tension between us.

We'd just ordered our drinks when he swept into the tiki-adorned dining room and greeted us all with French-style *bises*. 'Man! There's no parking anywhere near here tonight,' he said, pulling out his chair. 'I had to drive around forever, and finally found a spot about six blocks away.'

'Uh, huh.' Nichole, who'd known Eric for as long as I – the three of us having met at the Monterey College of Law – was not taken in by his theatrics. 'I said we should punish you by making you wait for your drink, but Sally took pity on your poor, dilatory soul and ordered you a Martini.'

'That's my girl,' he said, flashing that same charming smile that had captured my heart back when I was a first-year law student.

Our drinks served and our dinners ordered, Mei raised her glass of IPA in a toast. 'To us all being together once again. Because it's been way too long.'

'I'll drink to that,' I said, clinking with the other three. 'It has been much too long. So catch us up on what's been going on with you two.'

Mei told us about her new position as director of the gym up in San Francisco where she taught Pilates and yoga. It came with a higher paycheck, but involved fewer of the classes she loved to teach and more payroll and admin work, so she had mixed feelings about the promotion. Eric and I exchanged glances, then commiserated with her situation.

Next, Nichole, happy to have a lawyer and ex-lawyer with whom she could talk shop, launched into a detailed description of a case at the immigration clinic where she worked involving a Guatemalan client detained at the border for over six months.

'And how about you two?' asked Mei, once Nichole's sad story finally came to a victorious ending with the client having been granted asylum. 'What's new at the DA's office?'

Eric grunted. 'Just more of the same. But the big news is that I've been offered a position with Saul Abrams doing federal appellate work.'

'Dude!' said Nichole. 'I know that guy – he's awesome! That would be so rad to work there!'

The server arrived with our dinners, and there was a brief lull in our chat. Then, as we dug into the food, Eric explained his dilemma of whether to take what would probably be a more fulfilling job with Saul or stick with the better money and benefits of his rote, government job.

'I hear ya,' said Mei. 'It's a conundrum, all right.'

'So did Phillip help you at all with that question?' I asked, cutting off a slice of pork chop with sticky guava barbecue sauce.

Mei looked my way. 'Who's Phillip?'

'He's . . . uh, this psychic guy we're kind of . . . investigating . . .'

Nichole set her fork down on the table with a *thump*. 'No way, girlfriend. Seriously? You're on another case? And *Eric's* helping?

With a *psychic*?' She let out a hearty laugh. 'Okay, spill. All of it. Now.'

'Okay, fine.' I recounted everything I could remember about the case, with Eric interrupting occasionally to add tidbits I'd left out. I pulled down my turtleneck so Nichole and Mei could inspect my neck to assure I was telling the truth when I said I was all right, then told them how Kamila had texted me that morning to let me know Phillip and Meg were at Pages and Plums for lunch. 'So we rushed over there, and Eric got Phillip to do a psychic reading for him about his potential career choices—'

'I would have loved to be a fly on the wall for *that*,' interrupted Nichole. 'Just to watch your face while someone went on about your auras and past lives.'

'I only did it so Sally could talk to Meg alone, without Phillip there,' said Eric, betraying a hint of defensiveness. 'And the career advice angle was simply a hook to get him away.' He turned toward me. 'And so did she divulge anything interesting during your tête-à-tête?'

I nodded as I took a drink of my whiskey sour. 'She did. And I think it could be quite important, as a matter of fact.' They listened raptly as I recounted what I'd learned about Phillip becoming suspicious of Alan and following him one morning, and how Alan had never again parked his van at their house after that. 'Phillip told Meg that Alan had found another place to stay, and that's all she apparently knows. But I can't help thinking there's more to it, especially given the timing – only three days before he was killed.'

'I agree,' said Eric. 'Too bad we couldn't have been a fly on the wall for the conversation between Alan and Phillip.'

We ate in silence for a bit – unusual for this group – and then I asked, 'So how was your session with Phillip, anyway? Did he try to hypnotize you? 'Cause I think he tried to with me, but realized right away it wasn't going to work.'

'Yeah,' Eric said, 'I think he did try that, actually. So I pretended it was working – you know, getting a dazed look in my eyes, relaxing my body and stuff. I've seen those guys who come to the county fair with that hypnosis act, so I figured I could make him believe I'd gone into a trance. But he didn't fall for it and changed tack pretty quickly.' He smiled. 'Too bad, 'cause I would've loved to see what he'd have done if he thought I had in fact fallen under.'

'And what happened after that?' asked Mei.

'The funny thing,' said Eric with a shake of the head, 'is that he actually was kind of helpful, once he got past the mumbo jumbo and started talking about my job. He said I should consider what my own priorities in life are, think about what's important to me – happiness in my work, in my day-to-day life, or financial prosperity.'

'And?' pressed Mei.

'And . . . I don't know. Because truly, if I'm worried about money, how happy can I be in my day-to-day life? But on the other hand, if I dislike my job so much, what's the point of money?' Eric drank down the rest of his Martini, then turned to face me. 'But I do admit, Sal, the guy can read people – their personalities and emotions – pretty darn well. Maybe it's like you said, that fortune tellers are just super empathetic people? I hadn't ever really considered that before. If nothing else, the session was a bit of an eye-opener for me in that way.'

Nichole rolled her eyes at this, but Mei was nodding in agreement. 'I think you're right,' she said. 'Some people do have . . . how shall I say, *abilities* that are different – or more acute – than most others do. We think there are only certain senses, our human senses – taste, hearing, sight, touch, smell. But other animals can sense types of things we humans miss entirely. And in all sorts of ways. Like how the senses of sight and smell seem merged in dogs. Or what about those animals that see different wavelengths in the color spectrum, or geomagnetic energy, or sonar, for example? So those other kinds of senses must exist. And who's to say there aren't some people with the ability to sense things in unusual ways? Assuming otherwise, simply because it's not the same for all humans, is just pure, utter anthropocentricity.'

Eric, Nichole, and I stared at her a moment and then we all burst out laughing – Mei included. 'Try saying *that* after a couple more of these,' said Nichole, holding up the remnants of her Mai Tai.

Mei slapped her partner lightly on the arm. 'Well, anyway, you know what I'm saying. Maybe this Phillip guy *does* possess some sort of gift that we don't have and can't understand.'

'I guess it's possible,' I said with a shrug, then turned to Eric. 'So was there anything about him today that seemed . . . I dunno, suspect or odd?' I asked.

'You mean other than his "gift"?' He chuckled at his own joke, then pursed his lips in thought. 'No, nothing comes to mind. Though there was something kind of gross, now that I think about it.'

'Gross? As in disgusting?'

'Yeah. I kept noticing him reach down to his ankle and quickly pull his hand back. And then when he crossed his legs, his pant leg got kind of hiked up, and I saw this nasty rash on his leg.' Eric pulled a face.

'What kind of rash?' I asked.

'You know, rashy – red and splotchy, with ugly blisters. And some of them had broken open and were kind of weepy.'

'Yuck,' said Mei. 'Can I please finish my meal before we continue this discussion?' And then she saw my face. 'What? Why are you looking like that, Sally?'

'Ohmygod,' I said. 'It sounds like poison oak.'

TWENTY

Nichole and Mei stared at me as if I were cracked. 'So what's the big deal?' said Nichole. 'I got poison oak last year hiking out at Mount Tamalpais, and yeah, it wasn't pleasant, but it's not like having the plague or something.'

Eric's look, however, told me he understood.

'Hold on a sec,' I said, and pulled out my phone. After typing in a few key words, I scrolled through the Mayo Clinic page that had popped up, then set the phone on the table. 'It says it usually takes twelve to twenty-four hours for a poison oak rash to develop.'

Eric's face tightened in anger. 'It was *him*. That son of a—'

'Who? What?' said Mei. She and Nichole were now both leaning forward, confusion in their eyes.

'It was two days ago that I was attacked up in the Pogonip, and not only was there a ton of poison oak everywhere, but whoever tried to strangle me ran off afterwards through a big patch of the stuff. And also . . .' I paused for dramatic effect. 'The guy was wearing shorts.'

'Whoa.' Nichole blinked a few times, then frowned. 'This is getting gnarly.'

'Do you think he noticed you looking at his ankles?' I asked Eric.

'I don't think so. I was trying not to stare, since it seemed kind of rude.'

'And did you by any chance notice if he was wearing a belt?'

Eric shook his head. 'Huh, uh. But if he had been, it would have probably been hidden by that Hawaiian shirt he was wearing.'

'Right.' I drummed my fingers on the table as I considered this new piece of the puzzle. 'So we know Phillip was at Pages and Plums when I was on the phone with you about taking Buster for a walk up in the park, which means it's possible he heard our conversation. But he'd only just ordered his food, and I doubt he would have rushed out without paying.'

'He could have gotten it to go,' said Nichole.

'True. But it still would have taken a while for the food to be ready, so he couldn't have followed me right when I left the restaurant.' A server approached with a pitcher to refill our waters, but I waved her away.

'How long were you at home before you headed up to the Pogonip?' asked Eric.

'I dunno . . . probably twenty minutes or so? I ate a quick lunch before we left.'

'Which means Phillip could have shown up at your house after you got there and then followed you.' Eric swiped his phone to life and entered a query. 'Yep. I figured.' He handed me the device and there, for all the world to see on the White Pages app, was my name, age, address, and phone number.

'Dang. So much for privacy.' I stared at the screen for a moment before handing it back to Eric, then picked up my own phone once more and punched in the number for Pages and Plums. 'Hi, is this Sky?' I asked, switching to speaker mode so the others could hear. 'It's Sally Solari, and I have a quick question for you if you've got a moment. Do you remember when Phillip was there the day before yesterday for lunch? It was the day that detective showed up and talked to Lucinda and me.'

'Uh, huh,' said Sky, 'I do.'

'And do you remember how he changed his mind about eating there and decided to get his food to go?'

'Hold on a sec,' said Sky. 'I gotta take another call.' The others watched me, eagerness in their faces, as I held my breath and stared intently at the phone in my hand. There was a click, and I was worried we'd been disconnected, but then Sky got back on the line. 'Sorry,' he said. 'But yeah, I do remember that. It was weird the way all of a sudden he seemed like he was in this huge hurry to get out of there.'

'And do you by any chance recall what it was he ordered for lunch that day?'

'Yeah, I'm pretty sure it was the merguez sandwich. So why all this interest in Phillip, anyway?'

I mumbled some lame excuse about trying to win a bet with Eric, then quickly ended the call. 'He's gotta be our guy,' I said, setting the phone down next to my uneaten pork chop. 'Not only for the attack on me, but for Alan's death – and planting those cookbook pages in my car. I just can't figure out how he could have known I was going to be at Cruzin' Coffee that morning. Unless . . .'

The three others waited for me to finish my thought, and when all I did was stare blankly at the table next to ours, Nichole snapped her finger in front of my face. 'Unless *what*, girl? You've got us on pins and needles!'

'Unless Phillip *did* hypnotize someone. Someone like Lucinda, whose reading he did right before mine. That's gotta be it. She doesn't remember him putting her under, but you wouldn't know unless the person told you, right?' I glanced at Eric, who nodded.

'Yeah,' he said. 'Those people I saw at the fair didn't remember anything about it. In fact, some of them kept arguing afterwards that they hadn't really been hypnotized, even though we all saw it happen.'

'So Lucinda could have told Phillip all sorts of stuff – not just about our plan to meet Julian the next day for coffee, but also how we suspected him of Alan's murder.' I thought a moment, tapping a finger on the table. 'And for that matter, he could have hypnotized both of us, too, Eric, and we wouldn't remember it.'

He shuddered. 'That's a disturbing thought. If so, we need to be very careful from here out.'

'No matter *what*, we need to be careful,' I said.

Nichole sat back and folded her arms across her chest. 'I think the best defense at this point would be offense. Rather than waiting for this creep to come after you, why don't you go after him?'

'What?' I said. 'You have an idea?'

'I do.' Shoving her plate aside, she leaned forward, arms on the table. 'This guy clearly has it out for you. He's pissed off, and the whole thing has now become personal, I'd say, given all you've told us. So what about using that against him?'

'How so?' I asked.

'By using you as bait.'

'No way,' said Eric before I could respond. 'We're not putting Sally in any more danger than she's already in. Do you need to see her neck again?'

I'd been about to protest Nichole's suggestion as well, but hearing Eric's protective declaration on my behalf got my hackles up. 'Hold on,' I said. 'I think I'm the one to make that call.'

'You can't be serious, Sal.' Eric ran his hands through his shaggy hair, then spread his palms out flat on the table. He was pressing them down so hard that the veins started to pop out.

'Here's my idea,' said Nichole, clearly warming to the plan.

'Tomorrow morning, you go and park outside Phillip's house, pretending to spy on him. He'll totally notice you because of that classic car you drive.' But then she frowned. 'Oh, wait – you think he'll be home then?'

'It's a Saturday,' I said, 'so I'd imagine so. But Meg would likely be there, too.'

'No worries,' said Nichole. 'I bet that if you sit there long enough, he won't be able to resist coming outside to talk to you for long, and she wouldn't be able to hear anything from the car. And at that point, you accuse him of the crimes, and hopefully he'll spill something incriminating, which you will have recorded on your phone without him knowing.'

Eric was shaking his head as he stared icily at Nichole. 'I don't like this idea one little bit.'

'She wouldn't be alone,' said Nichole. 'The three of us can hide in my car a few doors down, and we'll make sure nothing bad happens. Strength in numbers, as they say. If he even tries to touch you, we'll be there in seconds and take him down.'

'What if he has a gun?' said Eric. 'Us being down the street wouldn't do diddly in that case.'

But Nichole waved aside this possibility. 'If he was the type of guy to have a gun, he would've used it on Sally up at that park – and on Alan, too. So no, I don't see that as an issue.'

'I really don't appreciate this cavalier attitude regarding Sally's safety.' Eric rose from his seat, his face flushed in anger. 'Maybe if it was Mei who was going to be put in the line of fire you'd be more—'

'Hold it right there, both of you!' I said, slapping the table with both my hands. '*I* don't appreciate being talked about as if I weren't even present in this conversation.' I took a few deep breaths. 'Thank you for trying to look out for me,' I said to Eric, my voice now soft, 'but this is obviously my decision.'

I turned to Nichole. 'Okay, I'm in. Let's do it.'

Fortified as I was by several cocktails the night before, my agreeing to the plan had seemed reasoned and logical at the time. While it clearly involved some risks, these were easily outweighed by the excitement of going on the offensive, as Nichole had put it. Far better than merely waiting passively to see what would happen next.

By Saturday morning, however, the Dutch courage had worn off. In the bright daylight now streaming through the bedroom window, the idea seemed far more sketchy. Low voices and the smell of coffee floated upstairs from the kitchen, but I lay in bed a bit longer, staring up at the cracks in the ceiling, each telling part of the story of the many earthquakes the old house had experienced through the years.

Did I really want to go through with this?

But then a vision of Phillip – a man who could preen about his 'gift' for seeing into my soul, yet the very next day attempt to throttle me with a belt – made me sit up in bed.

Yes. I did.

Joining the others downstairs, we formulated our plan of action. Then, forty-five minutes later, the four of us set off in two cars – Nichole with Mei and Eric, and me in the T-Bird leading the way. As I drove down the street toward Phillip's house, though, I slowed. A car was backing out of his driveway. Was Phillip leaving?

But no, it was Meg, alone in her car. And Phillip's red Corolla was parked on the street in front of the house. *Good.* Hoping that Phillip's partner didn't recognize my yellow convertible, I turned my face away as she drove past. I watched her in the rear-view mirror as she turned the corner, and only then did I pull up behind Phillip's car. Nichole continued further down the street, did a U-turn, and parked at the house one door down and across the street. The tint of the windows on her Prius prevented me from seeing the three of them inside, but I was comforted to know they were there.

I, on the other hand, sitting in the T-Bird with the top down, was completely in the open. Which was, of course, the plan, but the visibility still made me nervous. Especially since I now knew that Meg – who I'd counted on being at home and acting as a damper on Phillip's anger – wasn't there. Nevertheless, I sat stoically in my car staring at the front door, willing Phillip's curiosity to finally get the better of him.

After fifteen minutes, I'd seen no sign of any activity inside the house – no pulling back of the curtain, no lights going on or off. I was starting to worry that he wasn't home after all, or that he either hadn't seen me or, if he had, he wasn't going to rise to the bait.

'What do we do now?' I texted Eric.

I watched as the dots bounced on my screen. The three of them in Nichole's car were no doubt arguing about what to write back. 'Hold tight,' the reply finally came, 'prob hasn't seen U.'

So I waited. And waited.

Pulling out my phone, I saw that it had now been over a half-hour. *Damn.* What if he was in the back of the house streaming *The Sixth Sense* or watching YouTube videos on how to hypnotize your cat? Now that I'd leapt into the fire, I was set on seeing this thing through till I could stamp on its charred, smoldering remains.

'*Manache!*' I muttered, invoking Nonna's favorite swear word, and opened the car door. My phone buzzed before I'd even made it to the curb: 'what are U DOING?' came Eric's text. Then, 'NO!!!!'

Shoving the device in my pocket, I strode to the front door.

It opened before I had a chance to knock. 'Sally,' said Phillip, all smiles. 'What brings you here? Would you care to come inside?'

'No thanks, I'm good here. I wanted to ask you about something.'

'Okay . . .' He was still grinning, as if in on a joke only he was party to. We'd soon see about that.

'I know what you did,' I said.

'My, that's awful cryptic. And dramatic, as well.'

'I know you followed and attacked me up in the Pogonip on Wednesday,' I said, pointing to my neck, today once again concealed by a turtleneck jersey. 'The poison oak on your ankles gave you away.' This prompted a glance by him down toward his feet. 'And the merguez sausage you ordered at Pages and Plums, but then took instead to go and used to distract my dog while you tried to strangle me.'

His face was unreadable as he stood there returning my gaze.

'And I know it was you who stole those cookbooks the night of the dinner and then planted the ripped-out pages in my car. You clearly learned from Lucinda where I'd be that morning when you hypnotized her during her session.'

Was the smile starting to fade?

'And, most importantly, I know that you're the one who killed Alan – which is, of course, the reason for the other two incidents. But my only question is *why*? Why kill Alan? You two were on the same side politically. And you seemed to be so close. How could you do that to someone who was your good *friend*?'

Phillip continued to regard me, the smile now completely gone. 'You have no idea what you're talking about,' he said and, with a shake of the head, started to close the door. Not willing to have the conversation end so quickly, however, I blocked the threshold with my foot.

'Then set me straight,' I said. 'Because as far as I'm concerned, you're simply a sick sociopath, someone who – although he *claims* to be this marvelous spiritualist out to help humankind with his so-called "gift" – in fact has no qualms whatsoever about harassing his good friend at night in his van while he slept and then murdering him in cold blood for no reason whatsoever. So is that it? *Are* you simply a sick sociopath?'

I was clearly getting to him, because the muscles in his face had now tightened, and he was slowly clenching and unclenching his fists.

'Alan *was* my friend,' Phillip finally said, his voice rough. 'Or so I'd thought.' He gazed at me a moment, his jaw working, and then seemed to come to a decision. 'Here, give me your phone and come inside, and I'll tell you the *true* story about Alan. Because he's not the saint you thought he was. Nothing you've accused me of constitutes real proof of anything, but nevertheless, I don't want you recording me. Which is obviously what you're up to.'

He held out his hand, which I stared at for a moment. 'Okay, you can have my phone,' I said, 'but no way am I coming inside. Not after what you did to me the other day.' It took all the emotional strength I possessed not to reach up to touch my neck once again.

He shrugged. 'Fair enough.'

I pulled out my phone, turned off the recording app, and handed it over to him. After inspecting the device, then switching it off entirely, he shoved it into the pocket of his khaki slacks. Despite my anxiety levels being sky high, I couldn't help noticing his Hawaiian shirt. This one featured sea turtles swimming through a green sea and looked to be from the '50s, complete with vintage rayon with carved wooden buttons.

'Okay,' said Phillip, leaning against the door jamb. 'I have no idea what you're talking about with regard to my harassing Alan at night, for I did nothing of the kind. But I will give you points for being right on several counts. Figuring that out about the sausage was clever, though that was only an afterthought after your dog heard me in the bushes and came over to investigate. As was deducing that I'd hypnotized Lucinda.' He snickered. 'What an easy subject she was. Unlike your friend Eric, who thought he could fool me into thinking he'd fallen under. Or you, who didn't even try. As for the poison oak,' he glanced down again at his ankles, 'that was my bad. I should have known to keep it covered up.'

He was clearly enjoying this, being 'on stage' and having me hang on his every word. I just needed to keep him talking. 'So why kill Alan?' I asked. 'It makes no sense. You said you were friends, right?'

He actually had the decency to look sad. 'We were,' he said with a sigh. 'Which is why what he did was so incredibly painful.'

'What exactly did he do? What did you discover that morning you followed him?'

Phillip leaned out the door to look up and down the street, but apparently seeing nothing to raise his suspicions, he rocked back on his heels, then shook his head. 'Now that really annoyed me, you dragging Meg into all this and interrogating her about me. Yeah, she told me about your conversation, afterwards. But hey, I get it. We're similar, you and I – both like sharks, in constant forward motion till we achieve our goals.'

I didn't much like being compared to him – or to a shark, for that matter – but I let it slide. 'Uh, huh . . .' I said by way of encouragement.

'So what I found out was this. It had been nagging at me, the way Alan seemed so comfortable in his life, even though he was sleeping in a van every night and had no shower or place to chill when he needed to relax. It was completely off from what I'd seen in other people without homes. So, like Meg said, I decided to follow him one day. And lo and behold, he drove downtown to this quiet street, pulled into the driveway of a huge, Victorian home, and let himself in with a key.'

Phillip's hands were now clenched once again, his eyes cold. 'All of a sudden I realized the guy wasn't homeless at all – he was simply *playing* at it. Like it was some kind of game of *make-believe*.'

'Whoa,' I said, 'I can imagine that was quite the shock.' And I meant it, too. It was a bizarre story and certainly not what I'd expected Phillip to have found out. 'Why do you think Alan was pretending to be homeless?'

'What he *said*,' Phillip went on, making clear he didn't believe

a word of it, 'was that all he wanted was to gain a better understanding of what it was actually like to be homeless. He said he
wanted to have more empathy for the community so he could
better help their cause. But as far as I was concerned, all he'd
done was take advantage of me and Meg, using us – both emotionally and physically – for his little play-acting at being a poor little
rich boy.' Phillip was staring out at the spot in front of his house
where my car now sat as if it were a toxic waste site.

'Because you were so generous to him,' I prompted, 'letting
him use your bathroom and shower—'

'And laundry and kitchen and backyard,' he jumped in. 'We
completely opened our home to the guy, out of the goodness of
our hearts. And then it turns out he's been lying all this time?
Completely indefensible.'

Like what you did is defensible? was my thought, which I kept
to myself.

'So after Alan told me this ridiculous story, I reminded him that
money was truly tight for Meg and me – unlike for him with his
big, fancy house – and said I thought he should pay us some back
rent for his use of our home over the past two months.'

'Which I'm guessing he refused to do,' I said.

'Worse. He simply laughed. Like he thought the whole thing
was funny. So then I told him that if he didn't agree to pay us
some money, I'd let it be known all through the community exactly
what he'd done – how he found it amusing to masquerade as an
unhoused person yet go whenever he wanted to his beautiful
Victorian house with its perfectly manicured rose bushes and
bricked-in patio.'

I said nothing. Obviously this blackmailing threat had not gone
well.

'But he still refused,' said Phillip. 'So I left and drove back
home, steaming mad the whole way. He of course never came
back to our house, and I brushed it off with Meg and tried to let
it go. But then I saw that he was putting on this fancy dinner at
the restaurant to benefit the Teens' Table and I couldn't stand the
hypocrisy of it all. I decided I had to confront him once more, to
try one last time to get him to agree to make things right. But by
that point, it had become more than about the money. It was the
principle of the thing.'

And your principles are obviously so very high and lofty, I thought. 'I'm guessing that the argument he had with Raquel Santiago didn't do anything to change your mind,' I said.

His snort provided the answer to that question.

'So you followed him into the bookstore afterwards to confront him.'

'Right you are again. But he still thought the whole thing was funny and refused to reimburse our expenses. I told him I'd take those autographed cookbooks instead, since they were clearly worth a bundle. He said he didn't have a key to the cabinet and added that even if he did, he wouldn't open it for me. Which is when I lost it.' Phillip shook his head with a sigh, and I got the impression that maybe he did feel at least a little remorse about what he'd done.

'You pushed him, and he hit his head on the corner of the cabinet,' I filled in. 'And when he collapsed on to the floor, you broke the glass and stole the books.'

He nodded. 'Though I hadn't meant to *kill* the guy, so after I grabbed the books, when I saw him lying there on the floor like that, I just freaked out. I hid in the wait station till his body was found, and then when Lucinda came through the kitchen into the bookstore, I was able to sneak behind her and get out through the kitchen door into the parking lot during all the ruckus. But as soon as I was out, I realized I had to ditch the books – they were too big to hide. So I ripped out the signed pages and tossed them under the dumpster, then joined the rest of the crowd till the cops arrived.'

'Very clever,' I said. Without thinking, I glanced over my shoulder toward Nichole's car.

Which is when Phillip yanked me by the arm inside. Slamming the door shut, he locked the door, then grabbed me around the waist and hissed into my ear: 'Now you'll see just how clever I truly am.'

TWENTY-ONE

I wrestled Phillip's arms from my waist only to have his hands immediately grasp me about the neck. They were large, strong hands and, try as I might, I was unable to pull them away. 'Nobody to come to your aid this time,' he said as his grip grew stronger. 'Congratulations on solving your last crime. Too bad no one will ever know it.'

'Gahhhh,' was all I managed to articulate in response.

At a fierce pounding at the door, his hands loosened. 'Police!' called out a deep, male voice. 'Open up *now* or we'll break our way in!'

'What the hell? How did they know . . .?' Phillip released my neck, managing to shove me to the floor in the process, and darted toward the back of the house. I crawled to the front door and stood to unlock it, and there was Eric, a look of horror on his face.

'Ohmygod, Sal, are you okay?'

I managed a weak smile. 'Yeah, I'm fine,' I said, pulling down the top of my turtleneck collar.

Eric laughed. 'Dang. Now why didn't I think of that?' He reached out to touch Buster's thick, leather collar which I now wore about my neck. 'But I gotta say, it looks pretty good on you – very punk.'

A scuffling sound coming from the back of the house made the two of us look up, then head quickly that way. Through an open window, whose bent screen now lay on the dead lawn along the side of the building, we saw the tall, athletic Mei holding the struggling Phillip down by the shoulders. She was being assisted by Nichole, who had a red hightop sneaker atop the man's chest.

Eric and I ran out the back door to help them. I thought Eric was going to punch Phillip in the face when he leaned over his prone body, but instead, he extracted a handkerchief from his back pocket and used it to pull off Phillip's belt. Holding it up like a trophy, he said, 'I'm guessing this will prove useful, especially if – as I'm betting it does – it has evidence of Sally's blood on it.'

With a grin, I reached my hand up my shirt and extracted

Nichole's phone from where it had been nestled inside my bra. 'And the recording on this – though not allowed as evidence in a criminal court – surely won't hurt, either.'

At the sound of an approaching siren, Phillip closed his eyes and ceased his struggling.

Nonna's eyes positively twinkled when Eric showed up with me at her house the next day for Sunday dinner. 'Ooooo,' she said, pinching him on the cheek, 'ees *so* good to see you, my boy! Your head all better now?'

'It is. A hundred percent better, now that I get to see your beautiful face once again.' Eric leaned over to plant a pair of *baci* on her cheeks, which caused my grandmother to break out in a fit of the giggles. Nonna adores Eric, and I sometimes think that, if not for the fifty-plus-year age difference, she'd try to steal him away from me in a heartbeat. And Eric's shameless flirting with her only makes it that much easier to imagine.

There were seven of us there that afternoon, including my father and Abby, as well as Evie and Evan. I'd been worried about Nonna's reaction to Evie's new beau. She could be highly critical of any newcomers to our traditional Sunday meal, whom she would, more often than not, view as suspicious interlopers. But when introduced to Evan, my *nonna* was nothing but sweetness and charm, taking the young man by the hand and sitting him down in the seat right next to her own. Perhaps seeing Eric again had flipped some sort of internal switch, prompting this one-eighty from her normally brusque behavior.

After we were all seated, Nonna passed the antipasti platter, loaded down with cured meats, cheeses, and marinated vegetables. Then, once we'd moved on to the second course of pasta smothered in savory 'gravy' – the red sauce in which the meat for the main course had been simmered all morning long – my father turned to me and asked, 'So what's new, hon?'

I looked at Eric, who shrugged. Figuring they were going to hear all about it soon enough anyway, and hoping that my grandmother's increasing deafness would prevent her from hearing enough to get too agitated, I spilled my story. Dad, Abby, Evie, and Evan listened, engrossed in the tale, while Eric did his best to distract Nonna, complimenting her cooking and asking how on earth she managed to make such perfect al dente pasta.

'And so then the cops showed up at Phillip's house and carted him off to jail,' I said, having already recounted how Nichole and Mei had tackled the guy and held him down until help had arrived. 'After which Detective Vargas interviewed the four of us out front while the forensics people did their stuff in the side yard and indoors. He wasn't at all happy about the way we'd taken things into our own hands and gone to confront Phillip, but there wasn't much he could do about it at that point. And he even half-admitted that it would have taken his department much longer to get the goods on Phillip.'

Dad was shaking his head. 'I can't believe you did that, Sally. Or that *you* allowed her to,' he added, with a sour look at Eric.

'Hey, man,' Eric responded, interrupting his conversation with my grandmother. 'It wasn't my idea, and I did try to stop her.'

'Stop what?' asked Nonna.

'Oh, just Sally going to see this guy who's a bit of a jerk,' said Eric. 'But it's all fine now. Here, will you show me those canned Italian tomatoes you say are so good?'

'Thank you,' I mouthed as he pushed back his chair. Once Eric and Nonna had retreated to the kitchen, I continued with my story. 'So anyway, I talked to Detective Vargas this morning, and he says Phillip's fingerprints were on both those cookbook pages. They hadn't had a sample of his prints before yesterday, when he was taken into custody, which is why they weren't able to ID them till now. And the other good news is that they did find what looks like blood on his belt. It'll take a while for the lab results to come back, but it seems pretty likely that it's mine.'

'You think that's enough to get him for that guy's murder?' asked my dad.

'Well, he did confess to it on that recording I made, so you can be sure the cops will do everything they can to track down evidence to prove it in a court of law. Who knows, maybe there'll be some DNA or hair on the clothes Alan was wearing. Also, now that they know exactly what happened, they'll be able to interview the people from the fundraiser again to maybe find an eyewitness who saw Phillip follow Alan into the bookstore. It seems like, at the very least, they can prove Phillip stole those cookbooks, which places him at the time and location of the murder.' I shrugged. 'In any case, it seems clear they'll have enough to get him for attacking me – twice.'

Eric came back into the dining room bearing a mound of braised beef, pork, and sausage. 'Nonna's plating up the zucchini and potatoes and will be right out,' he said, setting the steaming platter on the table.

'There's another whole course?' exclaimed Evan, eyes wide. 'Oh, boy. Guess I shouldn't have eaten so much pasta.'

'Welcome to the world of Italian kitchens,' I said with a laugh. 'There's dessert, too – tiramisu. And if you don't take large portions of both, Nonna will remember your impudence forever more.'

Abby picked up the serving spoon and helped herself to a chunk of short rib and a fat slice of Italian sausage. 'So do you think Phillip was faking it all – that clairvoyance stuff?' she asked.

'Beats me,' I said. 'I mean, I don't believe that people can actually "communicate" with the dead or anything, but he did a really good job of making me, I dunno . . . *aware* of Letta and how – having spent so much time with her over the years, and because of all those memories I retain – she's an integral part of my *being*.'

'Letta was a good girl,' said Nonna, coming into the room with the remainder of the main course.

Dad placed a large, weathered hand atop hers as she took her seat at the head of the table. 'She was indeed, Mamma.'

'So I guess my answer is that, even though I don't believe in clairvoyance, Phillip does seem to be what you'd call an "empath". He's very good at reading people and being able to sense how they feel about things.'

'Yeah, it's too bad the guy turned out to have such a dark side,' said Eric. 'I thought he was great at helping me consider what it is I really want from my life.'

'And have you thought more about what your answer is going to be to Saul?' I asked.

After explaining his career dilemma to the others, Eric shook his head. 'I still don't know. I'm leaning towards going for it, but the money thing is pretty scary. Phillip, alas, didn't have any financial advice to give me – not that I'd have followed it if he had. By the way, did Lucinda ever tell you anything about her session with him? Other than the fact that she was convinced he didn't hypnotize her,' he added with a chuckle.

'Not much. Just that Phillip told her he had a vision of some guy in a dark coat killing Alan and stealing the cookbooks, which was obviously a fabrication. Oh, and I called her yesterday afternoon to tell her what happened and that she and Julian have now been cleared of any suspicion regarding Alan's death. She was, unsurprisingly, quite happy about that. And not just for her, but because it turns out she's actually become interested in Julian – you know, romantically.' I snorted. 'Whatever. To each their own. But anyway, ignoring the made-up story about the man in the dark coat, it does seem Phillip really does has a knack for "getting" people.'

'Except for Alan, of course,' said Eric.

'No, turns out he wasn't so good at reading him,' I agreed. 'But maybe their shared devotion to the whole homeless advocacy thing made it too hard. You know, like how it's not easy to be objective when you're super close to something – or someone?'

Abby was nodding. 'Yeah, that makes total sense.'

'Oh, and speaking of homeless advocacy groups,' I said, 'I was reading online this morning about food banks, and it turns out there's one sponsored by the Santa Cruz Restaurant Owners' Association – or at least they work with some local food banks by donating time and resources to them. So I've decided to ask Javier how he feels about Gauguin joining the program. I think it's time I got more involved and started giving back to the community.'

'That sounds great, hon,' said my father. 'I'd like to learn about that program, too.'

'Really?'

The surprise must have been evident on my face, because Dad had the look of exasperation he had a lot when I was a teenager. 'Don't stare at me like that,' he said. 'I have a heart, too, ya know. Just because I don't want people sleeping in the entryway to Solari's doesn't mean I don't care about their well-being. Send me the link, and I'll have a look at it.'

'Wow. Cool. I will.'

My father took a sip of wine, then sat back in his chair. 'And while we're on the subject of helping others, I have a proposal for you.'

'Oh yeah?' I said, trying to read his enigmatic smile.

'I see it as a win-win situation. Or more of a win-win-win,' he said, leaning forward again. 'I don't much like being a landlord, you want to stay where you're living, and Eric needs somewhere to park the money he's going to get when he sells his condo. So, what if you two bought Letta's house from me?'

'What?' I glanced at Eric, who was regarding my father with narrowed eyes. 'But I have no money saved for any kind of down payment,' I said.

'I'll loan it to you or, more specifically, I'll carry back your half of the note. I'm sure we can structure it so that nothing much changes financially for you. You continue to pay me money each month, except now the money goes toward loan repayment instead of rent. And you,' he turned to face Eric, 'will use the money you make selling your condo as your half of the down payment. Of course there are a lot of details to work out, and it'll obviously take Sally a lot longer to pay off her half of the house, but I'm sure we can make it work.' He paused, a serious look in his eyes. 'That is, if the two of you are serious enough about this relationship that you think you're ready to invest jointly in real estate.'

I turned to Eric. 'What do you think? You want to invest jointly in real estate and buy Letta's house with me?'

'I'd love to live with you at Letta's house, Sally – for the long term. And not having a massive mortgage from a bank would also make it far easier for me to take that job with Saul.' He took my hand in his. 'So yes. I do.'

And that's when Nonna just about lost it. '*Oh, giorno felice!*' she exclaimed, jumping up from her chair and clapping her hands in glee.

'No, no, it's not that,' I tried to explain, but Nonna just kept on grinning. 'Oh, well, whatever.' Returning her smile, I walked over to my grandmother and took her in my arms. 'She's right about one thing, though,' I said. 'It is indeed a very happy day.'

RECIPES

Salade Niçoise
(Serves 6)

As with so many regional foods, there is a fierce debate over what constitutes an 'authentic' salade Niçoise, with many purists insisting that it should contain only uncooked vegetables along with tinned anchovies, and no lettuce or vinegar. It was apparently the famed chef, Auguste Escoffier, who first popularized the use of boiled potatoes and green beans in the salad, but since he was from a town a full twenty minutes away from Nice, many 'true' Niçois still turn up their nose at what they consider to be heretical additions.

But virtually any salad Niçoise you order these days – be it in Nice or in Nantucket – is bound to consist of pretty much the same thing: a composed salad featuring tuna, hard-boiled eggs, blanched baby green beans, boiled potatoes, olives, anchovies, tomatoes and onions, all tossed in a light vinaigrette and arranged atop a bed of crisp lettuce. And although it may not be 'traditional', I think you will agree that it makes for a delightful and delicious combination of ingredients.

Though the dish is commonly prepared with canned tuna, the version here – the one served at Pages and Plums – showcases seared bluefin tuna, which is caught in our very own Monterey Bay. Either fresh, sushi-grade tuna or a can of high-quality tuna packed in olive oil, however, would work equally well, depending on your preference.

Ingredients

6 eggs, at room temperature
¾ lb. fingerling or red potatoes
¾ lb. French beans, the smaller the better
2 tablespoons salt, for cooking
1 head butter (i.e., Bibb or Boston) lettuce
¾ lb. tomatoes, sliced into wedges
1 cup Niçoise or similar olives such as kalamata

1 cup sliced red onion
1 can anchovies packed in oil (optional)
1 lb. sushi grade tuna steaks, or 2 cans tuna packed in olive oil
1 tablespoon olive oil for searing the ahi
1 tablespoon red wine vinegar
3 tablespoons extra virgin olive oil
Salt and freshly ground black pepper to taste

Directions

Place the room-temperature eggs gently into a pot of simmering water and cook for 8 minutes. Remove the eggs to a bowl of ice water. Once cool, peel the eggs, then slice them in half and chill until use.

Get a large pot of water boiling (you can reuse the egg water if you like) with 1 tablespoon of salt added. Place the potatoes in the boiling water and cook until a fork can pierce them (10–15 minutes, depending on their size), then immediately drain. Once cool, peel the potatoes if you like, then cut into bite-sized pieces. Chill until use.

Snap the ends off the beans and de-string them, if necessary. Get another large pot of water boiling with 1 tablespoon of salt added. While the water is coming to a boil, fill a baking pan or large bowl with ice and add water. Drop the beans into the boiling water. As soon they change color (which should happen right around the time the water comes back to a rolling boil), drain them and then place them in the ice water. Swish the beans around with your hands until they've cooled, then drain them again. (This icing step is important because it stops the beans from continuing to cook after they're removed from the hot water – you want them to still have a nice *snap* when you bite into them.) Pat them dry with a towel and keep chilled until use.

Wash and pat dry the lettuce leaves, then tear into bite-size pieces and spread them out on a large platter or individual plates. Arrange the potatoes, beans, tomatoes, olives, onion, eggs, and anchovies (and canned tuna, if using) atop the lettuce.

Heat 1 tablespoon olive oil over high heat in a heavy skillet till shimmering, then lay the ahi tuna steaks in the pan and cook until nicely browned (1 or 2 minutes). Flip them over, then remove from the pan as soon as the bottom of the fish starts to brown. They should still be raw – yet warm in the center – and nicely seared on the outside. Cut the ahi into slices and arrange on the platter/plates.

Drizzle the vinegar and extra-virgin olive oil over the salad and season with salt and freshly ground pepper, to taste. Serve immediately.

Seared Bok Choy with an Asian-Inspired Glaze
(Serves 4)

Bok choy (also known as pak choy), a member of the mustard family, is commonly chopped up and added to stir fries and soups, or eaten raw in salads. But it's also delicious roasted or fried, especially when its slightly peppery flavor is complemented with a sweet and savory sauce such as the one used here. Served with grilled meat and steamed white rice, this dish makes for a simple yet tasty meal.

Look for baby bok choy, which range in size from 5 to 8 inches in length. But if you can't find them, feel free to use the larger heads: Simply separate the stems and leaves and cook the stems first, then add the leaves at the end.

Ingredients

3 tablespoons soy sauce
2 tablespoons rice wine vinegar
2 tablespoons mirin
1 tablespoon roasted sesame oil
1 teaspoon sugar
1 clove garlic, minced
1 teaspoon ginger, minced
Pinch chili flakes (plus more, for garnish)
3 tablespoons canola, or other neutral oil, for frying bok choy
8 baby bok choy, or 4 large ones
Black sesame seeds, for garnish

Directions

Mix together the soy sauce, vinegar, mirin, sesame oil, sugar, garlic, ginger, and chili flakes in a small bowl.

Cut the baby bok choy in half lengthwise, and wash away any grit that's collected between the stems at the base. (If using large heads, separate the stems from the leaves.) Pat the bok choy dry with a dish towel.

Heat half of the canola oil in a large, heavy frying pan over medium-high heat until shimmering, then lay half of the bok choy, flat sides down, in the pan and cook until starting to brown. Flip them over and brown the other sides, then remove to a dish. Add the rest of the oil to the pan and brown the rest of the bok choy on both sides.

Return the first batch of bok choy to the pan, pour the sauce over it all and continue cooking, covered, until the white parts of the bok choy are tender (about 2–4 minutes).

Serve drizzled with any sauce left in the pan, and scattered with black sesame seeds and more chili flakes, if desired.

Risotto with Chanterelles and Peas
(Serves 4–6)

Risotto, though fairly labor-intensive, is actually a great dish for a restaurant – or dinner party – as most of the preparation can be done in advance, leaving only the last few minutes of cooking until right before service.

This is the recipe Kamila used for the vegetarian main at the Pages and Plums benefit dinner, but chicken stock works equally well. And if you can't find fresh chanterelle mushrooms, feel free to substitute another kind, such as crimini, or even canned mushrooms.

Ingredients

    5–6 cups vegetable or chicken stock (unsalted)
    2 tablespoons extra-virgin olive oil
    1 small onion, finely chopped
    ½–¾ lb. chanterelle (or other fresh) mushrooms, coarsely chopped (or 2 4-oz. cans sliced mushrooms)
    4 cloves garlic, minced
    3 teaspoons fresh thyme or sage, chopped
    1½ cups Arborio rice
    ½ cup dry white wine or white vermouth
    1 cup peas (fresh, or frozen and thawed)

Salt and black pepper
1 cup finely grated Parmesan and/or Pecorino Romano cheese
Chopped chives or parsley, for garnish

Directions

If using canned mushrooms, drain them and add the mushroom liquid to your stock. Heat the stock in a saucepan and keep it at a simmer as you prepare the risotto.

In a large, non-stick skillet, heat the oil over medium heat till it shimmers, then add the onions and cook, stirring occasionally until they start to soften, about two minutes. Add the garlic, thyme or sage, and mushrooms, and continue to cook until the mushrooms have softened (if fresh), or until they start to brown at the edges (if canned).

Turn the heat up to medium-high, then add the rice and stir well, so all the grains are coated with the oil in the pan. As soon as the rice starts to crackle, pour in the wine and continue to cook, stirring often, until the wine has all been absorbed. Ladle in enough simmering stock to just cover the rice, and keep stirring until the stock is absorbed. Continue to add one or two ladlefuls of stock, stirring until absorbed, then adding more stock. Once the rice is par-cooked, i.e., it still has quite a bit of bite to it (which should be after about 10 minutes), you can turn off the heat and let the risotto sit until ready to finish cooking right before service.

About ten minutes before you want to eat, add the peas to the risotto, then reheat the stock and the rice. Taste for seasoning, and add salt and black pepper as desired. Continue to ladle in stock and stir the risotto until absorbed, repeating the process until the risotto is done: the rice should be cooked all the way through, but still slightly al dente.

Stir in the cheese and one final ladleful of stock, then remove from heat and serve immediately, garnished with chives or parsley.

Sally's Grilled Steak and Veggies with Creamy Garlic-Lime Sauce
(Serves 4–6)

This is a terrific meal to make for an outdoor dinner party, because – other than the sauce and marinade, which can be made in advance – everything is cooked on the barbecue. So rather than being relegated to the kitchen, you're able to hang out with everyone else in the backyard as they sip cold beer or a robust Zinfandel and kibbitz as you tend to the grilling.

It's best to fire up the grill a little in advance and get the first batch of vegetables cooking, and then do the second round shortly before you want to eat. The first batch will do just fine keeping warm in the oven until it's time to eat.

If you can't find Cotija cheese (a mild and crumbly Mexican cheese, similar in texture to feta), you can substitute feta or finely grated Parmesan. I prefer ribeye steak for grilling, because of its high marbling and great flavor, but feel free to cook whatever cut of steak (or pork, or chicken!) you like.

Ingredients for Sauce

1 teaspoon minced garlic (about 1 large clove)
1 cup sour cream
¼ cup mayonnaise
½ cup crumbled Cotija cheese
2 teaspoons lime juice (or more, to taste)
½ teaspoon chili powder (or more, to taste)

Ingredients for Marinade

2 tablespoons lime juice
1 teaspoon minced garlic (about 1 large clove)
1½ cups olive oil
¼ teaspoon salt
Pinch black pepper

Ingredients for Grilling

4 medium russet potatoes, skin on
4 medium zucchinis (courgettes), cut lengthwise into half-inch slices
2 medium yellow onions, peeled and sliced into rings
4 large bell peppers (a mix or red, yellow, and green), cut into 8 wedges each
4 cobs of corn, husk and silk removed
1 bunch green (spring) onions, roots cut off

2 large ribeye steaks (or enough steak/meat of your
preference for 4–6 people)

Directions

In a medium bowl, combine all the ingredients for the sauce and
mix well. Taste, then add more lime juice and chili powder as
desired. Cover and refrigerate until needed.

In another bowl, combine all the ingredients for the marinade
and mix with a wire whisk. Set aside. (No need to refrigerate if
using the same day.)

Either microwave or bake the potatoes until a fork can just go
through them (i.e., until almost ready to eat). Let them completely
cool, then cut lengthwise into half-inch slices.

Prepare an outdoor grill, letting it come up (if gas) or down (if
briquettes/wood) to medium-high heat. Oil the grate lightly so the
food doesn't stick, then grill the peppers, onions and zucchini until
desired doneness, basting with the marinade as you cook them.
(Use a grilling basket or narrow grate for the onions, so they don't
fall through into the fire.) Remove the vegetables to a baking sheet
and place uncovered in an oven at 200°F to keep warm.

About 20–30 minutes before you want to eat, grill the rest of
the vegetables (the potatoes, corn, and green onions), basting them
with the marinade as they cook. Remove to a baking sheet as they
brown to your liking, and – if you're not going to eat them right
away – add them to the other vegetables in the oven.

Grill the steaks to your preferred doneness, basting them as
they cook. Remove them from the grill and let rest for 5–10
minutes, to allow the juices to be reabsorbed into the meat. Slice
the meat against the grain, and serve it with along with the grilled
vegetables and the creamy garlic-lime sauce.

Grilled Peaches with Balsamic-Plum-Black-Pepper Reduction
(Serves 6)

If you're going to be grilling your dinner anyway, it's easy to
simply throw on some peach halves after the main course is cooked,
to allow their sugar to caramelize with beautiful grate marks and
for them to take on a lovely smoky flavor. Once grilled, the peaches

can be kept warm in the oven until time for dessert, then served with a rich vanilla ice cream and drizzled with this flavorful balsamic reduction.

And don't worry that this recipe makes more sauce than you'll use on the peaches, as it keeps well in the fridge, and can be reheated and used later for a delicious glaze for anything from pork chops to chicken to tofu.

Ingredients

1 cup balsamic vinegar
2 tablespoons sugar
½ cup ripe plums, cut into chunks
¼ teaspoon black pepper (or more, to taste)
6 ripe peaches, pitted and halved
Olive oil to brush on peaches
Vanilla ice cream
Kosher or flake salt for garnish

Directions

Make the sauce: Combine in a medium saucepan the vinegar, sugar, plums and black pepper. Bring to a boil, then lower to a simmer and cook, stirring often so it doesn't burn, until reduced by half (about 20 minutes). The sauce should be thick enough to cling to the back of a spoon, yet thin enough to pour.

Strain the sauce through a fine sieve, pressing down with a spoon to get as much of the plum flesh off the skins as possible, then cover and store in the fridge until needed. The sauce can be made several days in advance and reheated in the microwave or on the stove before serving.

Brush the cut sides of the peaches with olive oil and place them, cut side down, on a medium-heat grill. Cook until warm through and grate marks appear.

Serve the grilled peaches with a scoop or two of ice cream, drizzle everything with warm balsamic reduction, and garnish with a sprinkle of salt.

About the author

The daughter of a law professor and a potter, **Leslie Karst** waited tables and sang in a new wave rock band before deciding she was ready for a 'real' job and ending up at Stanford Law School. It was during her career as a research and appellate attorney in Santa Cruz, California, that she rediscovered her youthful passion for food and cooking, and she once more returned to school – this time to earn a degree in culinary arts.

Now retired from the law, Leslie spends her time cooking, cycling, gardening, enjoying cocktail hour promptly at five o'clock, and of course writing. She and her wife and their Jack Russell mix split their time between Santa Cruz and Hilo, Hawaiʻi.

In addition to the Sally Solari mysteries, Leslie is also the author of *Justice is Served: A Tale of Scallops, the Law, and Cooking for RBG*.

www.lesliekarstauthor.com

ACKNOWLEDGMENTS

Once again, I am indebted to my fearless beta readers, Robin McDuff and Nancy Lundblad, for identifying plot holes, inconsistencies, typos, and other issues in the original manuscript. This final version is a better book because of you. Thanks also to Nancy for advising me regarding concussions, macular degeneration, and hospital lingo and protocols (though I take full responsibility for any errors that might remain); to Susan Woolley for her input regarding white collar crime/First Amendment appellate practices; and to Shirley Tessler for once again acting as my intrepid recipe editor.

I wouldn't be where I am as a published author without the assistance of my agent, Erin Niumata, and the help of many others at Folio Literary Management. And eternal gratitude goes out as well to Rachel Slatter at Severn House, for rescuing Sally and bringing her back to life.

Finally, much love to my wife, Robin, and to my fellow Mystery Lovers' Kitchen and Chicks on the Case bloggers – you're the best posse a gal could ever have.